is part romp, part suspense, but
adored this fun yet poignant book."
—Diane Chamberlain, *New York Times*–bestselling author
of *The Stolen Marriage*

"*The Testament of Harold's Wife* is a glorious—and
unique—tale of tragedy, resilience, and one kick-ass
grieving widow and grandmother. I laughed, cried, and
cheered as Louisa talked to her pet chickens, splashed bourbon in her tea, hid 'Glitter Jesus' around the house, and
wrestled with revenge. Louisa captured my heart, and I
will never forget her."
—Barbara Claypole White, bestselling author of *The Perfect
Son* and *The Promise Between Us*

"At the center of this moving, transcendent novel is the
unforgettable Louisa. Perceptive, wry, full of righteous fury
and enlarged by deep compassion . . . I promise you will
miss her when you turn the last page. The story itself—
flawlessly written and genuine to the core—takes an
unflinching look at how we survive shattering tragedy
and pointless cruelty and continue to love the world.
Its startling, life-affirming conclusion will haunt me for
a long time."
—Patry Francis, bestselling author of *The Orphans of
Race Point*

"Perhaps the toughest and bravest way to survive tragedy is
by bearing up. In *The Testament of Harold's Wife*, after
losing her husband and grandson, Louisa weathers catastro-
phe through hard-fought wisdom, humor, and revenge
served cold—fueled by a side of hot bourbon. I never left
her side as she proved reinvention is possible at any age."
—Randy Susan Meyers, author of *The Widow of Wall Street*

"*The Testament of Harold's Wife* is a richly told tale that explores the human-animal connection and the journey to get past tragedy. Louisa, the spunky, elderly narrator, delivers a tender hymn of hope and rebirth that stays with you long after the last page."
—Kim Michele Richardson, author of *The Sisters of Glass Ferry*

"Lynne Hugo's delightful page turner, *The Testament of Harold's Wife,* is fast-paced, unexpectedly poignant, and fun. Louisa's utterly winning voice propels us at breakneck speed. As a woman who has seen it all and lost it all, Louisa will take her place in the pantheon of unforgettable characters. You may never see an older woman in quite the same way again. This gorgeous new book, with its swiftly moving plot and subversive humor, will stay with you long after you have finished the final page."
—Laura Harrington, bestselling author of *Alice Bliss* and *A Catalog of Birds*

The Testament of Harold's Wife

LYNNE HUGO

KENSINGTON BOOKS
www.kensingtonbooks.com

KENSINGTON BOOKS are published by

Kensington Publishing Corp.
119 West 40th Street
New York, NY 10018

All Kensington titles, imprints, and distributed lines are available at special quantity discounts for bulk purchases for sales promotion, premiums, fund-raising, educational, or institutional use.

Special book excerpts or customized printings can also be created to fit specific needs. For details, write or phone the office of the Kensington Sales Manager: Kensington Publishing Corp., 119 West 40th Street, New York, NY 10018. Attn. Sales Department. Phone: 1-800-221-2647.

Kensington and the K logo Reg. U.S. Pat. & TM Off.

eISBN-13: 978-1-4967-1669-9
eISBN-10: 1-4967-1669-8
First Kensington Electronic Edition: October 2018

ISBN-13: 978-1-4967-1668-2
ISBN-10: 1-4967-1668-X
First Kensington Trade Paperback Printing: October 2018

10 9 8 7 6 5 4 3 2 1

Printed in the United States of America

For Tara and the Hughes family

In memory of
Henry Mannix Hughes
July 7, 1958–March 26, 1971

Acknowledgments

It's become nearly cliché to say that no novel makes its way to readers without the diligent effort of many people other than the author. But before that effort comes their belief and support, and I am so grateful to have been given that in generous measure.

Tara Gavin, thank you for reaching across the years, inviting my work, and raising it up with your insight, skill, and sensitive editing. Our conversations always inspire me. Diane Chamberlain, thank you for your friendship, for reading, and for introducing me to Susan Ginsburg and Stacy Testa at Writers House. I can't imagine better, more responsive and caring literary representation.

First readers providing helpful feedback and suggestions on the manuscript were Laura Harrington and the late Nancy Pinard, both outstanding authors, along with Jan Rockwell and Alan deCourcy. Susan Ginsburg's editorial note was a guiding star. Alan saved my computer from unnatural death on numerous occasions; technology is not my best friend. More than that, his encouragement and faith have nurtured me through multiple books.

I'd like to express my gratitude to the members of the Kensington Publishing Corporation editorial team, headed up by Steven Zacharius and Lynn Cully, all of whom were instrumental in the acquisition of *The Testament of Harold's Wife*. I have special appreciation, too, for the people who have worked with such care on the preparation of the manuscript, especially Monique Vescia, copy editor, and Paula Reedy, production editor. Vida Engstrand, director of communications, and Lulu Martinez, communications manager, handle publicity with enthusiasm and creativity. Kristine Noble is responsible for the beautiful cover.

Grateful acknowledgment for permission to include his work is made to Tom Merrill, author of "Come Lord and

Lift." The poem first appeared in *The Lyric* in the Summer 1992 issue.

Amy, Beth, Jo, and (the deceased) Meg are based on real chickens of the same names raised by Dr. Diana Davis. The nuggets of experience that start a novel are so interesting sometimes. No, Diana's not a farmer, she's a university provost; the chickens have been known to wander into the house, and Diana does have a cat, too. Those are the only facts behind the novel, but I hope the story resonates with truth for my readers.

Come Lord, and lift the fallen bird
Abandoned on the ground;
The soul bereft and longing so
To have the lost be found.

The heart that cries—let it but hear
Its sweet love answering,
Or out of ether one faint note
Of living comfort wring.

—Tom Merrill

1
Larry

Sometimes in the shower he'd think of it. Or it would get going in his head at night if he got up to pee and didn't fall back to sleep quickly. Like a movie rerun with no stop on the remote. Blinking and shaking his head sometimes worked, but he had to do it right away. If the movie got past the thud, the steering wheel fighting his hands, he had to let it play to the end to hear how he'd shouted, "There was a deer! It was a deer," at the back of the do-gooder woman who'd stopped at the accident.

"Honey, what's the matter?" LuAnn said once when he hadn't known she was awake, and she went up on her elbow and wiped his face with her finger. "It's okay to cry."

"What the hell are you talking about," he said, not a question. "Shut up, will you," not a question, either. He'd been looking at porn to get his mind on better things, but then he long-armed the magazine under the bed, switched off his lamp, and shimmied down with his back to her. If he hadn't, she'd have kept talking.

She'd made it worse saying that crap when he might have still been able to get it to stop. And then he'd had to let it play to the end again, to hear what he'd yelled, even though he'd seen the movie, hell, he'd made the damn movie, and he knew how it went:

A heavy thud, and then another, something recoiling off the hood. He jerked the wheel to an overcorrection back across the center line, off the shoulder. Get the truck under control, get it stopped. Goddamn, he'd dozed and hit something.

Prob'ly a deer. Rut season. They were all over the roads in the damn early dark. He'd never hear the end of it from LuAnn. Not his fault, dammit. He hadn't had that much, not that much, he'd get Chuck to tell her.

Don't just sit there, get out, check the truck. Shit. Front end a mess. Headlight and . . . oh Jesus. Jesus. What *is* that? Oh Jesus. No. No way. Don't look. A random sneaker and papers is all that is.

Gotta be a deer, there's deer all over the roads now. Rut season. Gotta be a deer. Truck ought t'drive okay. Get outta here, then figure what to do. Lose the empties outta the truck first, walk 'em t'the other side of the highway, other side, throw 'em in the brush. Lotta highway trash. Farther away. Don't trip. Wipe 'em clean. LuAnn'll see the truck. Probably look inside. Thinks she's smart.

Okay. Cross back, get t'the truck. Go, steady. Keep your eyes open.

A long lull in traffic. Lucky.

He was just checking the truck so he could get it straight to tell LuAnn what happened.

Wouldn't you know the damn do-gooder in a six-year-old blue Civic would pull up right then. "Are you all right? Oh my God! Did you get 911? Have you checked him? Where's the other car?" Bitch freaking out, holding a cell phone to her ear, running toward what lay crumpled on the gravel shoulder of the highway, the sun bleeding all over the blackening sky by then.

"It just now happened. Call 911! It was a deer! There was a deer!" He yelled at her back, yelled it twice, then followed her.

He could make the replay finally stop if he turned up the volume on how he yelled it again, too, as he caught up to the woman with the cell phone, to get it right in his head: "It was a deer! There was a deer!"

2
Louisa

I am Louisa, Harold's wife. Or I was. Now the last best friends I have are Jo, Beth, and Amy. The four of us still mourn Meg. I'm the only one who's finished *Little Women*, but when we have tea out in the yard, I read it aloud to them from the battered copy I bought at the library sale. I have all the classics now.

They don't care to hear more than a paragraph at a time, but so what? They're beautiful, my friends, my comfort. My looks are closest to Beth's, a brownish blond, but hers are wholly natural while mine are compliments of Miss Clairol. Amy is purely white but for a couple of stunning black streaks that also run in her otherwise cheery temperament, while Jo is a quick-eyed, pretty, russet auburn, like my sister down in Georgia. All of us are old, I suppose. My mind rebels at the word. Old is something that I once thought I'd never have to worry about because time took forever to pass. I won't think about it now, and you shouldn't focus on it, either. None of what's happened had to do with age anyway. It was all set in motion by two selfish men, one of them my son and one a stranger to us both, neither more than half my years, so if you're one of those people who think it's youth that matters, you've been warned.

I thought about changing my name to Meg, after my husband killed her, which was right before he killed himself. That doesn't sound good, does it? Well, it was quite the right thing to do. She was sick and it's wrong to allow suffering. We all miss her terribly. I didn't change my name, even though it would have made us a more coherent group again, because I thought my sainted mother would be upset. That's an expression Mom used to indicate someone was dead, calling them sainted. My sister, CarolSue, and I say it now as a joke. But my son, Gary—a name I would surely reconsider if I had the opportunity since I've learned it means "spear carrier"— would claim his departed father is definitely *not* sainted because he died on purpose. He would say it as a black-or-white fact, too. After everything that's happened, he cannot stand to look in the shadows. I'll never be able to count on him to kill me when my time comes. But I can take care of myself.

"This is crazy. They're chickens, Mom. They're chickens, and they don't belong in the house." Gary had dropped by without calling and caught me having tea in the living room with the girls. It was raining outside, and much as I love them, I don't sit in the rain to have tea. *That* would be crazy.

"They have names, son. Please be polite. You were raised better. Look, here's my pretty Beth. Say hello, Beth. You know Gary." Beth was already clucking quietly. She's quite the conversationalist. "Gary, tell Beth how pretty she is. Notice how my hair is the same color as hers?"

"Mom, no, I came to check on you, see if you need anything. I'm not talking to chickens. I'm going to get them out of the living room and back into the coop. Besides, Marvelle will kill them." Marvelle is a retired barn cat who looks like she's wearing a fluffy tuxedo. She came to us complete with her unfortunate name. Once a living legend mouser, I brought her inside to the soft life after she quit caring what the mice did. As the words spilled from Gary, she was curled up under my green ottoman, ignoring the hens *and* him. I thought it gracious on my part not to point this out. Gary started to chase down JoJo, which was a terrible way to start since she's the fastest, but I wasn't going to tell him. He wouldn't have a clue how to round them up anyway. All the farm has long leaked out of my boy, who no longer sees the life spark in creatures or feels its force in the land. You'd think, perhaps, that had to do with the way his son, Cody, died, because of that terrible drunken stranger, and Gary's fault in it, too, but it had happened well before then.

"Technically they're all hens," I said, very calm. I crossed my legs at the ankles as if I were entertaining the Prince of Wales, not that Gary looked all that royal in those baggy khakis. "You know, your father never did get another rooster after Bronson died. The girls were past their prime. I'm thinking of enlarging the flock again now, though, and then I might get one. Do you think a rooster would understand if I name him Laurie?"

My son was not looking engaged in this subject at all as JoJo flew up to the hanging light fixture in the dining area to escape him. "Don't you remember that male character named Laurie in *Little Women*? I read you that whole book—how old were you? Gary, please, will you please just sit? You're getting the girls stirred up. There's room next to Beth." I pointed to the couch. "Move over, Beth." Beth, obliging girl that she is, flapped her gold wings and half hopped, half flew up to the couch back on the other side. She couldn't have possibly created more room for him without entirely abandoning the couch.

"Mom! What are those holes in the wall?" Gary, who'd backed off his silly chicken roundup attempt and started to sit when Amy advanced toward him in a menacing way—she and I like to play good cop, bad cop, and she'd certainly not appreciated his comments—hoisted himself back up, and scrambled behind my chair away from her. I had to crane my neck to see him finger two small holes chest-high in the wall to the right of his high school graduation picture.

Oh crap, I thought. Well, it's my own fault. I could have

fixed those a long time ago, and at least he hadn't noticed the ones under the window. For a moment, I wished he'd notice that the walls need painting—once a cheery buttercup color, now they're more like a dying dandelion—but on the other hand if he noticed he might do it, and that would mean he'd be here in my house, and we haven't been getting along that well lately. He worries about me all the time now and it just brings out my worst side.

"Those have been there since last summer. Will you please sit down and have some tea?" I pointed to the china teapot in the cozy my mother knit. "Shall I get you a cup or a mug?"

"You know I don't like . . . Never mind. They *look* like bullet holes. Do you have something to tell me?"

"For heaven's sake. Were you raised on a farm or weren't you?"

"This is hardly a working farm, Mom. The chickens don't even produce eggs anymore. You need to get rid of them."

"I don't produce eggs anymore either, son. Are you going to get rid of me?"

"Mom!" he said, and put on his shocked look.

"You just don't remember all we did on this land. Your daddy hoped you'd take over, but he always suppor—"

"Wait a minute. How did those holes get there?" Gary was raised not to interrupt, but he does regularly. I stopped talking entirely to make a point, but it didn't sink in.

"That's just a couple BBs," I finally said, because he wouldn't let it go.

"*What?* What happened? Was someone breaking in?" Gary's face reddened deeper than its usual shade. He thinks all my business is his to know.

"Four or five deerflies were in here so I took them out. Back in August. I couldn't find the flyswatter. I wish you'd put things back where they belong when you come over."

"Jesus, Mom. I didn't move your . . . wait a minute. You were shooting deerflies? That's *insane*. You could kill yourself." He stopped for a few seconds, his mouth hanging open and his eyes widening as the idea took hold. He gathered steam and blew. "Wait a minute. Wait just a minute here. *Were* you trying to—?"

"Gary. You of all people shouldn't take the Lord's name in vain, I'm sure. I occasionally miss a deerfly. If I were aiming at a person, *any* person, I assure you I wouldn't miss."

Do you see what I mean about my worst side just popping right out? CarolSue gets all over me about it. "Stop, Louisa!" She says it all the time. "You're not helping him or you heal."

Gary's oval eyes went down to mail slots. "What's that supposed to mean?" he said, all this time standing over my chair, looming. I could feel my neck stiffening looking up at him at that bad angle, and I didn't appreciate it.

"Nothing, son. Would you like to give the girls some grapes? They'll eat right out of your hand. They love their grapes." Very glad to rest my neck by having a good reason to look away from him, I picked up the plate of green grapes I'd cut in half. Amy hopped into my lap right away, proving my point. Gary backed up, knocking the floor lamp into the wall and startling everyone. It hit the wall, and he caught it before it hit the floor. The rag rug might have kept it from breaking, but I think the shade would have been toast.

"Mom," he said louder, enunciating as if I was hard of hearing. "We need to think about getting rid of the chickens. They're too much for you now. They can't be in the house. I've been thinking about the farm anyway. This place has gotten too much for you to handle."

"Gary, I love you, son, but over my dead body will my girls leave." I wouldn't dignify the rest of his opinion.

"Is that a threat, Mom? If you feel like you might hurt yourself, I'll put you on the crisis prayer list and take you to the hospital until God makes things right. It sounds like a threat to me. I'll find a safer place for you." He felt around the holes again, stared at me, and without saying anything more turned and went down the hall toward the bedrooms.

Oh crap, I thought. Here we go.

Within a clock minute, he was back. He didn't loiter getting to the point.

"Where is Jesus?" he said, his whole self in agitation. I was going to get smart with him about how being a reverend, he should know, but I decided to be kind and give him a straight answer.

"Jesus is in the closet."

"Jesus is in the closet? You cannot be serious."

"I think maybe it's why he never got married," I said. Poor judgment on my part, but I couldn't stop my worst side. She does love the openings Gary gives her.

"That is *blasphemy*. Something *is* wrong with you. Why is the *picture* of Jesus in *your* closet?"

Here's the story on that picture: last year, after he became Reverend Gary, my son gave me a painting he'd done himself. He got offended almost to tears when I said Elvis looked good as a blonde in drag. I had to apologize many times and explain that all the paintings involving glitter that I'd seen before were of Elvis, which was why I didn't know this one was Jesus. I pointed out that no one knows what Jesus looked like. This hurt his feelings because the glitter halo was Gary's creative depiction of holiness, which was the point I was supposed to get. He is so sincere it would never occur to him that glitter might not be a good idea. Mollifying him backfired, though, because he carried out his plan to hang it in my bedroom, to be "the first thing I saw in the morning and the last before I closed my eyes."

I knew where that idea came from, and it's an example of chickens coming home to roost. My Harold would say Glitter Jesus on my bedroom wall now is exactly what I deserve for what I made *him* suffer (he claimed damage to his retinas) during our son's adolescence. Gary was miserable as a teenager, bony wrists and knees and ankles all going in wrong directions, plus he had trouble making friends. In ninth grade, after writing a report on Van Gogh, he decided his isolation was related to an artistic temperament. He'd always enjoyed art class, too. Like any mother, I ignored his father and evidence—anything for your child to have self-esteem, right?—and built him up with praise as gaudy and ill-conceived as his projects. What else would I do? I loved my son then, and I do now. Different as we are, I know I mustn't lose sight of all that is good and kind in him, and you mustn't, either.

Anyway, while death threats from me kept Harold's mouth shut, I'd display Gary's dreadful pictures in our bedroom, telling our boy I wanted his art to be the first thing I saw in the morning and the last thing at night. (Anything to keep them out of the living room.) You should have heard Harold when Gary applied to LaGrange Community College to "jump-start" his professional career with an Associate in Studio Art degree. "Now, there's a surefire moneymaker," he said in private, way more times than I cared to hear. That man could roll his eyes as well as any woman. Remembering little things like that crumples me inside like the wadded-up tissue that's stuck in my every pocket to fight the sneak attacks of memory.

Harold had to admit it turned out all right, though he never did give me any credit. After one semester, Gary's tactful instructor redirected him: had he ever thought about the amount of artistic vision computer graphics required? I'd hoped he'd get a Bachelor's, and Harold wanted him to study Agriculture, but at least Gary eventually got an Associate in Computer Science degree. And a job. When he married Nicole and then our grandson, Cody, was born, Harold and I thought we'd run the big bases and were home, safe. Life was finally so good that Harold and I joked how great it was that Nicole, not Gary, had decorated their house; we could visit without being blinded.

But I digress. The point is, now I was a widow and had this Glitter Jesus on my bedroom wall, as if arthritis and a double dose of grief weren't enough to make a body tremble and cringe. I'd never tell Gary that I wanted to remember Harold there beside me, especially horny and passionate and tender, the way he used to be. That I couldn't possibly, what with Jesus' hand raised up like a stop sign and a dot of glitter on the pupils of his eyes, giving a woman absolutely no privacy for trying to remember the best times. We all went over the edge after Cody died, but Gary thinking Glitter Jesus was a great gift shows a lot of his brain cells drowned in his tears. Once I even had the thought of getting another goat in hope that an accidental kick to the head might bring Gary to his right mind. Does that sound bad? When you live alone you have thoughts like that and you stop bothering to chide yourself for them.

How *could* any sane mother tell her son who's pushing forty-five that she was trying to give herself a little satisfaction, and Glitter Jesus' eyes staring her down were an inhibiting factor? It would have been about as natural as mentioning it to a stranger stocking shelves in the grocery store. Gary and I have never been alike, but back when we were all of us a family, all of us living our real lives, I'd watch and listen to him and smile, recognizing myself and Harold and our parents in him, the sum different from the parts, yet adding up to our son with an acceptable, even beautiful, logic. Now I couldn't find anyone or anything familiar in him. Ever since Gary got religion after Cody died, sometimes he looks like Glitter Jesus himself, little pricks of fire centered in his eyes.

On the other hand, what mother *should* tell her son anything about herself and sex? Even if he hadn't become Reverend Gary, I'm not that far gone. So I did the next worst thing to telling the truth. I stood up, gave him a kiss on the cheek, and lied. "Gary, this has been a lovely visit," I said. "Bless your heart." (CarolSue taught me to say that.) "I'm so glad you stopped by. I hope you remember to call first next time, because you know I've started to get out quite often with my friends. I really need to be getting my supper in the oven about now, and CarolSue is calling at five." As I said this, I was moving toward the door with my hand on his elbow. His face was a kaleidoscope as I talked, but I never let him get a word in. I might have been actually pushing him to the door. I realize that great mothers don't do that, but I'm trying to be honest and let the chips fall.

He called the next morning a little after ten, but I didn't answer the phone. I love that Caller ID gadget. And wouldn't you know, it was Gary signed me up for it. I know he really tries to be a good son.

I wasn't surprised at all when the sheriff's car bumped down my driveway soon after I didn't answer Gary's call. My son is nothing if not predictable. He was probably up until midnight hot-wiring the crisis prayer lists. But I was ahead of him: the hens were in the coop, the yellow kitchen was scrubbed, floor swept—even the cabinets wiped down—dishes out of the drainer. This isn't easy to do because so many things in my kitchen—oh, say, the red-handled paring knife, the cast iron skillet, the daisy spoon rest, the good spatula—were my mother's, and I remember them all the way back to when Harold and I were engaged. My mother was making me learn how to cook, and Harold would come early to sit in our kitchen, which just made me nervous because Mom would correct my every other move. Later, he'd praise what I'd made so lavishly that I knew it must have been terrible while he managed to hang around until Mom and Dad couldn't stay awake anymore. Oh, his kisses were so gentle, like he was afraid I would break. Believe me, I convinced him I wouldn't. And not that I could say it, but it would have been all right with me if his hands had wandered farther than they did before we were married. It was plain embarrassing, the way I wanted him touching me all over.

Anyway, I'd prepared everything today for unwanted company, even made my bed, and picked up the bedroom in case of a prying glance in there. But I left Harold's good shoes where they were, still half under his side of the dresser.

Really, I should donate them to the Goodwill in Elmont, but the idea of someone filling my Harold's shoes, well, I just cannot. The bathroom's cleaned, and I remembered to move Harold's straight razor from its place on the side of the sink where he'd left it that last morning. I'd replaced it there practically the minute CarolSue left for home after we got through Harold's service and settling his affairs and she'd satisfied herself that she'd boxed up his things so I wouldn't have to look at them.

Never an electric shaver for my Harold, not ever since we were first dating did that kind, good man give me beard burn. He'd shave a second time before we went out. He used to bring me daisies because he thought they were my favorite flower. I let him think that: he could pick them for free from the side of the road on his way to our house. Really, I love the scent of Peace roses and when we bought the farm and I ordered a bush from the Burpee catalog, Harold planted it for me. It's strong and healthy, fragrant with a tinge of lemon like his cologne I loved to breathe in. Oh God, where is my sweet Harold?

The usual ghosts appeared when I dusted the living room, each object reminding me how it came to be part of Harold and me. The pewter-base lamp that was a wedding present from Harold's aunt Elsie. A polished wood picture frame my parents gave us for our tenth anniversary. The picture of us in it is long faded. The green ceramic bowl I made in a college ceramics class for my father; my mother gave it to Harold when Dad died. And there's the white afghan that his mother knit for me; I refolded it over the back of Harold's empty chair. Everything in my house tells the story of what's gone forever.

Holes in the walls are filled with toothpaste and touched up with yellow highlighter. No, you're right, it didn't match the walls that well, but men don't notice something like that, now do they? I made sure that I had a calendar out on the kitchen table with some fake engagements written in. My hair pinned up with little tendrils left out, and even a makeup job: eyebrows, a touch of shadow, mascara, blush, lip gloss. Carol-Sue isn't my sister for nothing. I do so wish she had told her second husband that she hadn't signed on to leave her family and no, she wouldn't move to Georgia with him. It's almost a thousand miles from southeastern Indiana.

I opened the front door and stepped out on the porch when I heard the patrol car tires crunch on the gravel as Gus put on the brakes too hard. He is really full of himself. A mistake to go outside, though. I wasn't thinking of the heady scent in the air to bring *When lilacs last in the dooryard bloom'd* to mind and then, *O Captain! my Captain!* even though it's a full year now. Or will be next week. The first dark purple buds formed two weeks ago. Another thing I do wish is that Harold hadn't killed himself in April, right when the earth was rising up a hopeful pale green, bursting into pink and white and lavender, awash in yellow sun after the darkest winter we'd ever known, the winter I was surprised to outlive. It was the insult of spring Harold could not abide. It made me feel guilty that I could, and now I feel guilty that I've gone on a year without him, though every day I find another corner of life empty. *O Captain.*

I can stifle tears. Gus, maybe two hundred sixty pounds of him, labored out of his patrol car. *Sheriff* was emblazoned along the side of the car in black and gold on a white panel, and I couldn't help but notice how it contained the word *riff*. Shorthand for "reduction in force," the *Elmont Herald* explained, as half the county was laid off or let go in the past couple of years. Why couldn't Gus have been? Yes, I blame his interference for driving Harold to kill himself. But maybe it was my fault.

"Morning, Gus. Thought I heard a car out here." I threw my voice in his direction from the porch as I cleared up my eyes and arranged my mouth into a welcome.

"How're you doin', Miss Louisa? You're lookin' fine!"

Miss Louisa. That's rich. "I *am* fine, Gus. How 'bout yourself?"

"Can't complain." All the while Gus kept coming, right on up my worn porch steps.

"What brings you, Gus? Something wrong?"

"Just comin' by t'see how you're doing is all. Know it's comin' up on the anniversary."

Puffing fat men don't pull off casual all that well. He was wearing his glasses today, and they looked tight on his face. I remember when Gus was almost too skinny and not bad-looking even if he did have some acne. Oh, didn't we all. Even the boys in Vietnam then, like my Harold.

"Well, that's nice of you, Gus, but I'm okay. Of course it's hard. I miss Harold and Cody like both my legs have been cut off, but what can you expect when you lose your husband and grandson within six months? I'm doing all right."

Gus didn't say a word about how Gary had called him and sent him out here to confirm I belonged in a lunatic asylum. Probably told him that his poor mother was clearly losing her marbles, triggered by the anniversary of her husband's suicide. Out here the sheriff is the law and the social service system. We don't have a great tax base in this rural township. What Gus said was, "Mind if I come in and visit a minute?"

I made a point of staring at his waist. "Not comfortable with that gun coming into my house, Gus. Perhaps you can understand since I've lost both Cody and Harold." Now, no gun was involved in either Cody's or Harold's death, but I doubted Gus would think that fast. I truly think Gus showers with that gun on. But Gary probably told him he needed to see for himself that the house was filled with guns, chickens, and wanton disrespect for Holy Glitter. I was starting right out by throwing him a curveball about the guns.

Oh, how the struggle wrote itself across his face. It was just like teaching my fifth grade again when one of the boys was looking for a loophole to wriggle through. "Well, now,

Louisa, you know it's my job to be armed. I can assure you I won't touch . . ."

"Then we can just visit out here, Gus. Nothing nicer than a porch on a spring day." I felt the seat of the painted rocking chairs, then turned to the door. "No worry, chairs are nice and dry. I'll bring us some coffee. Be right back," I trilled over my shoulder.

"I think it's kind of chilly for you out here. How about I just put the gun out in the car while I come in. I'll be on my own time without it, of course," he said. The agony of defeat.

"Oh my! Bless your heart, I thought you already were. Anyway, I appreciate that."

I waited while he lumbered back to his car and watched him put the gun in the trunk. When he returned, I opened the door and let him follow me inside. I couldn't wait to see his face.

"How about that coffee?" I said. I was going to let him have a good look at the house and try to figure out where I had stashed the ungodly menagerie. "Come on into the kitchen and I'll put on a fresh pot. It'll only take a minute."

"I'd love a cup. That's a glorious picture. Is it new? Don't remember seeing it when I was here for Harold. You an Elvis fan? I always thought he had black hair. . . ."

His mentioning Harold, meaning how he kept coming here to arrest him—not that there was ever one indictment, not in this county—set my teeth on edge. "Oh yes, it's a beauty," I said. "Bless your heart. Gary painted that for me after Harold died. That sweet boy, bless *his* heart, too, hung it in the bedroom for me, but I'm just not in there all that much, and I decided to put it out here in the living room where I'd see it all day." Marvelle twitched her tail in amusement from her throne on the back of Harold's recliner. She and I share a sense of humor, something my son sorely lacks. Sometimes it makes me doubt everything I learned about genetics in biology class.

Gus followed me too slowly to the kitchen. He must have been scouring the place with his X-ray vision while I started coffee in the four-cup electric pot Gary got me for Christmas. Gus got to the kitchen table and sat down. He thought I didn't see him inch my calendar closer to himself and pretend he wasn't looking at it. The FBI missed a brilliant operative. I don't understand how he was able to thwart Harold's schemes to get revenge on the man who'd killed our grandson, but he did. Or what made him so determined. Did he have to prove that he was a big man because he didn't go to Vietnam and Harold did? What would Glitter Jesus have to say about that?

"You sure look pretty. Haven't changed in forty years. You been keeping busy?" Gus said.

This was just too easy. "Oh my, bless your heart. Well, I have my girlfriends and activities. Actually, I've been think-ing about doing some volunteer tutoring back at the school. Those farm boys still need to learn to read." I put on my ultra-sincere face, and brushed the hair CarolSue had taught me to leave loose on my forehead to the side as I pretended to worry what to say. "I didn't work over Christmas at the Toys! Store. Too hard to go back there after, you know, get-ting the call about Cody. Hard on the legs, too, all that stand-ing, too far to drive to Elmont. Not that my friends don't keep me running. But I need a solid focus."

"Seems like a fine idea."

"So, how have you been? What's been going on? I know you've got a big job on your hands. Practically a one-man force. I haven't really seen you since . . ." Believe me, I didn't care how he was. This was to divert him into talking about himself so he'd think he'd learned all about me. And if the slant reference to Harold's funeral made him uncomfortable, so much the better.

"Oh now, I do have a deputy, and some part-time help. But you know, we have more DUIs than we used to, and you'd be surprised, I don't know what we'll do exactly to manage, more drugs coming in. People don't realize. Even our own, you know, couple smart alecks growing . . . Hey, you don't want to hear this stuff. Would you mind if I use your bathroom?"

"Not at all. Down the hall, first door on the right." So he felt he needed to check the rest of the house to see if I was keeping the zoo—or maybe growing pot—back there. I know I can't grow pot, though. Not without buying grow lights first. I wonder if they're difficult to install?

After a ridiculous amount of time, the toilet flushed and the bathroom door opened with unnecessary loudness. I wondered for just a few seconds if Gus had really peed, and if his was like my Harold's had been, damn prostate pee, he called it. I used to lie in bed and listen: a tiny stream, then silence, then a little more. Fits and stops. Sometimes I'd fall back to sleep before Harold even made it back to bed. If I was awake, he'd take my hand and apologize. He didn't need to. After that bad fall he took in the dark making his way to the bathroom, I'd made him start to put on his glasses and turn on the bedside light when he had to get up in the night.

Gus's coffee was cooling on the kitchen table.

"See everything you wanted?" I said as he re-entered the kitchen, my tone innocent.

"Oh sure. Nice bathroom. Real nice." Blocks of sunlight rested on the table then as the earth turned toward noon. That morning they looked almost solid, like something I could use to smash him, this man who'd come to spy on me, doing my son's bidding. But it had been our Cody and my Harold who were smashed. Wishful thinking didn't do a thing to Gus.

"Miss Louisa, perhaps you would go to dinner with me sometime at the Lodge? The hunting club has a dinner, you know, the second Friday of the month, and we bring the ladies to that." Luckily for me, I don't have a partial plate like Harold did, because I'd surely have swallowed it when

Gus invited me out in the middle of my murderous thoughts. Some men have an astounding inability to read women, don't they? Thank goodness.

"That's a . . . lovely, Gus. That you bring the ladies, I mean . . . I'm sure they are very . . . honored."

"For sure. They love it. So, what do you say?"

"Thank you for asking me, but it just wouldn't be right so soon after Harold died. It wouldn't be respectful, Gus. It's hardly a year." And it would take me a hundred years to want to go out with you, I added to myself. Make that a thousand.

"I can wait," he said with a chuckle, and wiped a faint sweat sheen off his forehead with a chubby ringless hand. "You just call me when you're ready," he said with the great confidence of the clueless.

I changed the subject and we discussed the riveting topic of his arthritis (he has a bit of it in his knees that worries him). Then I had to be fascinated by his speculation about whether the county would patch or repave the rural route leading to the bridge that's out again before he went on to guessing how long the bridge will be out this time. Later, when he'd finished his coffee and left, Glitter Jesus stuffed behind the couch, I was tickled knowing Gus was burning up the phone line to Gary. He had to be secretly thinking Gary the least credible eye witness who'd ever asked for an *unofficial* official investigation in the twenty-seven years since Gus had first been elected sheriff of Dwayne Township. Miss Louisa was not only normal, she was kind of hot. Maybe CarolSue's remedial lessons in hairstyle and makeup for the harried woman who lived on a farm and taught fifth grade hadn't been entirely wasted.

There was one true thing I'd said to Gus, though. It was about needing a solid focus. After a year at a standstill, something about having to rev my engine to put one over on him gave me an idea. Something I could do for my Harold, in Cody's name. Sometimes you finally see something down the strangest, most out-of-the-way back road and you know it's time to take that route. So while Gus was trying to find a smooth way to tell voter Gary that maybe *he* was the crazy one because his mother is just as fine and normal as pot roast, I got on the phone to CarolSue to say, "I need your help because it's time to pick up Harold's cause and get revenge on Cody's killer. Only difference is we're going to do it right. We're going to have a Plan. None of that haphazard crap that didn't work."

And CarolSue said to me, "Well, of course we will. And I've been bored to tears lately. Charlie's always out in the garage, not that I want him underfoot, and I've already got the garden mulched. Annuals go in so early down here."

"Thank you, sister. I knew I could count on you."

"You have nothing to thank me for. You and I have to take care of each other, don't we? I'll be there. Haven't I been saying you've got to find something to take hold of? And maybe there's a little spark between you and Gus—"

"Have you lost your mind? That just pisses me off, I mean—I am Harold's wi—"

"Okay, okay. I just thought . . ."

"Well, don't think about anything but a Plan."

It was the middle of the night, too late to call CarolSue again, when a different thought came to me.

After Gary's visit, I'd reassured the girls that everything he said about getting them out of our house was nonsense and they absolutely shouldn't trouble their minds. We laughed and drank a toast to what good company we are. And you know how the next morning went with Gus. I'd taken care of everything. I didn't replay what Gary had said until my eyes opened in the blackness of my bedroom and The Thought was there, like one of those insights that you get with total clarity before sleep, but it fades in daylight and then you forget it until it's too late. Months later I'd remember how Marvelle's yellow eyes glinted at me from Harold's side of the bed and The Thought had been sudden, strong. *Gary wants me out.*

I lay there with The Thought. I could have saved myself a lot of trouble if I'd paid more attention to my instincts. Too late, I'd remember that I hadn't been able to sleep for fretting. This is my farm, my land. Harold and I made it sing out its good heart year after year. Our sweat has been its best rain. Corn was its song and it sang and sang, through seasons of planting and harvesting. It fed our mouths, and through years of sunsets and dawns, it fed our souls. The animals we raised and loved are buried here. My Harold's ashes are in this ground, with some of Cody's that his mother was kind to give us. The land sings the only notes I still hear. And I hear, I still hear.

3

What took my Harold's life, or made him give it up, was that our only grandson was stolen from us. Cody had been walking home from football practice when a driver "saw a deer in the road and swerved to avoid it." That driver saw a deer, but somehow never saw a boy almost six feet tall with reflector strips on his backpack? It was Harold who'd stuck on those shiny silver reflectors, worried about Cody walking the state highway at twilight. There are poor shoulders, and trucks speed as they head for the landfill over in Okeana. The part about the deer was the driver's story, and he stuck to it like Gorilla Glue. Do you suppose the fact that he was drunk makes that deer in the road more than a little iffy?

Harold used to pick Cody up after practice whenever he could. He'd do it behind Gary's back; Gary was always fighting with the boy about something, and walking the distance home was one of Cody's punishments. Gary didn't have the knack for parenting that his ex-wife, Nicole, did, or maybe the way Cody looked like his mother kept Gary's shame high. Gary was always one to do anger way better than *I'm sorry*. Nicole had left Gary over something bad that was Gary's fault. I never knew what, although some gossip made it back to me from someone who thought I knew—or who righteously thought I *should*—that "fornicating" with Nicole's sister-in-law was involved. Nicole said she wouldn't drag us into it, he was our son, after all. She'd hugged me and cried and said *no*, he'd need his parents. That was the kindness and the goodness of my daughter-in-law. She said she knew he was truly sorry and he'd promised to prove he could be a good husband, but she couldn't get back her feeling for him. She went to her parents' home in Collinsville and got work there, a miracle considering that her family is practically the entire population. Oh, we were a family once. I loved that girl like I'd given birth to her, love her still. She and I used to joke just by catching each other's eye when one of the men said something clueless. Hers were a golden hazel in most lights, and the thin rims of her glasses matched them.

Anyway, at sixteen, Cody didn't want to leave his school friends and football team. Maybe the fact that he'd taken the darling Lissie Madison to the Spring Fling factored in. In a way it counted as his first big date because he really liked her. He'd been sweet on her for months, too shy to ask, and finally worked himself up to it with a note passed during Algebra II. Harold told him to ask her in person, look her in the eye, to invite her, and I'd backed him up—having been a teacher, I could hardly endorse note-passing anyway—but Cody was shy. Still, he got a note back that she wasn't allowed to date until she was sixteen, five months away, but since it was a school dance, her parents might let her and she'd ask.

Well, Harold knew her dad and, as it happened, he soon ran into Matt at the Tractor Supply (where the men around here practically live). Of course, Harold mentioned that he would personally be doing the picking up and the bringing home of Lissie and what a well-mannered, smart, and good-hearted young man Cody was, such a help to Harold on the farm. My Harold could sell ice at the North Pole, but what he said was true. Bingo, Lissie was allowed to go. I thought Cody was going to throw himself on Harold's feet and kiss them when he heard about it from Lissie.

Sweet Harold. After he and Cody picked up Lissie, he

swung by our house so I could see them all dressed up, too: Cody in his first regular suit and a red tie that went with her red dress. His eyes so blue that night, shining with embarrassed delight when I fussed over them, and hers dark and sparkly, with her dark curly hair put up like a grown woman and little rhinestones artfully scattered here and there in it. He'd given her a wrist corsage of three white tea roses with baby's breath and some green, and she had a white rose for his boutonniere. Nicole paid for the picture a photographer took at the dance and ordered an extra one for us. Wasn't that good of her? It's one picture of Cody I don't need to look at to remember, even though I do look at it on my dresser every day. He was lit-up excited, everything ahead.

After the Spring Fling, Lissie's parents let her go on group dates with Cody, and likely that, as much as his school, football, and his friends, made him want to stay instead of move with his mother. Maybe us and the farm, too, because he wanted to live with us during the week. He'd have some dinners with his dad, he said, and weekend time with his mom. Gary wouldn't have it, though. I'm sure it hurt his feelings. If Cody didn't want to change high schools, living with him was the only option Gary would allow, so that's what Cody had to do. But Gary was always on him like a burr. They were not alike, which was hard on Gary and hard on Cody, the boy so popular, athletic, and loving our farm, too, as Gary never had. Gary wanted his son to be like him as much as Harold wished Gary were like him. Such pain parents and children inflict on one another, even though we all want to do better, be better. But we don't, do we? Anyone you love and need that much; well, isn't hurt and anger just the unshiny side of that mirror?

But to go on . . . The second Friday of November in 2009, dank as cold mud, Harold was having his own argument with the early dark, still working to harvest the last of the field corn, so he didn't go get Cody. I'd gotten seasonal work at the Toys! Store over in Elmont. Since I'd retired from teaching, money got tight around Christmas, and the training class was that week, noon to eight each day, which meant I couldn't help either one of them. Harold was pressured without me, but Cody was going to spend Sunday helping him in the fields, and Harold said they'd get it done right, work past dusk if they had to. Nicole was always generous when Cody wanted to stay with us of a weekend, though it meant she saw him less. She'd come down for his games, take him out to dinner, and head back. Sometimes she'd let Harold and me take the two of them out to eat, and afterward, if we got a private moment to whisper when we hugged good-bye, Nicole would answer again, *No, I'm not seeing anyone, and I won't until Cody's out of school. He's had enough to adjust to.* She wouldn't stay overnight with us, though I always wanted her to; she said it would cause trouble with Gary, and she was right.

Anyway, Harold always used to keep on going right into darkness when twilight rose skyward off the earth. He'd tell me not to worry, he could see forever down the fields. "The headlights part that field just like a comb on my black hair," he'd say, joking because dark as his hair used to be, it had turned that aluminum grey. His eyebrows had gone grey, too, and bushy the way men's get.

The deer are real in the fields, not fake, the way the drunk driver made one up. Harold and Cody would spot them sliding through growing rows, soundless, or blending into the dun brown of the harvested land, and they'd stop to watch, awed by their wild glory. Because of Cody, Harold had quit hunting. He never went again after he took Cody that one time, the first time the boy had a permit, and saw it all through Cody's tears. Because of Cody, Harold got new eyes for everything that lives on the land and in the skies. That boy was our Grace.

When he was tested, that driver who killed Cody blew

drunk on the Breathalyzer. And he stammered, stammered, when the sheriff asked if the deer was buck or doe. The only witness was Cody, and he was dead.

I called my sister about Cody as soon as I could gather any sounds that made words out of my body, which had become a hoarse sob. She was the only person who said anything sensible. I wish she'd never moved south.

"Just listen to me, Louisa honey," she said. "We know about this. People are going to say a lot of idiot things to you." She meant I should remember what it was like when she had the stillbirth and her first husband left her seven months later. Her voice came soft over the phone. She still sounds like herself, hasn't picked up that Georgia molasses accent. "Just give them the bereavement face and say, 'Bless your heart.' Down here, they teach girls to say that instead of *bullshit*. This is one of the times when people crowd in, nothing anyone says is the least comfort, but no one has the sense to know to shut up. Hang up now so I can get to the airport. I'll be there to hold your right hand, which is the only one you could throw a punch with anyhow." She and Charlie made record time from Atlanta to Indianapolis, where a teacher friend of mine who had Cody for sixth grade picked them up.

CarolSue's quick, practical, and guided me through the motions. When she got here, she took Harold's pickup, drove forty-five minutes to a decent dress store, and bought me a basic black dress, pretty much the same one as she'd packed for herself. I wore her pearls, she wore my old gold chain. I wouldn't have cared if she'd dressed us in bathing suits and put links of sausages around our necks. A couple hundred times, she saved a life when I was struck stupid by what people thought was consolation. Like when people said, "Cody's in a better place," before I could flare and spout, "Really? That's lovely because I want to send you to join him right now," CarolSue would slide in with, "Bless your heart. Won't you excuse us a moment? I believe Harold needs Louisa for something." Her husband, Charlie, made himself useful for once by keeping Harold's ginger ale heavily balanced with bourbon from a flask in his pocket. Anything to get through. I had a few myself. Gary and Nicole were separately seeking strangers in the crowd, their faces like slammed doors.

I try not to blame Harold for leaving me with only Gary just six months after we buried Cody. Sure, I have the girls. Did he really think they would be enough? I can't sleep with them, after all. Maybe Harold figured a heart can only be shattered and left unmendable once, and that had already happened to me, so I'd either go on or I wouldn't. We'll see.

He was so mad at Gary, it made me think it was really at himself. I tried to be like green in the spring telling him it's not your fault, to grow that in his mind, but he kept dousing it with Weed B Gon. Harold tried to make a reason to live out of revenge, and maybe he'd have made a go of it if the sheriff weren't such an efficient imbecile, getting in his way all the time. But Harold didn't manage to be smarter than Gus, with his tin badge and precious gun and his waxed cop car. I should have helped my Harold. He'd have gotten his revenge on that drunk driver, simple revenge, after the law failed us. Maybe it would have been enough. Maybe Harold would still be alive today. I don't know if revenge heals, but maybe it would have let him go on and we could have tried to live again. Now I think revenge is how he got through Vietnam; once his platoon had losses, he got angry enough to fight. To survive. I could be wrong about that. But it's the only way I can understand how he became something he wasn't, did things that weren't in him to do. The war changed him. It was Cody that had changed him back.

With Harold spitting bitterness at Gary for making the boy walk the highway, a silence between them thickened. I knew Gary needed our comfort, but what was I to do? I saw it Harold's way, though my heart was crushed by Gary's mourning as well as Harold's. Where was the space for my own? In my anger over being so pulled between them, I was neither wife nor mother. It was my Harold and his schemes I could have helped when he got crazy with grand revenge notions. But I didn't. It's a wasteful shame I didn't know then how good I'd be at crazy thoughts. I wish I'd tried them sooner.

And this is true, too: I didn't wear it the way my Harold did, but I was mad at Gary, too. Sometimes he'd come, sobbing, and yes, I put my arms around my son, but my heart was cold and sick as I followed the twisting black thread of memory to how he'd first given Nicole reason to leave, and then put Cody on that highway to walk the distance home. Nicole had brought us close to our son in a way Harold and I had both lost for a while. She first, and then the gift of Cody in our lives, had made me—and Harold, too—feel the exquisite tenderness of the bond to Gary, that child we'd once gathered in our arms and held on our laps. Of course I grieved for Gary. *I'm so sorry,* I said, as I held him. *I'm sorry, I'm so sorry, son.* I said it over and over, and perhaps it stood in for I'm so sorry your heart is shattered, my son. And that was true. But did he know, in that way children have of divining a parent's intent, that I was also saying, I'm so sorry you did this, and I'm so sorry I can't tell you that nothing is your fault, and I'm so sorry you didn't do the right things?

So here we are on the subject of fault, and it's only fair that I look for mine. I knew Gary's need was excruciating. He turned to me as a stand-in for his father when Harold couldn't forgive. I can't say I didn't know what he wanted, what he needed. And aren't parents our first stand-ins for God? So maybe those things I couldn't say to Gary make it my fault that he started listening to preachers and revivalists until he found one who was certain, before his tent pushed on to the next county, just how much God liked big cash donations "for the needy" and that, having paid his way, Gary would for sure see Cody in heaven, big as life and twice as real, probably in his football uniform suited up for the Big Devil Game, *if* Gary gave double what he could possibly afford. Then after his father's suicide, Gary decided he better get or-dained on the Internet as an extra layer of heaven travel in-surance, since the Bible says the Sins Of The Father Are Visited Upon . . . et cetera, so it would be Harold's fault if Gary got Left Behind.

Now he calls himself Reverend Gary, and he's trying to start up his own church, with all kinds of new rules he makes up every day from this or that line from the Bible, generally out of some extra-useful Old Testament book like Judges. Or sometimes he jumps right over to Revelations. He's renting a farmhouse ten miles out of town and holds services in the barn, which he got permission to paint white to be more holy, especially since it lacks a steeple as barns generally do. He had a huge banner made for the outside that proclaims, IT'S ALL ABOUT JESUS! in big, black capital letters, because the owner drew the line at painted signage on the building.

If he had to get religion, I wish Gary had joined the Meth-odist church in town like a sensible person. But he was des-perate to expiate what cannot be undone, desperate for forgiveness. What good would it do for him to know what I think about cash donations to a cult that promises that in re-turn? Maybe CarolSue is right that silence is kinder than an indictment if you can't give someone what he wants. I can't give him what he wants, but I know I'm all that Gary has left. What will happen to him when I die? Will he watch me dwindle, giving the last of his money and losing faith because of the miracle that doesn't happen?

My son does all kinds of things to take care of me, most equally useful as Glitter Jesus, and he thinks I don't appreci-ate his efforts to set me straight. He's right about that, but I don't come out and say so. He's not strong, my Gary, with his oval blue eyes and too-red face, his curly blond hair that all makes him look like a raw, oversized, overage angel. People are more fragile than you think. People break. Who knows what could make Gary break? I try to be careful what I say around him even when it's hard. Under all his certainty, I think he might be brittle as cheap glass.

Come to think of it, I might be now, too.

4
Larry

Two guys had taken turns forever pounding on something before they put rubber sheeting over it and got it on a long thing with wheels that slid into the ambulance. It made Larry wonder if it was a drag cart and if they'd put a deer down. The do-gooder was still there, crying now, talking to one of the cops.

They were in the middle of nofreakingwhere, half into the divided highway with its yellow dashes down the middle, the brown stubble of harvested corn poking up as far as the eye could or couldn't see on either side. Cops had set out glow sticks and kept their lights flashing, which was another reason he had to close his eyes. He felt like a bad kid, like he used to when it wasn't his fault but his old man said it was, and his stupid sister and the stupid baby and the stupid dog were always just fine but he was supposed to stop causing trouble, stop doing this and stop doing that, and he got so mad, so mad he wanted to hurt someone for making him feel like crap. It wasn't his fault.

Three cop cars and an ambulance. Who calls an ambulance for a deer, for chrissake? He told the fat cop, told 'em, told 'em the same every time: it was a deer. Another cop, one with eyebrows like woolly worms tryin' to reach each other, got right into Larry's face, too, telling him to touch his finger to his nose, tryin' to shame him like he'd wet the bed, like he was a kid, like everything was his fault, like he coulda helped runnin' into a goddamn deer.

Eyebrows acting like he was the man, putting hands on Larry and cuffing him. Goddamn cop tryin' to make him feel like it was his fault. Reading him his goddamn rights like he was a criminal.

"There was a deer, I told you."

"Well, okay, then, maybe you wanna take a Breathalyzer and that'll show if you saw a deer?" That was Eyebrows talking.

"That'll show I hit a deer?"

"Well . . . that'll show . . . Over there."

"I can sit?"

"Yeah." Eyebrows took his elbow and walked him like he couldn't walk himself to the cop car. Lights glinted off his badge when Larry looked behind him at the ambulance as the doors were shut, blurring lights red, blue, red, blue, red, the last sun over the western field red, the do-gooder's coat, was that red? The light was confusing. The glow sticks were yellow and the ambulance moved. The fat cop was out directing traffic around Larry's truck, cattywampus on the side of the highway, half on the shoulder, who put it like that? A few rubberneckers slowed down. Larry couldn't even give them a one-finger salute because of the cuffs. Eyebrows put his hand on Larry's head like he was a kid and didn't know not to hit his damn head getting in a car. The backseat was caged off from the front.

"You can sit right here in the car. This part goes in your mouth and you blow. Hey, was it a buck? Or maybe a doe?"

"Buck . . . mebbe a doe. How should I know?"

The sun was gone and so was the do-gooder. But the blue and red lights on the cop cars kept spinning and Eyebrows and the fat cop and the other one were still there, and dammit, so was Larry. Larry had needed to sit, he'd just wanted to sit, and they'd let him stay sitting in the cop car while they finished, but they didn't take the cuffs off him and then they didn't let him go.

Fucking liars.

5
Louisa

I hope there *was* a deer in the road, even though I know it's about as likely as the Brooklyn Bridge with Christmas lights plunked down on old Route 50. But even though I know it was the driver's lie, sometimes I comfort myself by imagining that different end for Cody and that a deer was the last thing Cody saw, not the pickup truck careening toward him. I see a beautiful buck standing still for him, trusting, and Cody's eyes wide and soft with pleasure. We're here to teach our children and grandchildren, I know that. But sometimes we see things through their eyes and everything changes. Everything.

It's mainly farms around here, edged by creeks and woods. In deer season, men in orange hats and vests sneak around and lie in wait. Some of them set out corn as a lure. And Harold was one of the hunters. Gary would have been, but he'd quit when it turned out that he was the worst shot since the invention of firearms.

Even though hunting is a featured attraction around here, Harold had never held a gun before he enlisted, but they were a big deal in basic training, and he wrote me that he had a good eye and a steady hand. It was after he got home from the war that he started with the hunting. He said the time alone was good for him, and even though I thought there was more to it, because he still had those dreams, I tried not to argue because it made things worse. At least he never sat in a blind where corn had been set out as a lure. My Harold was better than that. After all, those deer weren't trying to kill him.

The year that Cody was twelve, two years after my dad died, Harold and I had to sell Mom's house and have her move in with us. Harold had taken Cody out hunting with him for the last few days; we were having the mysterious gift of an Indian summer in mid-November that coincided with deer season. I was banging around the kitchen slamming drawers with my hip and muttering, "Nothing lasts in this house."

I winced and looked around, hoping I was alone. Mom hadn't been living with us long enough for me to remember to shut up when I was searching for what she'd put in some bizarre place, say ketchup in the freezer. But what I'd said bothered me like a bad omen. All I'd meant—at least at the moment—was that the spatula had disappeared, but the whole point of Mom living with us was so that she would last. I'd said it to Harold: *If we don't take her in, honey, she'll never last.*

I was in a terrible mood. Nearly eligible for retirement and the great state of Indiana had decided that all teachers had to pass a CPR test in order to keep their jobs, never mind that I'd been working twenty-five years and didn't have the name of a single dead student posted under mine.

The Saturday morning I'm remembering was dismal, a grudging sky over the fields, and I'd had to grain our two horses after I made Mom's breakfast, which made me late to class. Like I was the fifth grader, the instructor made me demonstrate what he'd been showing everyone, which I didn't exactly know because I was late. But big, dumb Re-susci Annie was lying on the floor, just waiting for me to restart her heart. Wouldn't I love for someone to restart mine some mornings?

I'd read the manual, though, so I found the spot and crossed my hands a notch above her sternum and I pumped and blew my life into hers, like I did every day with the kids in my class and my family, my life right into theirs. I got tired, like I did worrying over them. And the chickens and the livestock, not that we had much. I felt like screaming at Annie to buck up, for God's sake, get up, go on, *live, live, live.* No such luck. The small green life light just flickered like a tease and then went out, meaning, I guess, that while I didn't exactly kill her, I didn't save her, either.

When I got home to Mom, she was all stooped over and looking like a sneeze would knock her to the floor. She was thick enough around the middle and the hump of her back, but her arms and legs were so frail they put me in mind of dry sticks. I look at myself naked in the mirror now and I see my body evolving or devolving into hers. Mom's palsy had gotten worse and worse. The way her head moved back and forth, it looked like she was saying, "No, no, no," constantly. It grated me like cheese back then. Now I wonder if she was saying, *No, I do not want this to be happening to me,* and I wish I could tell her that I finally understand.

"What's going to happen to me, Louisa? I'm all alone. Daddy's gone. I've got nobody," she used to say, which made me want to tear out fistfuls of my hair. Or maybe hers. But I always tried to keep my voice patient and nice when I answered.

"You're not all alone, Mom. You've got me and Harold. We'll take care of you. And you know how Cody loves you. A great-grandson, Mom. Now that's something special. You can't let Cody down." Which was sort of switching the point, I know. I just used whatever might work.

"You don't understand. You can't understand. But you're a good daughter, Louisa, and I'm proud of how you went to college. First in the family ever. My breasts are gone, have you noticed? See?" she said, running her hands down the front of her blowsy shirt and working her body toward profile. Her breathing whistled through her false teeth like a February wind, and her body was cold to the touch. Sometimes, I couldn't help it, I used to think of a chicken overly stewed and left to chill, the way her flesh seemed to be falling away from her body.

"No, Mom, I hadn't seen that," I'd lie, "but I think it's just normal." Oh, she was right, I didn't understand. I hope she didn't know what I felt.

Ours was always a random sort of a farm, acres of field corn backing up to Rush Run, the broad creek that runs behind it like a vein to the river, cutting its way through a mile-wide stand of old forest. Back then we had Alcott, Cody's roan gelding, my beautiful flock of laying hens, and Bronson, the rooster; Ralph, the sheep—don't ask me why—and Emerson and Thoreau, the yellow Labs. May and Marvelle presided in the barn. And our goat, Rose, had the yard much of the year. Harold could not abide mowing and we got her between the time Gary left home and Cody was old enough to mow. But by then Rose was taking care of the patchy yard grass well, and giving milk, besides.

You see how little remains. What's that expression? *Life turns on a dime.* Or a blink. Or a drink. A mistake. Someone else's. Your own.

But about the deer. The whole thing goes back to Mom and that same day after I got home from my CPR class. It had cleared to a gorgeous late sun. Harold was taking Cody hunting for the first time that year. He had taught him to shoot, and Cody had a gift with soup cans. *He's good,* Harold used to marvel. *What a shot.*

Harold had talked up how great it would be to hunt together, and Cody automatically wanted to do whatever his grandpa did. Mom didn't want Harold to take Cody, and told Cody not to go. She'd lived in town all her life and couldn't accept it. I tried to explain hunting to her the way Harold had first explained it to me, but the words weren't mine and got stuck between my heart and my mouth. The truth is I think he liked having charge over something, as men do. Maybe when you make something else die, you don't think about dying yourself, you think you're bigger than dying.

Cody was antsy. He hadn't gotten his deer yet; it was the last day of the season and there'd be no more chances until next year. Twilight was coming on and he was going to lose his bet with Harold, which probably was for all of fifty cents. I was out by the barn emptying the heads of dead flowers into the compost when he came trudging up from the fields toward the house. He'd been all day in the woods our back fields skirt, trying for his deer. Harold wasn't hunting then, just keeping an eye on Cody, which I'd been glad for, thinking that at least I knew he couldn't accidentally shoot Cody. I didn't know that it was the only thing I wouldn't ever have to worry about. After that day, Harold would quit hunting forever.

"I need bullets," Cody called to me, a slump of crimson dejection in no big hurry, his long shadow preceding him, rifle over his shoulder the way Harold had taught him. "Only one left in the chamber. Didn't bring enough." He'd taken shots and missed. I'd known about the shots; faint retorts had come from our south side much earlier when I was hanging wash on the line.

It was by pure chance that I spotted it, plainly out in the second field that drops down to our woods, where Rush Run hurries on to get to another world. I gestured to Cody, who was nearly to the back step by then. The deep-blue and purple-grey shadows edging out from the woods kept me from seeing whether it was buck or doe, and Cody only had a youth permit for buck—but later the boy said he'd spotted the huge rack shining as though by moonrise or last sun, like something not quite of this earth, as he reversed and turned toward his target in the russet of late autumn. I even prayed. "Dear God," I said. "Let my grandson get that deer; he's only got one bullet."

What was I *thinking*?

I went in. Then I heard the gun. It was close enough that Mom did, too, even upstairs in her room, and, of course, it scared her pale, until I told her what Cody was after.

"If he got it, have him bring it around so I can see it up close," she said. Mom was trying, I could tell, she was trying to keep a hold on herself, to listen to me and get used to it here, to put things in what I'd said were their right places. I even asked her again.

"Are you sure, Mom? You know, it's different from what you're used to." I didn't want to tell her that I'd never gotten used to *this*, only pretended to for my husband.

"I told you, Louisa, have him bring it around."

I watched between the yellow print curtains at the kitchen window for Cody to come back while I started supper. Our rooster, Bronson, was perched on the head of the cement goose Harold had bought at the fair, his idea of a joke because I'd said I'd like some geese in our little back pond. When Harold set it outside the back door, poor Bronson went mad, squawking and flapping and trying to mate with the goose every day. Even Mom bent over laughing. He'd give up after a while and sit on the goose's head or back, pecking at her every once in a while trying to rouse her, before he went back to the hens. He used to put me in mind of Mom, wattles beneath her chin and hanging from her upper arms, longing for what's not there.

Then Harold came running up toward the house waving to me.

"Cody got his buck! It's beautiful, it's beautiful! I saw him take it down. What a shot." The storm door slapped behind him. "He needs the truck to get it. Where'd I leave the ropes?" Harold was so happy for Cody, all sweating and flushed and breathing like a trumpeter gone to heaven. I told him when he had it, to bring the truck around underneath Mom's window so she could see it, too.

When I heard the truck bumping up the pasture, I went upstairs to get Mom over to her window. When Harold stopped, Cody looked like he tumbled out of the passenger side. He ran for the house, Mom and I looking out the window as he did. Mom stared down. I looked over her shoulder into the bed of the truck. We could see the size of the hole in the buck's neck, the crimson spread out on the brown. Thin forelegs bent at the joint almost as though he was still running. I could see the heart convulsing on the way it does, maybe forty minutes, even if it's taken out, but I didn't know if Mom's eyes were good enough to catch it. I couldn't get dumb Annie's heart going like that if I pumped her chest and blew her into tomorrow.

I heard Cody on the stairs. "Grandma?" he called, hoarse-voiced, and I didn't answer because Mom was falling apart, crying and crying on me like a stone dissolving in water, and I held her. I laughed at first; she'd *said* she wanted to see. I looked down at the old buck as I held her, and then Cody came into the room, his face a red blear, sobbing, "Grandma, I'm sorry, I'm so sorry, I'm so sorry." Mom melted into my arms, heavy, her tears all over me until I could hardly stand up. I looked outside at the old buck again, then at Cody, needing me, but my arms were already full and I felt her thick, ancient body on spindly legs giving out beneath her, and my tears now, all over her. The thready blue pulse in her neck buried into mine, as if all the water were blood and flowing together down to Rush Run where the deer drink.

6

I never let myself believe there was a connection, not *really*, but Mom only lived another nine months after Cody shot the deer and the sadness of it broke their hearts. I fought her the whole time. It was like a long, long losing battle with Resusci Annie. I never could pump enough air and life into Mom, though I'd passed CPR and kept my job and no fifth graders had heart attacks that year anyway. Mom perked up for show when CarolSue came for weeks at a time, but no smiles reached her eyes and we weren't fooled. It was a natural death and no one's failure, but then Harold took Cody's death as his and carried it into a dark secret place. "I should have gone to pick him up, let the goddamn corn rot," he said once after Cody was gone, and then, when it was pointless, he *did* let it rot, though he had a buyer needing it. After Harold was gone, too, I had to pay to clear the land so that it could be planted when the seasons came around again. It felt all backward, but I had to have income.

Back when we first bought the farm, and I mean put ourselves in debt for life, we had a learning curve that was perpendicular. The place had come with some leftover chickens. Yes, alive. Everything we knew about chickens was nothing. What were we thinking?

I can tell you exactly what we were thinking: Oh! It will be *great!* We'll be so *happy.* It will be good for Harold, get him out of the machine shop where it smells like the artillery he worked on in Vietnam. How hard can it be, after all? It's good land. You put in seeds and they grow, right? You get a horse for the boy, the horse grazes. Maybe you get a goat or two, because farms are supposed to have them, right? You feed chickens, they lay eggs. Right?

Well, we were right about some of that. We did end up happy. The rest was a little more complicated. We agreed that the chickens and whatever other animals we'd acquire would be my responsibility, because tending to them could be done after school. This turned out to be a good deal; the job of keeping chickens was the easiest farm chore to learn. Until it started to get really hard, but that was my fault: I named them and I tamed them.

It didn't take me long to tell them apart, and see how different their personalities were. The flock of thirteen was of mixed breeds, and believe me, a Rhode Island Red looks nothing like an Ameraucana, for example. They took to eating out of my hand, and letting me pat them. I started letting them out of the coop to roam the yard because I saw how happy it made them. Harold said I was delusional, thinking I knew when *chickens* were happy. "So, honey, do they show their teeth when they grin if they're happy?" he said. But I *did* know.

I learned how to manage the coop: how to water, what to feed, how much straw bedding was best for the enclosed roost and laying boxes, how they'd always go into the roost on their own, just before dark, and that I didn't have to worry about that! I learned about predators. The former owner had written a few notes that added up to "There's nothing to it; feed 'em and collect the eggs." But I was a teacher. Teachers know how to look things up.

What to do with all the eggs? At first it wasn't so bad because by the time we moved, it was November twentieth, and laying had fallen off because there was so much less daylight. I had failed to read up on this, or it just hadn't registered. We weren't getting too many more eggs than we could use in order to send our cholesterol counts through the barn roof, and the rest I'd just give to friends when I had an overflow of a couple dozen saved up. In January, the laying stopped completely and I relaxed. Then spring came. By March I was collecting eleven eggs a day, and on April Fools' Day—an irony not lost on me—it was thirteen. Seems the flock must have been young and productive, according to my hurried catch-up reading. I started taking eggs to school for other teachers. Pretty soon I was hunting for new gift victims.

Then Harold, wouldn't you know it was Harold, decided it was time to make some money on this operation, and for that, we'd need more eggs, not fewer. Instead of just getting additional hens, even though yes, it can be touchy to add adults to a flock, wouldn't you know Harold showed up with Bronson. In a borrowed *cat* carrier!

A rooster. Bronson looked darn happy to see his new harem. Flexing his monster thighs, Bronson strode into the run, red comb the biggest in the run, and started bossing the girls around. The hens didn't waste any time with discussing things or organizing nonviolent protests. Pandemonium.

"Just women fighting over a man," Harold said. "Your department. Don't get hurt," and remembered something urgent he had to do in the barn, leaving the resident chicken expert to deal with this mess.

And what a mess it was. When you really have no idea what you're doing and wade into it because you're dumb enough to fall in love with land, buy a farm, and think you can just work it out as you go along, well, maybe it's better not to know ahead.

I knew that Anna, my gorgeous blossom-white Ameraucana, was a dominant sort, but I'd never quite realized that she was the Queen of the Coop. Until Bronson strutted on in. His breed was Barred Rock, I later learned, and he'd been hand-raised by a farmer Harold had met at the Tractor Supply who didn't have enough chickens for his two roosters anymore and was smart enough not to want more. So he'd brought in his younger one for the first taker at the Supply. Bronson was a handsome, big, black-and-white boy with an impressive red comb; I could see why Harold had been seduced. Of course, as relatively little as I knew about chickens, I was at least reading and learning. Everything Harold knew, he made up on the spot and it would stand as fact until I caught on.

Anna had seven of the other hens backing her up. I have never imagined an Unwelcome Wagon of quite such a magnitude. Bronson probably hadn't been getting much action as the beta rooster where he'd been, because he pretty much took it. After the first day or so, though, Anna was in love and from then on, she and Bronson were an item.

And that's how I ended up raising chickens. So we—meaning I—could sell eggs. Of course, what Harold didn't know was that one rooster can only handle so many chickens. I mean, *really*. Even those guys out west who believe it's okay to have a lot of wives stop at some number, don't they? Harold also didn't realize that there's not two cents of profit in selling eggs if you take good care of your birds, or that Bronson's arrival meant that we'd need a brood box.

Harold built the brood box himself. We waited to see what would happen. Soon enough, my Buff Orpington hen named Lulu went broody again, irritable and pecking at my hand to drive me off when I went in to the nesting box to pick up her egg one morning. By the next day she seemed like she was in a trance on the nest, determined and immovable. So I put her in the brood box Harold had constructed in what probably used to be a tool room in the barn. He'd followed instructions: it had a wire floor and straw, a feeder and water, and room for her to move around when she wanted. What would I have done without the library? Lulu settled herself on top of some golf balls I borrowed from the gym teacher at school. The next evening, I snuck out the golf balls, and eased a clutch of nine eggs underneath her, two of them her own.

How fast new farmers have to learn. Three weeks later, I

called in sick to school because I could hear the faint peeps from inside the shells and saw the first cracks in two of them when Lulu briefly got off the clutch to eat.

"Oh my God, Harold, you can't miss this," I insisted. And he did come watch with me, but he didn't get obsessed the way I did. I couldn't tear myself away from watching the pointy end of the eggs be slowly punched out, and a damp, scrawny baby emerge in jerky fits and starts, unfolding impossibly bigger than the confines of the shell, resting open-eyed between motions, exhausted by the effort of birthing itself. Six of the nine eggs hatched. I'd candled them all on the tenth day, holding the egg up to a flashlight to check for the shadow of an embryo, but I must have seen a wish in some, or just been lucky on the rest. For most of the first few years on the farm, whatever worked was a matter of dumb luck.

I tell all this as a way of showing that I experienced awe and death, and then I thought it was a useful combination to know about. Of course, the first time Harold drove the combine was a disaster; there's an art to raising and lowering the head to avoid rocks while keeping close to the smallest rises of the land. A lot of it is instinct. Or talent, perhaps. There are combine drivers and combine operators. The operators are the ones so good at it that the head of the combine very rarely gets wrecked.

Harold became an operator. He loved it all, too: the pale green of the undulating land when the crop first broke through the dark earth. It was a life and it *was* life. And I know how ordinary it all sounds, and it was. The cycles were natural and we lived with them.

When Mom died, terrible as I felt, there was a certain timeliness to it. The losses then were painful but not enraging. Can you see how and why that life would heal a man who'd been to war? It did. Yes, he did hunt once a year, and I tell you now it wasn't something I understood—that he'd take himself back to those primal memories—but maybe it was how he contained and limited them.

In those years, life proceeded on a course that made a certain sense. Even the vagaries of weather. If you accepted the natural world, when erratic heavens heaved spring hail a month before white-sky heat seared the fields, you might worry and grieve, but you were part of it, and it of you.

You see now, don't you? We were in that life. We could still laugh, we could cope, we could always go on. Then a drunk driver killed a boy, and six months later to the day, a stricken grandfather waited until nearly five o'clock. He kissed his wife and left her in their yellow kitchen, where she'd just turned on the light, saying he was going to make a pickup. ("What are you picking up?" she might have asked, but didn't, being distracted by peeling carrots. Did she think at the time—had she *ever* thought?—how much she would wish she had truly kissed him back right then or said some soft good words to him before he left?) He drove in twilight to the spot on the highway marked with a flat white river rock, where they'd gone every Friday with a small baggie of soil from their own farm (their grandson's "best place in the world"), and emptied it at the spot where their grandson's broken body had been thrown by the drunk driver's truck. The potatoes had been peeled and were roasting, the kitchen gathering fragrance, when her husband parked his pocked Silverado near his intention. She'd made him a meat loaf with bacon on top that night. It had taken effort. He left the keys under the front seat, two baggies of soil on the passenger side his only message to her, and he waited for the moment he felt a deer's heartbeat somewhere beating with his grandson's and stepped out in front of the Dwayne County Waste Recycling truck.

Not one thing natural, not one thing natural about any of it.

7

"The Plan, CarolSue. I need The Plan. Ha. Remember how Oma used to say 'What's The Plan?' every day when she stayed with us?" I said.

"It drove Mom crazy. Used to call Oma 'Mussolini.' Not to her face. But close. Remember the time she asked her how the trains were running?"

"No. Was I there? I bet she *meant* Hitler."

"Would've been going too far," she said, her voice sure. "She knew right when to back off." Sometimes I think Carol-Sue remembers Mom better than I do. It scares me. I cannot lose my mind. What if I couldn't remember Harold? Who would I be?

I inspected my tea for depth of color, pulled the bag out, squashed it against the lip of the mug. Harold always wanted coffee. "I'm surprised she didn't do it, though." As if I, too, could still hear more than isolated snippets of Mom's words in my memory. "Anyway, I need The Plan. Help me. You're the one who got the Mussolini gene—you look just like Oma and got her brains, so this is your department."

"Do you want my help, or do you plan to continue insulting me while I run up my phone bill?"

CarolSue's voice is a consolation and I always keep her on the phone as long as I can, not caring much what she says. Or I hadn't until then.

I took my tea to the couch and sat, annoying Marvelle,

who had stretched to her full black-and-white length across the two cushions. She gave me the evil eye and I gave her one back, practicing for the day.

"Yes. I want your help."

"You're not gonna go limp? I mean, you haven't been exactly clear thinking since it happened."

"Well, now who's insulting who?"

"That would be *whom*, teacher. You're making my point."

"I *know* that. I correct *you* all the time. You're just making me mad now. I *am* clear thinking. Lord, CarolSue. So I miss a pronoun. Have *you* got Glitter Jesus leaving shiny specks all over your carpet, making you think you've got floaters in your eye?"

"I know, it's . . ."

"—No, you don't. Because you also don't have Gary's Ladies' God Squad members calling you every damn day. It goes like this, 'Sister Louisa, this is your prayer line calling. It's all about Jesus! Do you have any questions troubling your heart today?'"

"And I hate to ask what you answer. . . ."

"I *want* to scream, 'What are you talking about? *What* is all about Jesus? Exactly *what*? Is that supposed to be some sort of answer? Some sort of comfort? Because I have no idea what you're talking about and I don't believe you do, either. Nobody *knows*.' But I've learned it's a mistake to say anything. Because when people are convinced of something that's unknowable, there's no point. So I just say, 'No thanks, I'm fine.' And then they say, 'Donations for the prayer call line may be sent to 3526 Lords Way, Rossville, Indiana. Have a *great* day.' In a very annoying chipper voice. That's Gary's address, in case you don't recognize it."

"I recognize it," CarolSue said quietly. "Stop answering the phone. You can see when it's me. Just answer when it's me. Or Gary himself, I guess."

"You know that'll bring him out here. Or he'll send Gus. Or both."

"Yeah. I guess you can start by telling him you don't care to be God-stalked." She snorted her laugh. "If worse comes to worst, tell him it's all made you into an atheist."

"That might be true."

"Well, that's okay, too. I don't think it really matters what we believe. Doesn't change the nature of reality one way or another, does it? Say whatever you need to say."

". . . but maybe he loves me." I resettled the phone to my ear, closer in the silence. I heard myself sigh as if I were someone else.

"There's that," she said.

"Like you always say."

"He tries so hard to please you."

"Not with this cult thing."

She sighed. "I know. But he's completely sincere and he has a good heart. Look what he's been through, losing his only child." She didn't need to say more. From CarolSue, that's a loaded gun. Raised and pointed. There's a reason she defends Gary automatically, both of them life members of a terrible exclusive club they were forced to join against their wills.

My heart beat on for a few minutes. CarolSue waited. She always does. "There's so much to weep over," I said. "This morning I put on Harold's blue plaid shirt, the one that's maybe ten years old. He wore it the day before he died and it was still in the hamper. Thank God I hadn't done the laundry."

"Gratitude," CarolSue said. "For one small thing. You could just start from there."

"Yes. I know. Okay. I'll try that." And I did. I think I gave it an honest try after we hung up. I thought about it. I thought about gratitude. For certain sweet memories. For what remains. I ran it by Marvelle, and then I discussed it with the other girls. I even vacuumed, thinking that might clear the feathers from my mind as well as from the kitchen floor. In the end, though, I ended up calling CarolSue back.

"It's not enough. The shirt doesn't really smell like Harold anymore. I want The Plan."

My sister sighed. We both take after Mom with the sighing. But then there was her voice, chipper and strong. "Okay, then. First step is to clarify the objective beyond just saying *revenge*."

"I want The Plan that will make Larry Ellis lose everything. Like I have." Marvelle opened one eye to indicate *Finally*, something vaguely interesting.

"You haven't lost *everything*. And you are *not* going to kill his family. Or him." CarolSue, ever practical, ever literal.

"Spoilsport. Where are you right now?" I said. I always like to visualize that though I've been to her house just once, when she and Charles got married eight years ago. She's been the one to do all the traveling, to come home.

"Sunroom, and *no*, he's out messing with crap in the garage, bless his heart."

I could picture her then, curled up on the overstuffed sofa in my favorite part of her house, where she's got some of Mom's and Grandma's things: one of the cherry rockers, an end table, a braided rug Grandma made, and framed family pictures. The image was comforting. (I'm not so fond of Carol-Sue's living room, elegant, formal, graceful lamps, art and drapes picked by a decorator as was the upholstered furniture in fabrics and colors so delicate a farm woman is uncomfortable sitting on them, even knowing full well she's just showered and doesn't even need to check her shoes because there's no barnyard in a retirement community of fancy patio homes.)

I knew she'd be all put together, in slacks and a coordinating pressed blouse, because she's always coordinated and pressed and wears nice shoes that don't need polish or new heels like mine. Her eyes are hydrangea-blue, wide-spaced above high cheekbones that keep you from even noticing the normal lines around her mouth. CarolSue is two years older but looks five—sometimes ten—years younger than I do. She's strong, stands straight, and gets her girls up high with a good bra. She hasn't let herself get blousy with that rose-dropping-its-petals look that I've accidentally mastered. She's a looker, thanks to having her teeth whitened and a real knack for eye makeup. She's got fashion sense and can pull off that new kind of haircut that looks like a small animal chewed its way around the ends. Her hands are the oldest-looking part of her, though she polishes her nails and uses lotion morning and night.

"Okay," I said. "Just checking. I don't want to kill him. Well, yes I do. When can you come?"

"Louisa. Stop. Harold wasn't intending to kill him. He could have *done* that. Killing him has bad idea written all over it. No. I say, first thing you've got to find out is what Larry Ellis really, really cares about."

"Are you putting me off? Are you coming or not?"

"Well, of course I'll come as soon as I can. I have a doctor's appointment, I mean, Charlie has one. I do, too, actually. Let me get through those, and—"

"What's wrong? What haven't you told me? When's your appointment?" I swung my feet to the floor and Marvelle stirred.

"Oh honey, it's nothing. You know, the annual junk for me, next Wednesday afternoon. Charlie's PSA was a little high. It'll be fine."

"Are you scared?"

"It's just age," she said, meaning no. It scared me, though.

"Yeah. Harold's ran a little high, too. But you'll tell me what's going on, right?"

"Of course. But right now, you come first."

8

Probably I was distracted by worry, but I didn't focus right in on where CarolSue was headed when she said I had to find out what Larry Ellis really cares about.

I learned his name first from the newspaper the day after Cody was killed. No face then, of course. Someone saved the newspaper for me so I'd know about the arraignment for vehicular manslaughter and DUI. The judge let him post bond. I was so caught up with restraining Harold that I hardly noticed my own feelings. And later, as much as Harold was obsessed with Larry Ellis, I wanted no image of that man. I was hanging on to every mind picture of Cody, scared at how they were fading; I wouldn't cede an iota of space to Larry Ellis.

I didn't read the newspaper my teacher friend kept for me, and I shook my head and moved away when people talked about him. I was running scared about how to keep Cody's toothy grin in my mind, the dark hair that he'd started to gel, the blue of his eyes. What was the exact color? Was it really the same as CarolSue's, or had they leaned grey, influenced by the hazel of Nicole's? I was frantic going through pictures, trying to find one that showed the precise color of his eyes. To think he'd been so embarrassed when his voice was changing—like a road full of potholes—and proud when there was enough hair on his face to shave. That erratic, splotchy new beard, and his eyebrows thickening up, too. He'd started to get some pimples. Boy and man converging in his physical being, past and future in the moment of confluence. But he'd not churned mean in that way of teenagers, not with us, anyway. Not that look of dissatisfaction or scorn. (Not at Harold or me, though Gary complained about back talk and attitude, and said, "Of course he's not like that with *you*. You two don't see that side of him." I liked to think that we didn't give him reason, but maybe that's not fair. Nicole wouldn't have told us if he gave her a hard time.) I replayed my memories of his face—the interested, warm, happy, grateful expressions I'd read and saved at the time, but oh, not savored and memorized well enough. Not enough. And what had his hands looked like exactly?

So while Harold laser-focused on Larry Ellis, I buried myself in remembering. We might as well have been in separate states. That's why I didn't have anything to go on when CarolSue said I needed to find out what Larry Ellis cares about. Harold would have known exactly. I didn't even know what he looked like.

Sometimes you have to push yourself to do the very hard thing that part of you is determined to do and part of you has no faith you can accomplish. (Yes, that word should be *difficult*, as *hard* refers to a physical property, and I always insisted my students use language correctly, but oh! today it just felt so terribly *hard*.)

After my Sunday afternoon talk with CarolSue, I had a nice glass of sherry with Marvelle and the girls. Marvelle and I had seconds. She couldn't finish hers so I did, not to waste it. We all talked over the steps I need to climb. (Or stumble up—Beth politely suggested that could happen. Yes, as you've probably noticed by now, I do talk to the girls when CarolSue isn't available. Don't you talk to your pets and don't you think you know what they would say back? Try to remember that I'm really no different from you, except maybe more alone.) I wrote a list as we figured it out:

a. **Look up what happened to Larry Ellis in court.** I had never let anyone tell me, not really. I knew he'd basically gotten off. I couldn't help but get the drift. Harold had been in the courtroom willing every word out of the prosecutor's mouth, every word the judge should have said. He'd gone in breathing fire and been left cold and sooty until he started with his personal retribution schemes. But I didn't want to hear about it, not any of it. I've said why. But because I'd stuck my fingers in my ears, I never did have notion number one about the man who took Cody's life and then Harold's. Or maybe it was Gus who took Harold's, thwarting him the way he did. Or maybe it was I, who never helped him.

But I digress. I'm not myself. I don't know who I am, though. Once I was a teacher, even if I did have trouble sticking to the curriculum, which wasn't challenging enough, and was considered mouthy by the administration. And once I was a mother and a grandmother and a farm wife. Now I'm none of those. I've been aimlessly looking for the point of my remaining life somewhere between the canned soup and the boxed macaroni and cheese in my cupboard. Once upon a time I cooked meals, you see, but I have no interest in that anymore.

Amy and JoJo both cluck at me to get on with The Plan. Knowing what happened in court isn't a Plan, they coo.

b. Oh! I have it now: **Look up Larry Ellis's arrest record.** That will give me his address, his age, and his picture. When I came up with this idea, JoJo positively sparkled with pride. She'd been behind the couch, so there was a bit of Glitter Jesus residue on her enhancing the impression, but I could tell from her excited flaps as she hopped onto her favorite wingback chair that she thought this was a dandy.

c. **Follow him.** How else can I find out what he cares about? Marvelle opened one yellow-green eye when I came up with that, an idea so good it roused even her. If you secretly watch someone's life, doesn't he show you what he cares about whether he means to or not?

9
Brandon

Ever since Larry, his mother's boyfriend, had killed a kid Brandon's age, his mother had been crazy. For one, she'd cleaned out her savings to get him an expensive lawyer and pay his fines, even though that money was supposed to help Brandon go to the community college after he graduated. She'd always said it was for him, because his absentee father occasionally paid her off when she threatened to take him to court. Not only that, but the other way she went crazy was how she cried a lot about the kid who died, saying she felt so bad for his mother, who she found out was single, too. Her face would be all wet against Brandon's and her arms around his neck, which was pretty uncomfortable, but he didn't pull away because she couldn't exactly cry on Larry right then. But it wasn't like she knew the kid or his mother; they lived in another town. Still, if he let himself think about it, which was why he didn't, Brandon couldn't fathom himself being here one minute and wiped-out-dead the next because of some random guy. There was no point to it. Brandon thought about how his English teacher had suggested he read *The Catcher in the Rye* for his book review, and the part of the opinion he'd written was that Holden Caulfield was way too cynical, but now he thought that he'd been wrong. He heard the kid Larry killed had been a football player and Brandon was, like, so not one of those. But when you're dead what difference does that make anyway?

His mother wanted to go to the dead kid's funeral, to pay respects and tell the family sorry, sorry, sorry, but Larry's attorney got wind of it and said absolutely not. That made his mother cry more. He said she couldn't even send a card. Nothing.

Brandon figured it was obvious Larry had been drunk again; his mother even knew he'd failed the Breathalyzer, but Larry told her those were way off all the time and he'd swerved because he'd seen a deer in the road. Bullshit, Brandon thought. He didn't say that to his mother. She was upset enough, and for a while didn't want him leaving the house, not even over to Dudley's, which was plain ridiculous. She was scared something random and pointless would happen to him, too, he guessed, even though Brandon was pretty sure it doesn't work that way. It wasn't like he and Dud were doing anything wrong. The dead kid hadn't been doing anything wrong either, so maybe it didn't much matter what you did. Dud had a PlayStation 3, which was still cool even though the PlayStation 4 had sixteen times the RAM. Brandon's mother said, "I don't like having you on the road, is all. Have him over here. You can order pizza." Finally Dud's mother called after Dud told her what was going on.

"Hey, LuAnn, my computer froze up again. Can I borrow Brandon to come fix it? Dudley doesn't know what's up this time." The truth was that Dud could fix their computer just fine since it wasn't frozen, but his mom was nice to do them a solid. Brandon's mother had relented and that sort of broke the spell, though she wanted him to call when he got wherever he was going. That wasn't so bad and he got his own cell phone out of it. Finally.

Larry was out of jail in three days. To hear him complain you'd have thought he'd been locked up for three years. Personally, Brandon would have been fine with it if Larry had been locked up forever—he deserved it. When she was rushing off to pay Larry's bond, his mother said Larry was going to pay them back. "He owes me big-time, honey. He'll be good to you, and you need a dad," she said.

Two counts of bullshit, Brandon thought to himself. Never gonna happen, either one. For one thing, his mother had also told him it would be "helpful" if he'd get a job as soon as possible. "That way there's more time to save for college," she'd said, so Brandon knew he was right about the money. He didn't say it out loud. He really tried not to upset her. She was always wanting him to spend time with Larry, be pals, do things together. She'd spent Brandon's whole life trying to find him a dad, for God's sake, a role in which Brandon could see Larry had zero interest. Not that Brandon wanted him in it. Personally, he didn't like Larry. The guy had a mean edge his mother didn't want to see. Larry wasn't smart either, like he wouldn't know a hard drive from a remote control but thought he knew everything.

Brandon didn't mention any of these things to his mother after the beginning when he realized she needed him not to. It made him sad that she was sort of desperate and went for creeps. Like that time she said she'd tripped and fell right on her face. Whatever. Maybe. He didn't know what to believe about the bruises but he had his suspicions, and if he ever knew for sure that Larry hit his mother, Brandon would kill him.

Brandon loved his mother. The noise from the master bedroom a lot of nights meant his mother liked Larry. A lot. Or needed him. And Brandon didn't particularly want to move again. He'd been talking to a girl named Emily at school and now that he had a cell phone he could text her, which was cool because he could read what he was saying and think about it before he pushed send. It helped him avoid embarrassing himself by saying something stupid like he had in the cafeteria when Emily said she was going to the Girls' Room.

If Larry actually made Brandon's mother happy like she claimed, Brandon could deal with it.

10
Louisa

In Indiana, driving under the influence is a Class A misdemeanor. A first offense can result in up to a year in jail, up to
a five-thousand-dollar fine, plus court costs and fees, and up
to one year probation. A violator also gets a ninety-day license suspension. But that suspension can be for pleasure driving
only if the violator has a decent attorney, one who gets it changed
to one hundred eighty days of a probationary license for
work, education, and probation purposes after the first thirty
days of more serious inconvenience.

That's all Larry Ellis was found guilty of. Not drunk and
"causing serious bodily harm" (yes, I'd say *dead* would qual-
ify as serious bodily harm), making it a Class C misdemeanor. Because he said there was a deer in his way, and he'd
panicked and swerved—just a bit, but it was enough because
Cody was walking with traffic instead of against it—that he
hadn't known what to do, "being more a city type," as his
lawyer put it.

I know about this because I paid in the courthouse for a
recording of the trial. Oma was right about the necessity of a
Plan. I just got up and went to the Dwayne County Courthouse and found someone to ask. A middle-aged woman
whose roots needed touching up told me where to go. She
was sitting in an office by herself and when she looked up she
smiled at me, like it was fine to be asking for this information. The scarlet lipstick on her teeth made me feel strangely

all right. I straightened my posture, hoisted my purse back up on my shoulder, and found the clerk's office. There, a brown-haired girl with wire-rimmed glasses around eyes too much like Cody's, blue and long-lashed, made the disc for me. She looked like she was sixteen herself, though she wore a small diamond on her left hand. (Take off those glasses! I wanted to beg her, and let me look at your eyes, but of course, I didn't.)

I brought the disc home and listened after supper. Sherry and company helped; I propped the kitchen door open so the girls could come in or not as they pleased, and all three chose to be with me, making their soft noises in comfort as it progressed, and I wiped my eyes and face over and over. The defense lawyer was just smarter and faster than the prosecutor. There was a substitute judge in from Elmont because Judge Kane's wife had died of cancer on the sixteenth of the month. He wasn't expected back on the bench until March. I'd known Margie in high school. Even knew she was sick. Why hadn't I sent a card?

"No wonder Harold lost his mind. Three days? Larry Ellis was sentenced to time served, three days? Probation? Who cares about probation? A hundred and eighty days of only driving to work and probation? Who cares? He probably has friends and a family to take care of the rest, if he even stuck to the restriction. A five-thousand-dollar fine? Bless someone's heart, that helps out the Great State of Indiana, I guess, but doesn't do a damn thing for Cody now, does it?" I ranted to CarolSue after twilight when I'd closed the girls into the coop for the night. I'd stayed to watch them head to the roost, as all chickens will do at the brink of darkness, their reliable and unfailing instinct to keep themselves safe. Oh my Cody, my Harold.

"A civil suit was the obvious thing to do," CarolSue said gently. "You know, like Nicole Brown Simpson's family after that O.J. travesty."

I knew I must have gotten her out of bed. She was probably in her bright pink lounging pajamas, the ones with the matching zipper jacket. I imagined her pulling it on while she held the phone tucked between shoulder and ear, then switching it to the other side. She'd never tell me that, though. She'd lie and say she was still up and pad out to the family room in her fuzzy mules, switching on the ginger jar lamp that sits like a fat Buddha on the rattan table out there. She'd sit in the soft half-circle of amber light the lamp lays on the red loveseat.

"I'm really sorry to call so late," I said. "You knew all this, I'm sure."

"Yes. I asked and Harold told me."

"Did you ask him about a civil suit, too? Oh, never mind. What's that about but money? Does money bring Cody back? It's too much like being paid for . . ."

"For all I know, he did."

"File a suit?"

"I wouldn't *know*. Harold mentioned it before he died."

"You always say 'before he died.' Instead of 'before he killed himself.'"

"I guess that's how I think of it. That he just died after Cody did. And now you're keeping yourself alive. Whatever it takes."

"So you think Gary might have a suit going on? Or, I guess it might even be over? I haven't seen anything about it in the paper. But then there's probably been weeks and weeks I haven't read the paper, if you want the truth. And I'd be the last person he'd tell. So much I don't know, huh?"

"Does it make a difference?"

"If Gary sued? Not one bit."

"Do you think you can sleep now?"

I didn't, but I could take care of her, too. "Yes, I'm getting pretty tired."

"What are you going to do tomorrow?" she asked, a final check.

"Start finding out what Larry Ellis cares about. So I can make sure he loses it."

"Ah ha. The Plan takes shape. Details shall be forthcoming as She Who Will Not Be Thwarted sets upon her task." Carol-Sue's always been able to capitalize words when she speaks and she's a tease. I used to be, too.

"Yeah, well, the only thing you've contributed so far is the brilliant insistence that I not actually kill him. Big deal. Do you think you'll be coming soon?"

"Soon. A few more things to take care of here, then I'll make reservations. Meanwhile, you know what to do."

11

I wouldn't marry my Harold when he first proposed. I was so mad that he'd enlisted that I lobbed my whole self at him like a live grenade. "No, I will *not* marry you now, Mr. Selfish. Exactly what am I supposed to do if something happens to you? Wait, maybe you're deluded enough to think you'll knock me up before you ship out, so I'll have something to remember you by?" (We'd scarcely rounded second base at the time.)

In a white heat, I went on like that for days. "This is just *stupid*," I raged. "Two years! That's how long an associate degree takes! And you refused do *that*. It's not too late for something that makes sense, you know!"

He was very smart, my Harold was. Maybe books weren't his strong point, but to avoid his being sent to that war, I could help him with his classes. I'd write the papers for him if he wanted. Of course, it was pointless blather; he'd already enlisted, his parents could never have paid for even community college, and his high school grades hadn't been scholarship material. There was a lot I didn't want to admit. High drama was easier than reality.

It was early 1964. He was staring ahead to his twenty-first birthday, and had already spent more than two years going nuts waiting for the *Greetings* letter from the Selective Service. "I'll go ape," he said. "They can get me until I'm twenty-six. Don't be bummed, I'll just go in, get it over with, and then I can start my life. Besides, when you enlist, you can get a better army job." As it was, he was working in a machine shop. He was good with his hands, but he wanted more than that. Maybe his own shop someday. "You know, when I get out, there's the GI Bill. You'll have your education, then maybe I'll have a better job, and I can take a few classes, too. And maybe I'll be in the Reserves afterward. That's good money and benefits."

Well, so much for that great plan. If he'd enlisted when he'd turned eighteen, if Johnson hadn't ramped up the war, if the Gulf of Tonkin hadn't happened, if, if, if . . . then, yes, Harold might have been on active duty for two years, and gotten out clean. The worst that would have happened is that maybe he'd have really learned how to make a bed well instead of having it look like three or four people were still sleeping in it.

As it happened, his timing couldn't have been worse. He was assigned to Fort Benning from where his unit, part of the 1st Cavalry Division Airmobile, was sent, in July of 1965, to Camp Radcliff, plunked in the central highlands of Vietnam and named—naturally—for a dead American pilot. He was supposed to repair small arms artillery like he had at Fort Benning, but then he was sent out to another unit, where he didn't know anyone. He carried an M16 for some time, on search-and-destroy missions. I know that much.

If I had it to do over again, my anger when he enlisted would be all about seeing that it was going to turn so wrong. Just so wrong. It would be about having read history. Or it could be about having a moral stance, about civilians or napalm, or something other than what it was: my being mad that he *chose* to go instead of waiting to see if he *had* to go. But I see this now: for Harold it was all about taking control. Nobody likes the feeling of having no say over his own life or what he cares about. Isn't helplessness what we all fear most? Maybe that was the foretelling of his decision to enact his own justice when he set out after Cody's killer, when it became evident that no one else was going to *do* anything. I don't guess I ever really understood until now, when I've decided I can't sit around any longer myself. It's a shame I can't tell him that I finally forgive him for enlisting. You're probably thinking that he knew, since I married him after all, but believe me, he never made the mistake of thinking I fully forgave him for that. It was a far distance from point A, when he left for basic training, to point C, that being our wedding.

In basic, Harold learned how to run at a stuffed dummy with a bayonet while shouting *kill* and practiced his shooting. I worked at staying mad. For a while I didn't even answer his letters (holding a grudge is a special talent of mine). That was during the time I dated some other boys. I wanted to be able to say *I told you so* when he got killed, and feel especially smart. But of course, I finally thawed. What melted my resolve was his telling me that he wished he'd listened to me, and that no matter what the other guys did, he wanted me to know he was being faithful because he had to believe in something, and a future with me was the only good he could see from there.

I realize it doesn't make me look exactly wonderful that I got over being mad because he said he should have listened to me, but you'll probably figure out I can be like that, and if I tell you myself, at least you'll know I'm honest. I started writing to him every day, and Harold wrote to me every day he could—often not about what he was doing, but about what he wanted to be doing. He was shielding me from the worst of it.

It took years for me to hear what he did tell, in dribs and drabs, about the pigs—he refused to have a pig on our farm—the sticky, stifling heat, the leeches, the blood, the mud, the bodies, the hunger, the foot rot, the constant fear firing intermittently into rage as they stalked and were stalked in the jungle. The terrible length of nights. We were married a long time. Most of it he never told. But he couldn't hide the night terrors, which came back every now and then for a long time. He never did use the GI Bill.

Like so many, he came home changed. I hardly knew him. But I'd promised, and there were all those plans we'd made in writing. There was no way to back out, not then. And I was lucky. Over time, he found his way back to himself. Maybe he took what had happened and locked it away, just like he'd first had to lock away the kind boy who'd put on the uniform, learned to shoot, and used that skill. So much he kept from me. Maybe it helped that he had me to come back to.

I finished college just before he got out. He didn't make it back for my graduation, but we waited and had the party three weeks late so he could be there. Now I wonder if it felt like another world to him, like I was some naïve, even spoiled, rich girl celebrating herself. Which I wasn't—rich, I mean. Naïve, yes, compared to what he'd seen. I know that now. And as spoiled as most Americans by having running water and flush toilets, enough food and clothing, and not being in fear for our lives.

It was just as well my mother and I needed some time to put together a spring wedding because his first year back as a civilian was also my first year teaching. Fifth-grade boys are brutal to control on the playground for first-year teachers (I was pretty, and wanted them to like me, a deadly and dumb combination that I didn't put together in my head). Harold was impatient with himself and everyone else, trying to understand life at home.

You already know we were married a long time. There are things a wife knows about her husband that no one else knows. My Harold was never a hunter, never a killer. He had the same heart as Cody once. After the war, some nights he'd jump up in a dead sleep, cold yet sweat soaked. Suddenly he'd be across the room, crouching. Wide awake, yet not. Terrified. I would be afraid of what he'd do. "Harold! Harold! It's me!" I'd call. Once he threw a lamp. It hit the wall behind me and then the floor. Glass as broken as he was around my bare feet. I'd learned that if I screamed, it made things worse, the screams of women everywhere sounding alike. Slowly, he'd come to. And sob. Sometimes he would not let me touch him.

He'd healed slowly, but there was still that part of him locked away. And then, when Cody shot a deer and felt what he'd done, Harold saw everything through Cody's eyes and felt it with Cody's heart and it unlocked that last part of his own. It changed him as much as going to war had changed him. I saw it happen. That's what such love did.

12

Every fall, deer hunting starts up around here. There are firearm, archery, and muzzleloader seasons, all with their different dates and licenses. The hunters' bright hats dot the woods like apples still hanging after the frost. Some even climb trees to hide in, men waiting for the creatures to leg their way into their sights, noiseless except for the small rustle of leaves. I can see that part in my mind without much bother. But then I see the deer, its enormous eyes knowing and uncertain at once, picking its way along, just trying to live another day, and I wonder when is it that you can't stand what's about to happen? I blink and flinch, hearing the simultaneous explosion and kick, like a hoof deep in a shoulder, and the stutter of a second shot. Maybe someone else's shot, from another side. It happens, that close. Harold used to say the first shot is life, the way things are, the second shot is the mercy.

Maybe for him. Maybe stepping out in front of that truck to die was a mercy for him. I have tried to think of it that way, although I really think he was punishing himself for the unbearable weight of failure.

I would never listen to Harold's revenge schemes for Larry Ellis, but for sure Gus never caught him with a weapon; he never touched his gun again after he promised Cody he wouldn't. I know this much, though: he knew exactly who Larry was, where he lived, where he worked. He made it his business to find out everything about him as completely as I refused to know anything. But Harold was careless. I don't think he gave a damn what busybody might realize he was out to get Larry. Of course it got around to Gus—it probably took all of ten minutes, everyone here knowing everyone's business the way we do—and naturally Gus made it his business to catch him at it. Not that anyone, probably including Gus, much cared what happened to Larry Ellis; everyone knew what he'd done. No, it was all Gus's misguided attempt to protect my Harold from himself. Gus didn't get it: how much better it would have been to let Harold have at Larry. Harold could have lived with whatever happened. Even six months in jail. But when Gus kept stopping him, it took away his hope, time after time, and finally he had nothing left to live for. People have to have hope. I realize it's the same for Gary. Sometimes people make up the craziest things to put their hope in. I ought to be all right with that, having lost Harold when he lost hope.

Even CarolSue says she doesn't know the details of Harold's intentions, although the two of them always did get along, and Harold started to go after Larry while she stayed with us after Cody's service. She knew I needed her. I could have saved myself a lot of trouble now if I'd just helped my Harold, or at least let him tell us what he was doing. I wouldn't have to ferret out every piece of information about Larry Ellis now. I'd know the enemy the way he did.

CarolSue says that at first Harold set out to torment Larry. He wanted to make his life miserable, have him never know what was coming. I think it must have started as vandalism. Men out here love their trucks, and Harold would have known how to mess with one. Not only that, he knew how engines work. That would explain the misdemeanor arrests for whatever Gus either caught him at or pulled him in for but somehow made sure there were no charges, or none that stuck. Instead of being relieved or grateful, Harold was furious and depressed. He must have ramped it up, because then there were Class D felony charges, one for criminal confinement and one for theft. In this state, those are "wobblers" that can be charged as either a felony or a misdemeanor. CarolSue was the one who found that handy information. When Harold upped the ante, Gus took a new tack trying to stop him; he didn't intervene, figuring on the judge's discretion to choose the short jail stint to cool Harold off. But the prosecutor couldn't get an indictment, not around here, didn't much matter what evidence he had. I don't think he even really wanted one. Like Gus, he just wanted Harold to quit.

Harold wasn't about to quit. He was about to double down. So Gus pretty much took to tailing him, to cut him off at the pass, to make sure he didn't succeed. Doesn't say much for how busy we keep the sheriff out here, does it? Makes you think we could get along just fine without one, doesn't it? Well, as you know, Harold finally did quit for good. I hope Gus is happy now.

I ponder winners and losers sometimes in the evening when darkness comes so slowly that I forget to reach up and turn on the floor lamp by the blue chair. Maybe I nod off and on and off. Marvelle doesn't remind me. A voice in my mind that is not my own says, *Oh, Louisa, how your life rode, glorious, toward a mysterious horizon on the edge of an upright rolling dime. And out of nowhere, your dime wobbled with the first news you couldn't absorb, then careened and plunked down flat. You didn't really think it would roll on forever. And yet you did.*

I come to. I take stock: am I in my right mind?

The world is as utterly changed as Dorothy's when she wakes in Oz. Except for three chickens and a cat, I am alone. A blond Elvis in drag festooned in glitter is in my house. Five miles down the road, two of our neighbors' farms are being laid out for a subdivision, asphalt and concrete eating the land. When did they sell? How did I not notice?

I remember before Cody died, the first diminishments. I had no idea what had been set in motion when Gary gave

Nicole reason to leave him. I still didn't feel the dime tipping when Rosie had to be euthanized. Was the first tilt when Mom died before Emerson and Thoreau, those sweet yellow Labs who were littermates? I miss their eager kisses and tails. Before it was time to find a new puppy, our Cody, gone. Gone. Harold couldn't bear to keep Cody's horse, but we found him a good home with a 4-H family. Oh, the sheep has been gone for years; that was a failed experiment. My Harold, gone. When the land returns to life like this, the May trees covering their arms in blossoms like open laughter, and enough rain for now, I see them all as they were: moving, believing, eating, squabbling. Laughing as if it would always be the springtime of our lives, as if a dime could stand on end and roll and roll and roll.

CarolSue called right after supper, said she hadn't wanted to let it get too late. There was a soft rain falling through late light that made me think *almost planting time*, and how Harold would be antsy that the fields be dry enough to plant and then get enough rain for the corn to grow. How the fifth graders would be hitting growth spurts in the spring, and getting crazy for school to end.

CarolSue was right about one thing. Her mammogram was fine. She was sorry she hadn't told me that Charles had had a biopsy. They'd been called in to meet with his doctor, the last appointment of the day today. When she said that, she didn't have to say any more. Prostate cancer.

I don't know how long I sat holding the phone in my hand after we hung up. Marvelle jumped in my lap and jumped back off after a while. Sometime after dark I remembered to feed her.

13

When we were kids, CarolSue was the one with the charmed life. She was Dad's favorite, and the pretty one, that was obvious. Not only had she gotten the hydrangea-blue eyes and the best eyelashes, she had a way of making bad decisions work out for her. She went to a secretarial school instead of college, though she was smarter than I—at least at math. Oh, she *could* have gone, she said she just didn't have the patience for years more school and anyway, she didn't want to be a nurse or a teacher, which was what she saw a college woman would end up doing. She said she could be a secretary by going to school for six months, for heaven's sake; she had aced business typing in high school and she figured she could pick up shorthand pretty fast. So she did that, and she *did* get a decent job, and then she married early. To a guy with a heart murmur, which had made him the winner of a golden 4F ticket.

He was her first husband, Phillip, who'd been her high school boyfriend, the one Dad thought was a loser, "with or without a lousy heart murmur," as he muttered out of Carol-Sue's earshot. Even Mom had never taken a great shine to him, I could tell. But somehow, she was all set up for a great life, while I was doggedly making my way through college to become a teacher (she was right about what women were steered to be then: secretaries, nurses, teachers), and just as doggedly staying mad at Harold.

At first Phillip didn't even turn out to be such a loser, which was a surprise because Dad was often right about people. Then, of course, he turned out to be right, but that came later.

In the early years, they both worked, they both saved, they bought a nice house. If they weren't happy, they put on a damn good show of it. Back then, CarolSue and I weren't like we are now with each other. I wouldn't have instantly known her sterling "I'm fine" from the silver-plate one. But I think she really was. Even Mom and Dad warmed up.

And then she was pregnant. I was crazy jealous, unmarried still, while she had everything we both wanted. So of course, I immediately organized an enormous baby shower. Mom said *wait*. I mailed invitations. "It's not like she waited to tell people, Mom," I said. "Honey, it's early. You never know. The time for a shower is at the end," she said. I rolled my eyes. She didn't roll hers back, but she did shake her head while she made tea sandwiches, which just annoyed me.

The shower had an extremely original color theme: pink and blue. We played every silly game women have ever invented, and CarolSue loved it. Three days later CarolSue was spotting, then cramping. Bed rest didn't help. She lost the baby at thirteen weeks.

I didn't make the same mistake with the next pregnancy. Or the next. She stopped telling people—including me—when she was pregnant. She'd only tell Mom. Mom would let it slip to me, so I'd be careful what I said around her, I think. Not ask her anything, for one. And then Mom would tell me when she lost another one. Sometimes it was right away. Sometimes she'd carry it longer, six or eight weeks. As long as nine or ten.

Phillip wanted to "take a break," so she said they weren't trying when Harold and I got married, and I admit, I was glad of it. She was my matron of honor and only attendant. I thought it would distract her and she'd be able to celebrate with me. Even though as far as I knew she wasn't pregnant again then, she hadn't given me a shower, and she was wan as a lily on a coffin in the pastel pink gown I'd thought was so lovely, devoid of expression. My wedding pictures were spoiled. I knew it was selfish, but when I saw them, I wished again I hadn't asked her to be in it at all.

I turned my attention to making my own home. We were living in town then, and Harold—back from Vietnam, of course—was working in the machine shop, and still trying to get himself grounded again in America. Which wasn't proving easy. Now I could tell you that he was haunted by what he'd seen; what did we know of that then? What did we know of what soldiers needed to heal? I thought just I could be enough! One of my hundreds of mistakes.

Maybe Harold and I would have waited longer to have a baby. But I was so scared that CarolSue's story would be mine that I had to find out. Especially after she lost yet another one. I think most of us had lost count. Maybe it was the sixth—or perhaps it was the seventh. You might think, *Louisa, how could you possibly not know how many babies your sister lost?* But it's true. When something painful happens over and over, your mind doesn't *want* to keep track of how many times it's already happened. How could you go on if you remembered that?

As you might guess, because it's the way these things go, I got pregnant the second I tried and never even threw up.

But here's what you wouldn't guess, and how what should have been so happy—like my wedding—turned into a confusing forest, canopied with branches of sadness and fear. Just weeks after I spilled to the family that Harold and I were expecting, CarolSue told us all that she, too, was pregnant again. I admit, I was annoyed. I wanted this to be my time, and not have us all go through another depression with her. And, of course, it scared me. I was just clearing the end of the first trimester myself, and I well knew, from her experience, that even though the odds were now in my favor, I could still lose the baby.

But there was an upside. She hung on to that pregnancy, and as our bellies expanded, we grew close, planning how the cousins would grow up like siblings. We hoped they'd be the same sex, and pored over the book of baby names for ones that would sound cute together.

I imagine you can read the danger signs here. I'm the one who didn't. CarolSue's son was stillborn, a week before Gary, robust as a horse, arrived and latched on to feed like he'd been taking classes in how to do it for the past nine months. And gotten an A plus.

Harold and I had to scramble to choose a name that Carol-Sue and I hadn't considered. We settled on Gary because neither of us objected too strenuously and the birth certificate had to be filled out. Also, it sounded nothing like David, which is what CarolSue and Phillip named their lost baby, because it means "beloved son," he explained. So Harold and I made Gary's middle name David, in his memory. It was the only thing we could think of to do. She took it the way we meant it, to honor her lost son, and asked to hold her nephew. Handing Gary to her felt all wrong, like it would make everything worse, if that was possible, but I did it. CarolSue took some strange comfort in it, seeing something in my son then that she's held to ever since. (You'll notice the softness she feels for him, how she takes his side.)

It's only now, after all that's happened, that I think I understand what CarolSue must have felt as our family and Phillip's gathered in a ragged circle in the cemetery beside New Hope Community Church to bury her son's ashes, which were in a little white box that looked like marble, but might have been quality plastic for all I knew firsthand then about death. The hole had been dug and was covered with bright green felt that didn't match the patchy winter-burned grass around it. Everything looked wrong, all wrong.

CarolSue picked up the box and held it against her chest, while the minister read the service committing the baby's ashes to the ground and whatever else there was of him to

God's eternal care. Even back then, I wondered what that meant. We were supposed to put the first dirt on top of it at the end, when it was put in the prepared hole, each family member contributing.

That was The Plan, but I can tell you it didn't happen. The minister had to finally take the box away from CarolSue. I was afraid he was going to end up wrestling her for it, but she finally let go. I couldn't help; Gary was in my arms, swaddled in a blue-and-white blanket, wearing a little white cap against the grey chill of the day. Anyone I could have left him with was at the service. Mom and Dad half led, half carried CarolSue to the car, Phillip walking alone behind them until Harold dropped back alongside him, which I thought was kind. I walked by myself then, carrying Gary, like a guilty stranger who had the poor taste to bring an infant.

That baby was CarolSue's last. She told Mom—not me— that she couldn't stand to lose any more, she wouldn't survive it. Then Phillip left her, seven months later. Phil had had his "fill of sadness," which were his exact words, and I thought an ironic way to put it coming from him, but I managed to keep my mouth shut at the time since no one else was in the mood for a bit of levity. Had I taken my eyes off my newborn and really felt CarolSue's loss, the enormity of what anyone can lose, the yawning chasm would have swallowed me then. I know that because now it has.

Or it's tried to. But over the next years I saw how Carol-Sue managed by clutching the smallest twigs of hope that grew out of the sides of that chasm she'd fallen into. Some of them broke off, and she'd fall farther.

Some didn't, though, and then she'd cling and maybe get a toehold, too. She clawed her way toward daylight. I wasn't much help to her then, not nearly the help she's been to me since I've joined The Bereavement Club.

So, you see, I thought it was only fair that I might have to go on largely alone now, and sometimes tell her what I thought she could bear to hear. I'm sure that's what she did for me, when she'd lost her only child, and I was fragile with fear and guilt. Her attention needed to be on saving Charlie now, just as mine had to be on my baby back then.

If she wasn't coming to help me in person, then The Plan might have to be developed and revised without CarolSue. I figured I'd do what I had to do, tell her what I could, keep the rest to myself. There's a first for everything. I'd done my thinking; it was time to get serious.

14

Thanks to daylight savings time, the long shafts of late afternoon light stretched through supper hours. I was trying to get a look inside Larry Ellis's ranch-style house. I knew he and a woman left the house because I'd been staking it out since four o'clock. (Is that overage Barbie doll his *wife*? Is that a wig? Where do they even *sell* those ridiculous shoes? Who wears hot-pink stilettos? Lord, how I wish CarolSue was with me.)

I wished for CarolSue like crazy, but she'd have a fit if she knew I was skulking around Larry Ellis's house. She'd get on her high horse and say, "Louisa, this has bad idea written all over it." She can be impossible sometimes. She's the one who said I had to find out what he cares about, and how could I do that except by following him? And I tried, but I just didn't realize how hard it is to follow someone. I have no idea how detectives actually do this part.

By five thirty, I had to pee so badly I decided I simply had to get over to Jamie's Gas N'Go Market where I know the bathroom isn't disgusting because I've stopped there when I've driven to Indy. But before I even turned the key to start up the car, the twosome came out. I guessed it had to be Larry; it was his address, and he got into the truck that's registered to him. The Barbie got into the passenger side and they drove off.

That's when things really deteriorated. Not only did I have to uncross my legs to drive, I had the car facing south when Ellis turned north out of his driveway, so I had to find a place to turn around. A U-turn would have put me in a ditch. I *should* have backed up and turned in Ellis's driveway, but I didn't think of that in time, further displaying my lack of aptitude for the police academy. That maneuver must have taken me a quarter mile in the wrong direction. Then I got behind a mattress store delivery driver going twelve miles an hour trying to read numbers on mailboxes that aren't there. People way out here apparently think that if you don't know where they are when you're looking for them, they don't want you finding them anyway. I couldn't get around him because we were headed up a hill right then.

But once I could speed, I thought, Oh! Is that the tail of Ellis's truck making a right turn in the distance? It was a pickup truck, but far enough ahead that even making out the color wasn't possible. It might have been him, and I made the turn, but then within a quarter mile, there was a four-way stop, and I knew I was only guessing.

I thought I saw some dust settling and went to the right, thinking it might be a sign from a merciful God on my side. Don't we all think that silly way sometimes? Five or six or ten miles later I'd not seen a single vehicle, let alone a pickup truck. I'd have settled for a pink Cadillac to follow. But there was just the vast Indiana farmland, her old, old fields, their everlasting sameness now laid open again in endless wavy furrows to become inland seas of corn. It will rise bright green, be silvered by sun, be cut down. I pulled over near a stand of forest in front of a house and small cluster of outbuildings not all that unlike my own, I guessed, though the parcels of land out here are bigger. Where was I? On an empty, bisecting road in my old car, in my old body that had to pee, following something that had disappeared.

I was fairly sure the place wasn't deserted—it looked too well cared for—but for the moment no one was visible and I put my forehead on the steering wheel to gather myself. Already I had failed.

Is everyone like this? Your own sense tells you that a plan you've made is just not sensible, and yet you don't give up on it because there's another part of you that just pushes on, whether from stubbornness or a valuable kind of persistence. But you don't know which. Or whether it's because you desperately need to pee and pursuing The Plan takes you to the closest facility. As you age, you have to start watching yourself for this motive.

I drove back the way I was pretty sure I'd come, toward Larry's house, talking to CarolSue out loud. Or maybe I was talking to Harold. Defending myself. "So I let him get away. At least Gus didn't catch *me*. Unlike someone else I know. Oh Lord, I have to pee. Oh Lord, I don't remember passing that ugly blue house before. Am I lost?"

I wasn't. I calmed down and finally recognized the way to Larry's house and from there, I knew the way back to my own. But I was still upset, and I couldn't shake that "it's now or never" feeling. I had worked myself up to do this without CarolSue, had made myself strong enough and brave enough, and then I'd lost him. Of course, this might explain what I did: I really had to pee, and I thought I knew for sure that Larry's house was empty.

15

"You did what? Oh my God, Louisa. What were you thinking? That's breaking and entering. You'd go to prison for that. That has bad idea written—"

"I was thinking I'd wet my pants is what I was thinking. And she was dressed up like they were going out. From what I could see, anyway. She was wearing stiletto heels. *Hot-pink* stiletto heels. Most stupid shoes you ever saw."

"Forget the shoes! For all you knew they were going three houses up the road to drop off a casserole at a dead person's house. Sorry, bad example, but good grief, you have lost your mind."

I'd propped the kitchen door open before I called Carol-Sue, and as we talked, the long mid-May twilight rested like good cotton on my bare arms and legs. I sat at the table in a swatch of soft sunlight. I let it warm the sherry with which I was congratulating myself and closed my ropy fingers around the gold of it. Lovely, lovely. I was quite proud, and at the moment I did not have to pee.

"I know in your heart you are impressed," I said. "And you're dying to hear every detail. But you're not going to hear any of it unless you stop lecturing."

"For God's sake. Are you drinking? Lay it on me," she resigned. I knew she was rolling her eyes. We do that. Now she'd set a tone, and I had to hold back details to keep myself puffed up. Now you know why I wasn't going to—didn't want to—talk about how desperate and crazy I'd felt when I pulled up across the road from Larry's house, right where I'd been parked earlier. I'd cried a little bit, and said, "I can't do this," out loud. I sat there a few minutes just staring at my hands and thinking that they are my mother's hands now, the left with its thin gold band and old-fashioned diamond off-kilter next to it. Mom was lucky in one way—she had me to watch out for her when she was alone, with CarolSue as a spare. But this is what mattered: she could look in my eyes and see enough of a mirror that she knew she was home. When I look at Gary now, I recognize nothing anymore. Since he got involved with that cult, it might be easier for me to find people I could talk to if I do land in jail.

So I had that thought and it didn't go away as I sat there parked just beyond the home of the man who'd killed my grandson and then, effectively, my husband, and turned the son I'd known into a stranger. That fearful "I can't do this" dissolved, life changing again as if I'd stepped into a new skin. Believe me when I say this: there is nothing crazier than a truly sane old lady who can't lose more than she already has. I was still scared, but the fear wasn't enough to make me fail. I just wasn't going to fail.

So I left all that out and told CarolSue how he'd worn a blue Colts shirt and cowboy boots, I'd seen that much, and had a scrawny ponytail that looked to be the greyish-brown color of dishwater that badly needs to be changed. I'd glimpsed that when he turned to get into the pickup truck. (In his mug shot, his stringy hair had been raked back over his ears. His eyes were too close together and too low on his face, as if all his features had been pinched into too small an area.) I told her about his yard, scrubby, screaming to be mowed. Two more weeks and I bet he could hide a stolen car in that grass. Between the untrimmed random shrubs where I snuck up to look in the window—my heart thudding *what the hell are you doing*, but I would not turn back—thorny weeds prickled around my shoelaces and the bottom of my slacks. The white paint on the windowsill was badly cracked and offered multiple spots for long, satisfying peel-offs, tiny opening acts of vandalism, but I limited myself to one to save time and because I know there's not much point in vandalism if nobody knows you've done it; this house is such a mess, nobody would notice if I actually broke the window.

It turned out I was at a bedroom window—Larry's maybe, since there was a king-size bed with a thick, puffy green comforter on it. It looked like it was the color of grass. Of course I could have been wrong; I was peering through a dirty window. But the thought of my Harold under the greened-up grass came into my mind, and so did the thought of planting an explosive device underneath Larry's bed.

Oh my, how little we understand what the course of someone's life may make her capable of. This was another thing I didn't bother to tell CarolSue.

A pouf of breeze raised my hair and as quickly the breeze stopped, as if someone had blown on me. I looked over my shoulder and even turned around, but there was nothing. Just the big shed in the back of Larry's yard, a dark red scab on the property, and the empty fields. No dog barked, nothing to warn me off. I crept around the house to the messy concrete patio, where four lawn chairs with saggy green webbed seats, a rusted bucket, and broken plastic rake looked forgotten. There was a grill, too. Two big pots of flourishing pansies, yellow, purple, apricot, and blue, looked like pieces to a different puzzle. A single cement step led to a back door. I must have been CIA in a previous life because I sidled up to that door and peeped in as if I knew what I was doing. The kitchen. Why not? I'd come this far and had nothing to show for it. I had no idea what Larry Ellis cares about yet. I tried the door.

It was unlocked.

Yes. I did. I went in. Of course, that's what completely flipped CarolSue out when she heard it and it derailed the conversation for a while before I got to the good part. Or the bad part. Or the important part.

"Hey, if you don't like how I'm making a Plan, get on a plane and come help me," I finally said, and immediately felt terrible because she went dead silent. I'd hurt her. Charlie was having radiation every day for eight weeks. "I'm sorry. I guess all this sounds dumb now. Maybe it is. Let's talk about something else. Let's talk about you for a change. You always change the subject back. Tell me about what it's like taking Charlie for the treatments. What do you do while he has the radiation? I know it's got to be hard on you, all the waiting around." And really, going on with it all was like that dime balanced again on its edge and whatever CarolSue said was the nudge that would drop it down or keep it rolling.

The dime teetered a moment and then CarolSue said, "I just read when he's having treatments. I took out a bunch of books I was supposed to read in high school from the library. You remember, I used to get CliffsNotes, but the books are actually pretty good. Anyway, it doesn't sound dumb. I want to hear everything. Charlie's going to be fine. Harold would have been fine except for Larry Ellis because Cody would still be here, and Cody would be fine. Sometimes if we don't get mad and fight back I guess we'd just lay down and die. Charlie's fighting back, you're fighting back. I'm fighting back with both of you. It's stupid, I know, but I just feel so angry sometimes. And it helps to have someone to be angry at. *Damn* Larry Ellis. Cody was . . . such a good . . . he was a *good* boy."

The dime rolled on.

I still left out the more terrifying details. I told her what a revolting mess the kitchen was, dirty dishes crusty with food on the counters, unwashed pots on the stove, the sour smell, the way I could hear my sneakers peel heel-toe from the sticky floor.

"Get on with it," she said. "You're not going to turn him

in to the Board of Health for revenge. Obviously, having an immaculate home is not what he cares about."

She was right, but she was taking all the fun out of this. I scooped Marvelle under one arm and got up to pour myself some more sherry. There was a time I went for bourbon, way back, when Harold and I were young. On my next trip to town, maybe I'll get myself a bottle of that to improve my tea.

I could have used a belt of bourbon without the tea when I crept out of that kitchen, which was painted a pukey tan. Bam! Right there in front of me was a deer, staring me down. A deer with huge antlers. In the dining room, behind the head of the Early American table. A dead deer, I mean, the kind mounted on the wall, confronting me. No, that's the wrong word. The deer was asking for help. Begging. It broke my heart. And, oh my God, in what passed for a living room, there were four more. Those poor animals, those poor, poor animals. Their majestic heads, their enormous unblinking eyes.

As strange as it sounds for the years I've lived in the country surrounded by animals, I've never been near a trophy. Such a ridiculous word to use for something that meant you no harm, isn't it? I almost couldn't go forward or backward. The deer—it felt like a herd, or really, one of the groups of families I've seen so often on our land or running out of the woods between farms—looked magnificent, dignified and humiliated at once. "I'm sorry, I'm sorry," I whispered. My eyes filled and I was ashamed to be a human.

Finally, I lowered my head and tiptoed past the last of them into a hallway to look through the rest of the house, though I was sure I knew now what Larry Ellis cared about.

In the living room were big framed pictures of him, beefed-up by camouflage and boots, a rifle slung over his shoulder, with a propped-up dead deer, his cap jauntily tilted back to show an outsized grin. There were more lining the hallway. The pictures of this man who'd testified he didn't know if a deer in the road was a buck or a doe (though it was November, rut season, when bucks have full antlers and he's a trophy hunter) made me nauseous, which distracted me from fear. This was one time I should not have listened to my body.

The first room on the left was a bathroom, ordinary except that the shower curtain was a camouflage print. Carol-Sue went so silent I thought she'd fainted when I told her I went in and used it. "Well? I told you how badly I had to pee! I was desperate. It seemed like a good idea at the time."

"Tell me you didn't flush it."

"Of course I flushed it. You know what Mom always said about the filthy people who don't flush."

"Oh my God, I bet you washed—"

"—Well, of course I washed my hands. Did you listen to anything Mom said about people who don't?"

Later, of course, it would be apparent how close I'd come to being caught with my pants down, and I mean that literally, but it had seemed perfectly okay at the time. And I didn't have a head injury yet, either.

It looked like there were three bedrooms, light brown carpeting running down the hall and through each one. I thought I knew already which was the master, and I was oriented correctly—there was that king bed, more hunting pictures, I now saw, and its own bathroom. I scanned a small walk-in closet: his side, her side. Hers with a lot of pinks, reds, blues, blacks. High heels on shoe racks. Thick boots on the floor of his side. Jackets, camouflage, jeans. Heavy, dark bureaus and nightstands in the room, a lamp on each side of the bed. *American Hunter* magazine lying on the floor. Another magazine, open to a centerfold of a naked woman on the floor. Rumpled clothes on the floor. White socks, obviously dirty.

Nursing disgust, I stepped into the hallway and opened the door into another room, which was darkened by a shade pulled down over the only window. I'd taken only two steps into the room when I heard sirens in the distance. Roots shot from the soles of my feet through the thin carpet. Louder, louder. Someone must have seen me and called the police.

My car was right across the road, too. How could I have been so stupid?

At the same minute as these thoughts—which all jumbled and flew together much faster than I could have begun to enumerate them for CarolSue—if I had told her about the sirens and the boy who suddenly sat upright in a twin bed there, apparently startled awake by the screeching sirens. A shout: "Hey!"

I turned fast, bumping hard into the doorjamb, clutched my head where I'd hit it, and ran.

16

You might think a woman my age can't move all that fast. You'd be wrong, so wrong. I fled back down the hall, through the herd of deer, the tack of the kitchen floor seeming to grab my feet. Between the dining room and the back door I thought I heard either "Mom!" or "Help!" but it slid into the piercing sirens, that high-low high-low screech like adrenaline coming, coming, coming, and it was all just sound mixed into the explosive drumming of my heart.

My head thrummed with pain. As I made it to the back door, I had two impulses: do anything to escape, and to go out with my hands up, the way I'd seen trapped criminals surrender to cops in movies, to avoid being shot by the SWAT team that was doubtless surrounding the house right now. Panicked, I picked a middle course. I made a run for it with my hands up. Palms in the air like white flags, I ran around the far side of the house, away from the driveway, expecting to be confronted by drawn guns.

Nothing.

Only unmowed grass mixed with scrappy weeds. There was a stand of trees fifty feet to my right and I made a break for that, keeping my hands up just in case. Keeping trees between me and the house and the driveway as much as I could, I moved toward the road. The driveway was vacant. The noise of the sirens was raising the hair on my arms and felt like something physical in the air. I kept going toward the road.

Still nothing except sound. I pulled the car keys out of my pocket and made a break for it out of the trees across the end of Larry's yard. I almost ran into his mailbox because I was looking back at the house to see if anyone was coming. Just then a police car raced down the road toward me. I raised my hands to surrender. The police car flew on by me.

I couldn't believe it. My God, didn't I just hold up a sign for them? Another police car was coming, and this time I kept my hands down. But I was stuck, for the moment, at the end of Larry's driveway. Those guys must be lost, I thought. They hadn't even slowed down.

When the second one passed, I hurried across the road, got in my car, and started my getaway. Not a quarter mile down the road was a flock of police cars, two ambulances, and three fire trucks. A tractor trailer had collided with a farm tractor. The SMV—Slow Moving Vehicle—sign was visible, sideways and just off the ground above a jutting oversize tire emerging like a bent wrist from the wreckage. It looked like there was a car involved. I spotted some crumpled blue on the far side of one of the police cars, and realized more emergency vehicles must be coming because sirens were screaming, red and blue lights flashing, on that side, too. Something was spilled on the road. Twisted metal glinted in the slanting sunlight.

I braked and for once I thought fast. There wasn't a car behind mine and nothing coming toward me. Of course not; the road was blocked. One car was ahead, up near where the policeman stood in front of his vehicle. I just needed a little of the berm to do a three-point turn. I drove back past the scene of my crime and was only lost for about twenty minutes as the new person I'd become found a new way home.

17

They haunt me, the deer. That terrible trapped beauty, pre-served, hung on a wall. Gone but not gone, more real than my grandson or my husband. More real than memory that can't place details about the shape of teeth, fingernails, the placement of small moles, the exact color of eyes.

This is what a man does for fun: he kills animals that did him no harm and would have done nothing but run from him, and he hangs their heads on a wall. How many shots does it take him, the big man, to kill? Does he follow bleed-ing and suffering deer to the triumph? What kind of mother raised this man? I have agonized over my mistakes; my son has made bad choices, yes, and now he is vulnerable and foolish, but he would not kill and call it sport. He may not have absorbed my love for the creatures of the land, but he would not kill for sport.

I see a buck raising his head just as the bullet explodes. Cody felt the truck the instant before it hit him. I see them like movies paused in my head.

They haunt me.

18
Larry

The kid was playing on the Nintendo. It was pretty much all he ever did as far as Larry could tell. Although when Crazy Connie from down the road told LuAnn that she'd seen a strange car at the house while they were at work, LuAnn flipped out and accused the kid of having a girl there. Somehow she knew there was this girl he liked. Larry couldn't imagine that the kid had told her, even if he was kind of a mama's boy. How did women figure this shit out?

The kid denied it all, said some stranger broke in. Larry called bullshit on that because the guns were worth a lot and they were all there. Then LuAnn said her jewelry wasn't gone either and no stuff was locked up, so the kid's story made no sense, and she'd grounded him except for his job because she didn't want him getting some girl pregnant like happened to her. Big deal, Larry figured. The kid'll just play video games anyway. LuAnn made him put the sound on mute, but she'd gone shopping with Crazy Connie, the only woman alive who liked shoes as much as LuAnn. Larry let him have the volume on. Easier to get in LuAnn's pants if her kid tells her that her boyfriend's cool. Larry also thought: big deal if the kid did have a girl in his bed. LuAnn was always telling Larry how the kid needed a dad so he'd learn to be a man, wasn't she? Then the minute the kid acts like a man, she flips out. Women were always contradicting themselves. But maybe he should give the kid sex pointers. LuAnn could count on his father to be completely useless on this score as every other.

Larry smirked to himself. She'd owe him some dirty sex herself if he educated the kid about condoms. But it wasn't just about getting her to let loose her inner whore, even if it used to be. Larry hadn't forgotten about LuAnn getting him the lawyer.

She'd told him to just play a video game with the kid. She'd said, "You can do it. And, please, his name is Brandon, not Kid." He hadn't answered one way or the other, rather she didn't know he'd never played a video game in his life. She kept on about it, said it would mean a lot to her, and finally he'd said, "For God's sake, will you drop it." Usually, he didn't like it when she left him alone with the kid, but today, he was relieved not to have her watching him.

Now Larry finished the ham sandwich she'd left him, crumpled the potato chip bag and squashed his Coke can, pushed all of it toward the center of the table. He sighed, slid back the chair, hitched up his pants, and headed into the living room where the kid was on the couch fixated on the TV screen, his thumbs a blur on the game control. The sound effects were automatic gunfire, an AK47, no good for hunting.

"Hey, kid." Tried again, louder. "Hey, kid."

"Hey."

"Whatcha up to?"

"I did it already."

"What?"

"Got the wet towels off the bedroom floor."

"Oh. Yeah, well, that'll make your mom happy."

The kid was staring at the screen where he was getting guys to shoot stuff. Cars and bodies were flying into the air. It was pointless. It wouldn't even improve your aim out where it counted. You weren't looking down sights; there was no weight in your hands or against your shoulder. You sure didn't feel the kick of the shot.

"What's that called?"

The kid glanced at him suspiciously. "I got this for Christmas."

"Just wonderin' what it's called."

"*Mafia III.*"

"Looks pretty easy."

"Ever tried it?"

Larry didn't know how to take that—an invitation or a challenge. He looked around the living room for reassurance. The fourteen-point buck he'd taken down two years ago inspired him. "You ever done that for real?"

"Huh?" The kid looked away from the screen. Looked at him. Progress.

"Like what actual men do—tracking, shooting, for real. With a rifle."

The kid must have thought he hid that smirk. His voice was polite when he said, "Uh, no. These guys aren't cops, Lar."

"Nah. Not talkin' about cops. I'm talkin' hunting." Larry swung his arm up and pointed to the trophies mounted around them. "This stuff on the screen doesn't do crap to make you a man. You get out in the world, it doesn't do crap to put you in real control of anything. You wanna have power, learn how to hunt. Be a predator." Larry looked at the kid straight on. His hair was short, blond, but not as blond as LuAnn's, that was for sure. Maybe LuAnn's wasn't real, even if she claimed it was. The kid's eyes were sort of like hers, round and blue. He had the look of a yearling buck, scrawny and leggy, too delicate to be tough. With any luck, he'd fill out. Just a couple pimples. Patchy facial hair starting to come in. He did need a man to show him stuff, LuAnn was right about that much even if he was sick to death of hearing about her kid, her kid, her kid. She was freaking obsessed with her kid. That's what started the fights and the only way to shut her up was a good slap, sometimes a little more. Her fault.

He'd do her a favor and pay her back for the lawyer if he

taught the kid how to be a man. "Some time ya oughta try real hunting."

"Mom—"

"Jeez, does your mom need to know every time you take a shit? I mean, you're not a baby, are you? And besides, she says she wants us to have 'a good relationship.'" Larry put air quotes around the words, his tone mocking. "She ever tell you that?"

"Yeah."

"Well, you like it when she wants us to go shopping or sit on the patio with her? Or visit your grandma, my personal favorite."

The kid sort of rolled his eyes up and sighed at the same time, maybe a cross between disgust and fatigue. Larry wasn't sure if it meant he was bored with the conversation or sick of his mother, but then the kid said, "Not exactly."

Larry took heart and pressed on. "Yeah. Me neither not exactly." Then he stalled, couldn't think of another thing to say. The kid turned his face to the TV screen and fired his thumbs up again.

"So—see, it's a guy thing. Y'interested?"

"In what?" But the kid kept playing his stupid game now.

"Hunting."

There was only the sound of the fake AK47s, the fluid motion of his thumbs. Larry glanced at the screen. The kid was blowing up bodies. Larry wanted to blow up the kid right then for making him feel small when the kid didn't even know Larry was talking about something big. Screw him.

"So, you lookin' for a job, huh?" He vaguely remembered LuAnn saying something like that.

"I got one."

The kid didn't even glance in his direction. His arms looked thin as a fawn's forelegs. He definitely ought to work out. Or something.

"Yeah, I guess your mom mighta said that. She's cool,

right?" Larry figured she probably had said something. There was no point to this at all. He was just trying to pay LuAnn back. LuAnn was loyal, he'd say that about her. The big thing was paying the bond and the lawyer, sure, but she was good about driving when they went out at night, too. Anyway, no one had been loyal to him like LuAnn, but it was a weird feeling, not that he'd ever let her have something over him.

"How about you show me how you work that thing," he said, pointing to the Nintendo with his chin, "as long as you know it's not worth crap about being a man. Did'ja know hunting raises your testosterone? Keeps you healthy."

Larry put his fist up and the kid actually fist bumped it before he got a second set of controls from under the couch. Larry saw a brief half-smile on the kid's face. He thought he'd won until the kid beat him hugely.

19
Louisa

I was young yesterday, which was a quick forever lifetimes ago. I recognize myself completely and not at all. I might be like anyone who's old. How would I know? Some mornings I catch myself staring out the window and the yard looks unfamiliar. So I look down and wonder if that's a small tremor in my hand. So I set the coffee cup down. It's chipped. I need to throw it away. It clatters softly against the saucer. Marvelle winds herself around my calf, and I know she is real.

Sometimes there is a good reason for death. Old age, or to end suffering. Or, I suppose, both. When Harold killed Meg, she was sick. We'd thought she had a bound egg, but when I felt inside her, there was none. I held her in a warm bathtub for twenty minutes, talking to her the whole while, girl talk about which member of the family should get the Darwin Award for Least Evolved Behavior Of The Year (which we always awarded to one of the males, Nicole and I being the final judges, of course). We finally realized Meg had vent gleet, which is like thrush, and could have spread to the others. She was sick and suffering, and Harold wrung her neck and then he buried her and we mourned. We mourned while we shoveled all the bedding from the roost and scrubbed out the whole coop with a bleach solution. We mourned. I knew what had happened and the reason.

But everything does not happen for a reason. Or if there *is* a reason, as people, bless their hearts, kept saying at Cody's funeral, and then at Harold's, then there's not a good reason. That is something that human beings cannot abide: there really is not a *good* reason for everything. I am thinking about the deer hunted down by men creeping through cold woods in southeast Indiana, and men hunted down by men creeping through the hot jungle in southeast Asia. Some things happen for a bad reason, like hubris, or no reason at all. Or reasons so complex that trying to untangle them makes you stare out of windows and tremble and almost wish it *was* just a tremor in your hand.

"Mom!" Gary's shape and voice rose and loomed, sudden, into the peace of the back door I'd left open to the yard for the girls. I had the drapes drawn, the car in the barn, and hadn't answered the front door. I thought he'd left, but instead, he'd come around to the back and snuck up on me. Marvelle jumped off the kitchen table and flattened into an escape. Her back paw caught some of the papers I'd been reading, which fluttered up and then toward the floor. The girls flapped and scattered noisily, especially Beth, who is easily startled. Amy flew toward Gary but then reversed and ended on the back of the couch. "Get away," he yelled, with a dramatic show of unnecessary ducking and swatting. Now he stood—my big, raw-boned, blue-eyed, and earnest son, so well intentioned—come again, he said, to check on me. By which he *meant* another attempt to *fix* me. He was carrying a cardboard box in one hand.

"Get away, chicken!" Again. And more waving, although she was already perched.

"She's ten feet away from you. And unarmed."

"Chickens don't belong in the house! Why didn't you answer the front door?"

"Why didn't you call before you came? I never answer the door for strangers. Goodness, why did you have your hair cut like that? You got *fleeced*." I was pleasing myself with an underhanded reference to his giving all that money to the cult. Yes, I know that's not helpful in a relationship, and CarolSue would be sure to point that out to me later, but Gary didn't pick up on it anyway.

"I went to the same barber I always . . . oh no. You always do that to me. I did call. You didn't answer the phone!"

True enough. I'd seen it was him, but the girls and I were busy, discussing hunting. (Marvelle approves of it. The chickens are opposed.) I'd been telling them what I was learning; the sheets of paper covering the kitchen table were photocopies of Indiana and county hunting laws I'd looked up at the library. The discussion had gotten so animated that all of us were having some sherry at the time Gary called, and a touch more by the time he showed up.

"Then why are you here?" I'm sure my tone carried that I didn't want him to be. CarolSue says this is how I contribute to the problem. She's right, but I didn't catch myself in time.

It wounded him. "Mom, I don't think you get it. When you don't answer the phone I get scared. What if you've fallen and can't get up? There used to be this commercial on TV and I really understand it now." His eyes watered. "I can't let something happen to you. Anyway, look, I brought you a present." He opened the box and set a large wax bird with an impressive wingspan and a wick protruding from its back on the kitchen table. Then he pulled a book of matches from his shirt pocket.

"Oh my! It's quite intricately carved, isn't it? Is it a hawk or . . . a vulture? I'm not too good with birds of prey." Actually, I can identify them quite well in the sky where they belong. I knew I wasn't being nice to my son, but I don't like it when he treats me like a feeble old lady.

"A dove, Mom, a dove! It's a Light Of The World candle. I got it off the Internet. Look, I'll light it for you. As it burns, see, the dove's wings go down slowly as the dove brings you Peace."

"Until the light flickers and then poof, it goes right out?" Why don't I remember to shut up? I have to remind myself that I believe in tolerance.

His face reddened. "Mom, I'm worried about your mind. It's not good for you to be alone all the time. Sometimes you completely miss the point. See, it's about—"

"No, dear, I get it. It's lovely. I'm sorry. Really, I am. It's just that right now isn't a good time."

I wanted him to leave. For one, he ticked me off with the comment about my mind. But I also had to keep him out of the living room. And the bedroom and the rest of the house, because I'd stashed Glitter Jesus in the linen closet for the time being. There was still some sparkle in JoJo's feathers from when she'd tried to land on Jesus' crown when he was lying behind the blue chair in the living room. There may be some personal animosity involved since the girls have discovered that glitter is not edible.

But more urgently, in a minute he was going to notice that I was wearing Harold's clothes.

Too late. "*What* are you wearing?" Gary demanded. He had on a red shirt I didn't recognize. There was a time I knew all his clothes. There was a time he sat on my lap and I'd read him stories until my legs went numb. There was a time I thought I could never stand to be apart from him.

"I was chilly," I lied, cleaning up my tone to mollify him. "And you know, I've been out doing volunteer work, honey, so I hadn't gotten my laundry done." The truth is that when I got home from the library, I'd put on Harold's last un-washed shirt, the blue plaid. I can close my eyes and see his broad expectant face, planes of light resting easy on his wide cheekbones, his hair, needing a cut, touching the top of the open collar. The way his rimless glasses left a mark on the top of his cheeks: he'd put on weight and it showed in his face and his meat-and-potatoes belly. There was a faint sweat smell to him, and his breath would go a hint sour after meals. But I never had to make up a reason to love him, which is not the same as saying I understood everything he did or that we never fought. "Go ahead and light that nice candle, maybe it

will warm me up. That was thoughtful of you. I didn't mean
to be rude. I'm just tired. How have you been?"

Maybe you can tell I was torn between trying to be nicer,
trying to reassure him, and trying to get rid of him. I not only
had on Harold's blue plaid shirt, which Gary might or might
not have recognized. I'd also put on his khaki shorts, which
were pretty much calf-length on me, and held the whole
getup together with his dress belt, which rested on my hips,
its prong stuffed through a new hole I'd made with the point
of my kitchen scissors. I'm not saying it was a fashion state-
ment; I'm saying I wanted his arms around me while I
worked on The Plan For Revenge now that I knew what
Larry Ellis cared about. But I suppose the getup might have
given Gary some ammunition for his "Mom has lost her
mind" theory.

He didn't answer about how he'd been or even get side-
tracked into telling me the latest about his church; he was
eyeballing my outfit. I glanced at my wrist where I hoped he
wouldn't notice that I wasn't wearing my watch. Pulling
Harold's sleeve to my fingertips, I said, "Never mind lighting
the candle, dear. It's later than I thought. Look, son, I need to
change and get ready to go out. I have plans tonight. A . . .
date. The chickens just came in the back door a minute ago
because I left it open when I came in to get their . . . vita-
mins." Sometimes you just have to make stuff up as you go
along, something I used to get all over Harold for doing. As
you can probably tell, this was not my most shining ten minutes with Gary. I do much better with a little prep time.

"A *date*? You don't mean with a *man*?" Gary went right
over the moon. I thought his contacts were going to pop off
his eyes.

Of course I hadn't meant a date with a man. But Gary
sounded so outraged at the very notion that I got my back up
again, as I explained later to CarolSue.

"I guess I can date a man if I want to, son. It's not like I've invited him to move in with me. Yet," I added, that last word an afterthought while I narrowed my eyes to a dare.

As CarolSue pointed out when I told her about it, the God Squad was sure to go right into overdrive now. I could have been smarter. But the accidental advantage of getting him all worked up was that he didn't go on a Glitter Jesus hunt, and forgot all about what I was wearing. Fortunately, the girls and I take our sherry out of my fine china cups, because I took a couple of sips of what I'm sure he thought was tea while he ranted on. How strange it is to be a parent and the child of one: how strands of expectation and disappointment always braid over and over with love to form the uncuttable cord.

Anyway, I told CarolSue that I thought I'd kept Gary distracted enough that he hadn't paid attention to the photocopies and handwritten notes spread over my kitchen table. Along with a small dot of chicken poop from when Beth was alarmed by Gary's sudden entrance. I wasn't entirely sure, though, because he'd set the dove—which truly did resemble a turkey vulture—next to the poop, which I hadn't been able to wipe up right away, not without calling his attention to it. Don't get the wrong idea from Gary, who lives to criticize. Marvelle's litter box gets cleaned out every day and I keep a decent house. I was raised right. Of course, my mother never had a job outside our home, so I never quite met her standards, but I do keep up.

I've explained why I might not have told CarolSue everything, as The Plan evolved. Once in a while I also omitted something because our mother used to remind us that you can't shove words back into your mouth once they're out. I'm regularly reminded of this by my failures with Gary. After I hung up with CarolSue, I asked Marvelle if she agreed that Gary hadn't noticed Harold's old hunting rifle, brought down from the attic where it had been since his promise to Cody, propped in the hallway. And he hadn't gone into my bedroom, where Harold's camouflage pants and jacket, also rescued from the attic, were on the foot of the bed with his old orange hunting hat. She nodded her tail affirmatively, which is actually a more difficult maneuver than the negative switch, so I was sure she'd understood. Because Gary would have started an interrogation on the spot about the rifle rather than take a chance that Gus could get here in time to stop Bonnie from going on a rampage, even though Clyde was already dead. *You know that Bonnie,* Marvelle smirked. *She's wild.*

It was a good thing there was no interrogation, too, because it's hard to make up good lies fast when you're playing defense, although I'm a lot better at it than my fifth graders ever were. But I'm not telling CarolSue that since I saw those deer heads in Larry Ellis's house, it's brought it to my mind that possibly Larry Ellis himself needs to be hunted down.

Marvelle and I drank a toast to *that* idea. And she suggested that we switch from sherry to something stronger. Something Harold would like. "Good idea," I said. "But no driving. We never . . . ever." The very mention of that insulted her. She knows what can happen. She lives in the ruins.

20

I didn't tell CarolSue before I did it, but it wasn't because I was afraid she'd call Gary. She'd never do that, although she might have considered zipping past Go to have me committed. Most likely, though, she'd think I'd gone out and bought a fifth of bourbon before I made the decision. Well, she'd be right about the bourbon, but so what? Marvelle and the girls had some, too, while we discussed a reasonable course of action. Beth mentioned that perhaps I was in danger of becoming a bit obsessive about tracking Larry Ellis, and what more information did I really need? But then Marvelle, who'd maybe lapped up more of Kentucky's best than I thought, told Beth to shut up, that some good old-fashioned stalking was entirely in order, and that Louisa was entitled to learn all she could in order to develop an effective Plan. How did Beth think Marvelle had been the most renowned mouser in the Great Fucking State of Indiana, anyway? Amy positively cackled at that. She loves to see Beth get her comeuppance.

"Language, Marvelle! Just because Harold flew F-bombers once in a while after he came back from the war, there's no need for you to be coarse," I told her. "You do have a point about gathering all information possible. I know what that shithead cares about now, but it's not like CarolSue came up with an instant Plan about how to use the information."

"Language!" Beth cooed. I swear she channels my mother.

"Point taken. I bet you'd like a little more Wild Turkey. So anyway, we do need more information, I think, to develop The Plan. If we're not just going to shoot him in the street, I mean. The problem with that is practical, much as I'm drawn to it. I might not make bail and who would take care of you all? Gary?"

Marvelle and the girls looked alarmed. "Yes, my point exactly," I said. "I'm sure I'd get off on justifiable homicide in the end. But we know how long it takes for trials. CarolSue is totally opposed, too. She said as much and that was when it was only a hypothetical. Not that she's come up with anything useful. But what does this leave us with for a Plan? I mean, yes we know what he cares about, but it's not like I can take all the deer in the woods away from Larry Ellis. I'm just not sure how to use the information. Yet."

So, as you see, it's not like I didn't seek advice before I went back to spy on Larry Ellis a second time.

And I was so much better prepared. For example, I had the brains to bring an empty coffee can with its red plastic lid in case I had another pee emergency. I went at sundown, well slathered with mosquito repellent, even though I'm sure those chemicals kill your brain cells as effectively as they repel mosquitos. I dressed in grey, to blend in with the twilight. Carol-Sue would have said I looked like a bag lady, but the only grey clothes in the house were Harold's work shirt and my old dress slacks from teaching, but the point was the color, and it reassured me about my mind that I'd thought of such fine-point details.

There was no choice but to park on the road. It wasn't like I could pull into their driveway, for heaven's sake. I'd passed the house slowly twice, staking it out, and seen the pickup truck and a car both parked in front of the two-car garage, which was open and just as junky as the inside of the house from what I could see. Neither vehicle could possibly have fit in there with the random boxes spilling contents, strewn tools, bike, and an overturned sawhorse. Those people certainly make me look like Housekeeper Of The Year, which I truly wish I could point out to my mother. Anyway, I drove on past after turning around in a different spot each time and stashed my car maybe a quarter mile down the road, using the berm as best I could.

I snuck down the road. The houses are very wide-spaced out here; the nearest was well beyond where I parked and across the road. It's mainly cornfields with some land in soy and a few cow pastures here and there, mainly Black Angus. Big stands of uncut woods, too, of course. I felt like Nancy Drew, my heart beating too fast, skulking along the brushy roadside toward the Ellis house, but the truth is there wasn't anyone to see me. King Kong wearing a pink tutu and rhinestone tiara could have avoided detection as easily as I did. I thought ahead to how I'd omit that detail when it all worked out and I finally told CarolSue about this reconnaissance.

By the time I reached the corner of the Ellis property, I was sweaty in the dusk. I might have even been panting a bit as I stood in the brushy shadows of the tree line where I'd made my break from on my last mission. Elaborately trying to look casual in case a car came along, which none did, thank goodness. You might be thinking, "For a woman who's so big on making a Plan, what on earth is The Plan now? Is this nutcase just going to amble up to the Ellis house, sneak around, and try to listen in?" That's exactly what CarolSue said later, which is what she claimed any rational person would think. Well, I hate to say *yes* when the word *nutcase* is attached to it like that, and I have to say that while it might not sound well conceived as described, it turned out to be a stroke of genius. Pure genius.

Be patient, as I always tell CarolSue. I have to tell a story in my own way. So I crept from shadow to shadow toward the house until I was back underneath that master bedroom window, just like the first time. Of course I kept way beneath it, not trying to look inside. It didn't do me a bit of good, though. Even though it was a butter-soft twilight, clear, peach-colored, beautiful and edgeless, when anyone with a lick of sense has every window open, Ellis's was shut.

But then I heard laughter. A man's, harsh as barking. A woman spoke then, ending with a bell trail of giggles. Silence, then more talking. It got louder and a door slammed. A scraping sound. Other sounds I couldn't identify as I was frantically shrinking myself, trying to get behind and between two shrubs that were considerably smaller than I.

They had come out onto the patio. The door slammed again.

"Hey, kid," the man said. Was it Larry? "Take out the trash."

"Ma, kin I go over t'Dud's house?" Could I have heard right? Someone would name their child Dud? Stay focused, Louisa, I told myself. This must be the boy who was in that bed. Squatting in the bushes was awkward, and branches were in my face and neck, but I was afraid to move. A whine of mosquito approached my ear, and I raised my shoulder to shield it. No one was visible to me, but my memory of distance told me I was only ten or twelve feet from them.

"No way. You're supposed to see your father this weekend. So you need to get that history paper that's due Monday done ahead."

"He texted. He's got something else. Like always. I gotta work Saturday till two anyway."

"Oh. Maybe he'll be free next weekend."

"Uh huh. So can I go?"

"I guess. But don't be later than nine thirty, honey. Call me when you get there. And when you're leaving to come home. That's why I got you the—"

"I know, Mom. Don't worry."

"Hey, that trash needs to go out before you go," the man said. "Please." The please delayed and mocking.

A mumble that might have been "Later," and another door

slam. Maybe a minute of silence. I tried to make my huddle smaller, tucked in my hands, which looked stark and white against the shrubbery, dirt, and weeds.

"You spoil that kid," he said. "You shoulda backed me up. I asked the way you said to."

"Don't start. Please."

"Well, for chrissake, I'm trying, but the kid has an attitude. He needs a good—"

Her voice came in, a descant over his rising one, but I couldn't make out all she said until I picked up, "—even a job, so please stop. So, back to this weekend. I really want to go," she interrupted.

"Nah. It's gonna get hot soon. You know I hate hot weather. I wanna get out and scout new ground before rut season. Mine are hunted out." He barked his laugh. "I'm too good. Deer fear me. Women crave me, huh?"

"In your dreams," she said. (Personally, envisioning Ellis's mug shot and the brief glimpse I'd had of him with that ridiculous ponytail, I completely agreed with her although he was right about the kid and the trash, and she looked like a pygmy Barbie-doll imitation herself.) And then she spoiled it anyway with a flirtatious giggle.

"Gonna hang some trail cameras, but gotta go farther out. Might even find me a nice new home decor. I'll take the kid with me for ya."

"I've told you no on that. I'd really like you to do this with us as a family. You promised."

"What's the big deal?"

"Not explaining it again. I don't see why you have to do this year-round. Why can't you wait until deer season at least?" she whined. "This is a family event, and . . . you're gonna get caught one of these days. What's gonna happen then, huh? Wanna lose your hunting license? Can you go to jail for that stuff? I think I heard you can. I don't have the money to get you off again. Anyway, you should come be with me and Brandon." There was a pause, and, then, almost begging, "We need you, honey."

"It's your family. Oh, wait. Supposedly, he'll be with his *dad*, remember? Hah. Big fat chance of that one. You go, stay overnight, drink wine coolers, and talk about shoes. The kid'll go to Dud's the way he always does. You know damn well he's not gonna end up going with you or going to see that asshole. Don't say I didn't try. You've got this stupid thing about guns 'cause your dumbass brother shot his own foot. I'm gonna fire up the grill now." That's pretty close to what he said. He'd gotten up and moved so it was more difficult to hear him. The door creaked and banged shut again; I surmised that one of them had gone into the house, probably her, if he was lighting the grill.

But then I heard the door open again, her voice. "Honey, I know you're trying with him and it means a lot. You're right. He won't want to go with me, and there's no chance his father will do . . . Maybe you could show him about cars, something like that?—something useful. That'd be really good. . . ."

I didn't hear what came next because I'd started to edge backward slowly out of the bushes, careful not to make noise or movement, nothing that might attract attention. My knees and ankles had stiffened, my back was an ache that wanted to moan. Darkness was rising off the ground skyward, but it certainly wasn't enough to hide me. I unfolded as if I were ancient, willing myself not to be.

I turned toward the road, one careful, silent foot in front of the other, crouching, hunched as my mother before she died. I had just stepped clear of the house when there was a blast of thumping music from the driveway, and the sound of a gunning motor. Jerking myself back into the house shadow, I breathed in *please*, and then breathed out *thank you* for the oblivion of the young. The boy was in the car—it was red and sporty, although it looked old, and had several doodads dangling from the rearview mirror—and he wasn't paying the slightest attention, though he could have spotted me easily. I ducked back until I heard the car clear the driveway. Take out the trash, you young twit, I wanted to yell after him, but don't worry, I haven't lost my mind. Cody always took out the trash. Well, maybe not the first time he was told when he was with Gary. I don't think he had much respect for his dad.

Again, I did my casual stroll act to get back to my car, although I wanted to bolt like a deer. I didn't know whether I'd even learned anything useful. On the way home the moon was nearly full, hanging big and just above the trees. I had less trouble seeing the road than I do when the night sky is lightless. Still, I tried to concentrate on driving rather than excavate what I'd heard. I can't afford an accident. What if Gary tried to take my keys away, or the company raised my insurance rates?

21

Deer have always lived on our land. The field corn attracts them and the thick woods where they bed and make their trails to the ready water of Rush Run. Sometimes men have knocked at my front door and asked if they could hunt our property in season. I have always said no, and Harold didn't argue the point. But if he answered the door, he'd always ask if the man was a vet. If he'd served in Vietnam, Harold would say yes without asking anything else. He also said yes to men who needed meat for their families to get through the winter. That was before he took Cody out, of course, and when he was still hunting himself. I've told you how Cody changed the Vietnam-soldier side of Harold, the part of him that wanted to be out in the forest stalking with a rifle, perhaps exorcising demons, perhaps summoning an old, bizarre exhilaration he'd shared with his platoon. I didn't know. But I believe he saw what Cody saw; we didn't need the meat. We didn't need it, and Cody saw the pain with no need of the family's to either balance or justify it.

Once Harold asked me why I said no, and I shrugged and said I wasn't comfortable with strangers carrying guns on our land. He wouldn't have understood the truth because I didn't, either. I loved our animals too much and the deer seemed their kin, only a half-step removed. All the plastic-wrapped meat in the grocery store—yes, I thought about that when I bought and fixed it for the family. Would they have understood if I'd said, *no more*: I won't buy it, I won't eat it, I won't serve it? My meat-and-potatoes husband, son, and grandson? The only person who would have heard my heart was Nicole, and we lost her. Are you thinking there was no *we* to it, Louisa? It was Gary with his thoughtlessness that caused the whole family to lose Nicole. He broke a lot of hearts, that son of yours. I confess I've thought that, but let's stick to the point I'm making about how I cared for the animals and still served meat. Do you see how my mind set aside its own failures of logic? How difficult it is to live when we think.

It turns out that there are a lot of laws about deer hunting, even in a county as old-boy as Dwayne, Indiana. Harold knew them back when he hunted, I'm sure, not that it was a supper-table topic. As I've said, there wasn't a comfortable chair in my mind for the idea of hunting to rest in, so I closed the door and didn't think about it. Harold, Gary, Cody, Nicole, Mom, my students, CarolSue, my teacher friends, and the neighbors all had my focus. The chickens and Rose the goat, the Labs and the cats, and the horses had my attention.

Now, though, I was educating myself on the topic. My kitchen table was covered with the pages of laws. What kind of gun, say a rifle versus a muzzleloader, a hunter may aim and on exactly which dates. How many deer each hunter is allowed to shoot, with antlers and without. The season for the more quaint bow and arrow—and the crossbow, a distinction I'll spare myself reading up on, since Larry Ellis's guns were displayed along with the prideful pictures of him grinning over the posed bodies of his kill.

With the photocopies of the laws I also had instruction manuals. Illustrated Guides To Death. Of course they're not called that. They have names like *The Whitetail Huntsman* and *Successful Big Game Tracking*. There are primers and more advanced directions. And there are publications for expert killers. Men like Larry Ellis were evidently way out of

Harold's league, back in the day when he bought a license and a deer tag for himself and for Cody. Trophy hunting is an obsession for them.

Two pamphlets had especially caught my attention. One had worked like tumblers in the combination to Larry Ellis's mind state: *Scouting Big Game Before the Season.* The other one was the seed for The Plan: *Priming the Hunt in the Off Season.*

Harold hadn't been thinking nearly big enough when he hatched his ineffective revenge schemes. He'd had no idea that he was trying to take out Attila the Hun with a squirt gun. I wasn't going to make that mistake. I got back to my reading. Teachers know how to look things up, and how to make long-range plans. I should have helped my Harold. We'd have been unstoppable together.

Al Pelley, the farmer who had contracted to put in and tend the field corn this year, looked at me as if my mind were wandering dangerously near the void. The register of his voice was definitely higher than usual and I noted a flush on his face, which was impressive since he's ruddy-skinned anyway.

"You want me to *what?* First, it'll reduce your yield. There's no market for it, won't do a damn thing except attract all the deer in the state. That soil is fine for corn. No need for this, Louisa. And why would you want those waves?" He jabbed his left forefinger at the schematic I'd drawn for planting, which he held in his right hand.

I'd taken one whole field out of regular field corn. The edges of it will be let go, in curvy lines, back into the natural grasses that lead into the woods above Rush Run Creek. A section of it will be planted in clover; some in corn and oats that won't be cut; some in brassica, kale and turnips and winter greens, although those won't be planted until August to create a cold-weather food source. Al was entirely right that this would attract deer. That was the exact idea. The curvy lines were to provide the deer the cover they like; using the

field next to the woods was to put a food source near where
they bed and find water. I was extremely proud of myself. I
gave myself an A plus. I hoped every deer in the county would
come. I was still working on how to connect this up to Larry
Ellis, but first things first. I'd even told CarolSue the basic
Plan I'd come up with: to attract deer, somehow get word out
that they were abundant on my land, catch Larry Ellis hunting out of season, call the sheriff, and press charges, with the
result that he'd lose his hunting license. You might think
there are a lot of holes in The Plan, but as I said, it was a
work in progress and my sister hadn't been much help.

Al squinted at me and then looked down at the paper I'd
given him, which was eleven by twenty inches. He looked
back up at me with that look people give when they think
you're putting them on and don't appreciate being made a
fool of.

"Don't you think the lines are pretty?"

He stared, not a trace of my humor playing on his face.

"Well, Amy's the artistic one, and she's very impressed
with the design." I said this to annoy him more. The design
was all mine.

Although he's an inch taller than I am, I think it's fair to
say Al's one of those runty, bowlegged men who looks like he
couldn't handle a rototiller let alone a combine, but he's got
cowboy in his blood and he's stringy-strong because of it.
Harold told me that Al had come out of a rodeo and married
a farmer's daughter six months before their daughter was
born. That was a long time ago, and the union didn't last,
but what Al knows about farming did.

"I just want to try something different," I finally said into
his silence. "We can do two plantings of the oats, one in the
spring, and a late one. We'll sell the first cut, okay? And the
winter greens will cleanse the soil. I read that."

"That's not enough oats to be worthwhile, Louisa. And
the soil ph is already six point seven. Had it tested at the
County Extension myself. You talked to Gary about this?"

THE TESTAMENT OF HAROLD'S WIFE

Al scratched his cheek, leaving a white line next to his mustache, which was halfway between brown and grey, like his unruly hair. He wore overalls like the ones Harold used to favor. It was only nine, though; the dew was barely off the grass. Maybe he didn't realize how warm it would be by noon. I always told Harold those sorts of things, and Al lived alone.

"Are you worried about being paid, Al?" I came back at him quickly and Al looked surprised. "Because I'll write you a check for half right now. I don't expect you to wait." I probably should have told him the truth, made him an ally, but the business about asking Gary upset me. And I didn't want anyone but CarolSue knowing that I was out to make Larry Ellis lose what he loved. Hunting. As you know, I was still evolving Plan details, but teachers are good at revising Plans.

Al and I were standing on the front porch. Al had declined my offer of coffee. He didn't meet my eyes, which I later realized should have tipped me off that there was something I didn't know. "It's not that. I was jus . . ." he mumbled, but then he couldn't let it go. "Not right. Won't make the land pay what it should."

"It'll be all right, Al. Really."

"All right with you, maybe," he muttered, turning, tossing the back of his hand in my direction in a wave of departure, dismissal, or resignation, as he went down the two porch stairs and cut across the grass toward his truck. "Your grass is bad. Hired a kid for help on my own place. Got too much to do myself. Took on too much contract work. Want me to have him mow for you? Good kid, just gotta learn."

The grass was lush, weedy, and overgrown. Cody used to mow the grass. CarolSue asked me who was taking care of it, and I told her, "No one. I have no one."

I really didn't want another boy mowing the lawn. "Our Cody used to . . . he was the one who . . ." I had to look away from Al then. Some things you don't want another person to see. He had the good sense to give me a couple seconds. When I looked back, he shrugged.

"Up to you. But when Harold was here, he—"

I looked away again and then I gave in. Teachers are nothing if not practical. The old push mower is too heavy for me. Harold's riding mower had broken down yet again. He'd been going to get a new one after the harvest—that harvest that I wasted—after he died. I wanted to ask Gary to mow even less than I wanted a boy who wasn't our beloved Cody to do it.

"Yeah," I said. "Okay. Thanks."

22

I'll give him credit for this much: Al did not beat it back to his own place and call Gary before the highway dust had settled. He must have slept on it because it was a full twenty-four hours before Gary got wind of my plan (a wind that could only have blown out of Al's mouth), and bounced his rattletrap van down the ruts in my driveway so fast and hard, I'm surprised his head didn't go right through the top.

I didn't get what was going on at first, which scared me again about my mind, which I cannot afford to lose. But he showed up with a strawberry cheese danish from Diana Dee's Bakery over in Germantown—a particular weakness of mine—instead of some new atrocity like the bumper sticker he put on my car last week. GOT JESUS? it said, next to a picture of a glass of milk. I had to work with a pan of hot water and a razor blade to get it off after he left. The danish made him a son I could relate to again, like when he was married to Nicole, and the notion was so lovely it threw me off my game. In those few moments, he reminded me of Harold.

"Good coffee, Mom," he even said before he showed his hand. "Hey, cat, get off the table. Great weather we've been having. I guess Al must be about ready to put the corn in, huh?"

"That he is. Ground's dry enough now."

"So are you doing okay money-wise? I mean I know you didn't get the crop harvested after Dad died, and . . ." He trailed off, waiting for me to pick up the piece of yarn he was trailing and knit it into some information for him. Only I didn't. I hate knitting.

I took a drink of my coffee, which was still almost as hot as I like it. The light in the room was quietly full, clear, unyielding—not the kind to make you blink—but direct and true, unwilling to soften small flaws of my housekeeping. A couple of random crumbs on the counter, whitish dried droplets of water on the window above the kitchen sink, a smeary sponge line where I'd wiped the kitchen table, a small spiderweb I can't reach up in the corner next to the dish cupboard. In the same way, I could see the lines on my son's face. The angry parentheses around his mouth from the arguments he won with Nicole, and the war he lost when she left, how it surprised and nearly killed him and he didn't know it and might never. The grey-brown hollows under his eyes that must be the dried pools of Cody grief. I saw where he'd missed two spots when he shaved that morning, and how the collar of his tan shirt was slightly frayed. These scars of grief and failure put me in mind of my Harold, and I started to move my hand across the table to put it over his. Had it not been for that same expansive light, when I leaned into feeling *oh my son, my son,* and looked into his eyes, I'd never have caught how they hooded for an instant when I didn't answer about my finances, as if he were calculating what to say next.

I pulled my hand back.

"So, uh, Al mentioned you're not putting all the land back in field corn."

"Oh, did he."

"Can't figure why you're not."

"You or Al, you mean?"

"Uh, Al."

"He shouldn't worry. Doesn't affect him." I smiled at my son and took a sip from my cup. "How's your coffee doing? Want me to heat it up for you?"

"Mom. No, my coffee's fine. You're putting in crazy stuff that won't make money."

"Oh my. Poor Al. I'll have to have a talk with him. Have you heard when the repairs on the bridge over Three Mile Creek are starting? That's going to be a bad detour."

Gary's neck was red. He scratched his arm, then the back of his head. He closed his eyes in a prolonged blink, then wiped his forehead with the back of his hand. "The sign says the detour starts Friday. You couldn't have missed it, it's right—look, Mom. I'm glad you're not putting corn in that field. That's good."

This was a new tack. I decided to hold steady. "Hmmm."

"There's no need to put crazy stuff in there, though. Just leave it empty. Leave it empty. Since you don't need the income corn would have brought, well, don't put anything in. Don't lose money by putting in crazy stuff. Like Al says, I mean."

"Hmmm." I tried to read his eyes as I took another sip of my coffee, starting to cool and turning unpalatable. "I hate it when that bridge is out, don't you? I wish they'd fix it right once and for all instead of all this stupid patchwork. Going all the way around something instead of straight to it just drives me nuts."

"You should just leave the field empty. Al says."

This is Gary's way. He just keeps saying the same thing, as if to wear a rut in my brain that will come to seem familiar and I'll start thinking it was my idea. That's how he's trying to save me with his new religion, too.

"I get the feeling that's what you want me to do for some reason, Gary. But I can't imagine why."

Gary hesitated. I could tell I'd caught him. I just didn't know in what.

". . . Just surprised you don't need the money for corn, is all. Can't see throwing it away planting crazy stuff."

"Nice of you to be concerned, son, but I'm just fine. You don't need to worry about my money. Or my mind."

"I do worry, Mom. I'm trying to take care of you. And my church. You're all I have now." His eyes watered with emotion and I felt guilty, as I often do with him. "By the way," he went on, "one of the members said he passed you putting flowers by the crosses up on the highway."

"Actually, I planted them. I didn't like how the flowers would die so quick when I'd leave them there, so I had this brilliant idea. I put a border of rocks in front of the crosses and made a garden. That way when they mow the berm they have to go around the flowers or they'll break the blade." I couldn't stop myself from babbling. "It's Lou Anson does that mowing anyway, and he's a sweetheart. I asked him if it was okay. He said nothing's supposed to be allowed there, but go right ahead. Of course he knew Harold, and anything for Harold and his grandson. Said the spot was sacred. That was his word, too."

You might have guessed it was Gary who put the crosses there. They make me sad. I like my circle of round, smooth rocks, which I painted white and where I wrote words to my man and my boy that would be hidden where the cheeks of the stones kiss. I like them and the living brightness of the flowers inside the border: a riot of apricot, blue, lavender, and yellow pansies, planted in the dirt from the farm where Harold and I brought Cody every week. Cody so loved the farm, like his grandpa. Now I bring two little baggies more dirt every Friday by myself. As soon as the pansies get leggy and tired of heat, I will dig them up and put in every color of dahlias, those sturdy survivors. And whatever other flower I think of that will rise up and bloom a silent song of grief and joy and unspeakable memories.

"Do I know Lou?" was all Gary said, his voice serrated with suspicion. I should have paid attention to that.

"Sure, you remember Lou. Lives over behind the quarry. Big, outgoing guy, little bit hard of hearing. Used to be on a submarine, well, that was back during Vietnam, you wouldn't have known the family then, you weren't born, but that's when I first knew Bernice. When you were growing up he was on the fire department." I was glad to be off the subject of the land, just the biggest of the subjects I did not want to discuss with my son, which included everything except, right then, Lou and the weather. Or possibly the best way to make meat loaf. We hadn't disagreed about Grandma's meat loaf recipe yet.

I went on for another minute feeding him tidbits about Lou and Bernice and their gorgeous daughter, Christina, until it backfired. "Oh wait," he interrupted. "Didn't they send her away to that school for—"

"I don't remember that. Just how great Lou always was to your dad. There's a thing between Vietnam vets, but they just liked each other anyway."

"She was like a genius, and they sent her to that fancy college out east."

I pretended to search my memory for words like *merit scholarship* and *Princeton* and shrugged. "Knowing Lou and Bernice, such down-to-earth people, I doubt that." I didn't want Gary's animosity toward smart, successful people like Christina to have him take an attitude toward Lou. I especially didn't want Gary out there "checking" when Lou was mowing, taking any close looks at how those crosses had been pounded deep into the ground, until they appeared a sort of trellis for the living flowers rising all around and from that sacred ground. It had been either that or get them out of there completely, and this was my version of being respectful.

I was suddenly tired and out of material. It's a sad thing when you have nothing to say to your son and it's your own fault. I'd steered him away from what I was doing with my fields—for the time being. Now I had to distract him from his crosses and my flowers.

I knew I wasn't looking at him and made myself do it. I have always sniffed out Gary's dissembling, disliking the sneaky side of him that I thought had no genetic basis. But there we sat in that merciless light, me hiding my own secrets behind my eyes when I met his.

Gary had gotten the longitude and latitude of where Cody's

body was found from the police report. That's where he put the cross. Harold stepped out in front of that Dwayne County Waste Recycling truck right from Cody's cross. That's how he knew, or thought he did, where to find a portal to Cody. Sometimes I wonder what he would have done if Gary hadn't made it so easy for him. So damned easy.

I manufactured a smile and spread it across my face. "It's time I got outside and let the girls out in the yard. They hate being in the run when they can be loose. Need to get them fresh water, too. Want to come?" I knew he wouldn't.

"There's nothing wrong with chickens staying in a chicken coop." He shook his head. "No, I've got to get back to the church. Speaking of which, I was going to mow the grass but Al said he could spare the kid he hired for his own place for a couple hours, so I went ahead and gave him twenty bucks. Make sure he remembers I already paid. But the mower might need gas, sorry about that. And Mom, really, I'm counting on you to be sensible about that field. Leave it empty, it's what God wants, so do it, okay." It wasn't a question and I didn't answer partly because Gary stood up abruptly, leaned over, kissed my cheek, and headed to the front door. He didn't alter his path to avoid Marvelle, dozing in a swath of sun spilled from the kitchen linoleum over onto the living room carpet. His shoe grazed her back and she startled up, frightened that she'd been fooled enough to sleep while he was there.

"Gary imagines he's looking out for you, don't you think? It was nice of him to pay to have the grass mowed. We both know he loves you," CarolSue said during our phone time late afternoon.

I added more bourbon to my tea and shrugged for Beth's benefit as I tossed her a grape. Amy beat her to it, though. They are often not kind to one another no matter how I scold. Then I shook my head, knowing CarolSue would wait for me to find words.

"I know you're right. He's doing the best he can. He does love me. And I love him. But look at my family. How often has love made things work out all right? Hell, how often has it even averted disaster?"

"Oh honey. I can't argue with you there. It does take more than love, doesn't it?"

23

Gary stayed away for a while after that visit. I should have been suspicious about what that meant, especially because I took CarolSue's advice and stopped answering the daily prayer calls. Normally, that would bring Gary out to check up on me. I had prepared to tell him that sweet as the attention is, I'd tripped a couple of times running to answer the phone, and it was lucky I hadn't broken my hip—such a common injury for the elderly—so it would be best if the group's prayers for me were silent. I thought he might buy that. Of course I should have pondered why I hadn't needed this excellent story.

But it was only Al who showed up, to start the planting early Saturday morning. I handed him the same plan again.

"You sure about this?" Al said, squinting at it, although the sun was thin where we stood between the house and the barn. Al liked to get an early start, and I'd met him outside with a thermos of coffee and a new copy of the drawing. He held the paper as if it might detonate.

"Let me know if you need me to order any more seed," I said. "And when you take a break, there's some of those cinnamon rolls you like so well in the kitchen. I got them at the Stop N'Shop." There was a time when I baked cinnamon rolls for the men myself, and it did fill the whole house with such a sweet fragrance that lasted until almost noon, but with Harold and Cody gone, I've no heart for it even though

the ones from the store aren't much to speak of and I'm sure
Al knows it. He'll eat them, though. "I'll wait five minutes
before I let the girls out of the coop." This last was a reference to his threats to run over any hens that got in his path;
for some reason of his own, Al hates chickens.

"Make it ten," Al said, folding the plan and stuffing it in
his shirt pocket. "Kid's in the barn getting out the mower
now. He's catchin' on." He took the thermos, turned, and
strode across the weedy gravel. His feet were thudding in a
way that definitely wasn't happy, but they kept going. I
watched to see that they did, noticing how his jeans were
frayed around the heels of his boots. I waited to be sure until I
saw the plow heading out of the barn and then I went inside
and took a deep breath, poured myself some coffee, and smiled.

I knew how quickly early May would slide toward summer even though for the most part it was staying lovely and
cool. I wasn't going to sit around and congratulate myself,
even though I'd done CarolSue's job and come up with The
Plan, which, believe me, I pointed out to her. She did add one
decent idea, even if she did back into it, and it returned me to
the library for more research.

"So I guess other animals are going to like this pretty well,
too," she'd said. "You planning an entire banquet service?"

She was just being her version of funny, but I did start
thinking. By the time Al cut the slant along the woods' edge
in uneven curves, shaking his head the whole time, I'd found
a seed mix of native prairie grasses: big bluestem and little
bluestem, Indian grass, Canada wild rye, side-oats grama.
The area I was letting go into high grass could be more than
a weed jungle; it could be cover and food for other wildlife,
too. And I hadn't known that the old prairie had bloomed
purple with asters, pink coreopsis, wild indigo, but those
seeds were part of the mix, and the botany book said they
would attract butterflies.

"There's even milkweed, black-eyed Susans, and yellow

coneflower," I rattled on to CarolSue. "You should see the pictures."

"How much time are you spending out in the sun?" she said.

"I'm wearing that stuff. Sunscreen."

"Seriously? Because I was wondering if you maybe had a touch of sunstroke."

"Oh stop it. Of course Al is bitching about sowing the clover. So I'll do it myself if I have to. Can't plant the winter stuff until August, so there's no hurry with that. I wish you could see the deer. The fawns still have their spots."

I refreshed my teacup with some of the good stuff. It was five thirty and I hadn't thought about supper yet. The girls had been snacking on grapes and oatmeal, which they've come to enjoy over chicken feed. I'd needed to come in and put my feet up before tending to watering them and feeding Marvelle.

"What's happening with Gary?"

"Dunno. How's Charlie looking today?"

"Tired and peaked. I think he might be depressed, but maybe he's just worn out from the treatments." My sister sounded tired out herself.

"I know you're exhausted. We don't have to talk about The Plan right now, y'know. I'll tell you if there are any developments. Did you finish *Jane Eyre*?"

"Not yet. Don't tell me anything about what's going on in that attic. My eyes get too tired to read for very long and there's nothing but reruns on TV. I've seen all my shows already. The Plan is the best distraction I have. Unless Charlie breaks down and gets rid of HBO. I want Showtime."

"Gets rid of B.O.? What are you saying? Is the radiation affecting how he smells?"

"Oh Lord, Louisa. I want him to discontinue Home. Box. Office. On the cable television and subscribe to Showtime instead. They show different *movies*. We *pay extra* and it's hooked—"

"Okay, Miss High-and-Mighty Technology. Some of us don't—"

"I know. I'm sorry. Never mind. What's going on with Harassment By Prayer?"

"I stopped answering like you said, and I have my story ready, but he hasn't shown up for days. Hasn't sent Gus, either."

"That makes me very nervous," she said.

But I was enjoying my Plan For Revenge too much to pay attention to my sister. I should have.

Gary did show up again, of course. He brought me a giant loaf of white bread and a plastic stamp that would imprint an image of Jesus into an individual slice. I almost fainted when he showed me.

"Are you serious?" I shouldn't have said that, of course.

"Mom, I don't think you're trying to understand. Think about it for a minute, the meaning of daily bread, how we take things for granted, until maybe we don't have them. It's to remind us to give thanks for what we do have. You of all people—"

I could not have this conversation. Not with my son. Not as long as my memory of Cody and Harold was intact, for sure. "Well, thank you for the bread, son. The thing is, the doctor told me that I'm kind of borderline with my blood sugar, you know how older people are, and not to eat any white food."

"What? You never told me that. White food? What does that mean?"

"Oh, you know. It's stuff that's high in carbohydrates. I didn't want to worry you."

How I can make things up. It's wonderful what you learn listening to National Public Radio. I might even have borderline blood sugar for all I know, so it hardly counts as a lie.

"Well, I'll bring you another kind of bread next time I come. Un-white bread. Like brown bread, I mean. You know. Wheat. But you always used to serve white so I thought . . .

But, Mom, you need to tell me these things. I should go to your next doctor appointment so I know what's going on." He was sweet and earnest and I thought, CarolSue is right that he's trying to take care of me.

Gary ended up taking the bread (which I would have eaten) and leaving the stamp, because I'd lost the heart to persist and claim that I didn't eat bread at all anymore. I have to help him not to fail again.

Then he called and asked what size shoes I wore. I said I didn't need shoes, but he was relentless so I told him size 7, so I could give myself a point for telling the truth. A week later, he showed up with a fancy pair of new gardening shoes, saying he'd noticed that the ones I was wearing last time he'd been to visit were old and beat-up. "Where'd you get these?" I asked him. "They look waterproof."

"The Internet," he said. "They just started selling them on one of my favorite sites. They *are* waterproof. Try them on."

I did. "They fit. This was really thoughtful of you." I walked around the kitchen in them. It was midafternoon, and my feet had started to hurt. They always do by then. I get tired when I've worked since morning. "They feel very comfortable." It was true. "Thank you, son. These are wonderful." I hugged him then, and meant it.

He also brought whole wheat bread, the kind like cardboard, which I don't much like. The wheat bread made me realize that I wasn't going to get any more strawberry cheese danish from Diana Dee's, which was tantamount to having shot myself in the foot with the new shoe on it. And he pointed out that the stamp would work nicely on this type of bread. But Gary also brought some lovely fresh strawberries, which were in season, and I did truly appreciate the shoes. I told CarolSue I thought Gary and I might be turning a corner.

"Pretty soon you'll be able to have a yard sale of tacky religious artifacts, too," she teased.

"I'm running out of closets to stash the stuff in. You should see me run around trying to find it all to put it out when I know he's coming. But I think I've figured out how to . . . I don't know. Deal with Gary better. I'm trying."

Of course, later I would realize Gary thought the same thing about me. And later I would realize how I'd slowly let my guard down over the summer. And here's the kicker: I didn't even see it for weeks. I don't generally look behind me when I walk. Not until it rained one night and the ground was very moist when I was up early and went to the empty field to see if the clover Al planted had started to come up. When I was going back to the house, almost retracing my steps, something looked funny about my footprints and I stopped to look at them. Then I turned and looked at them sideways. My left foot was imprinting the word *Jesus* into the soil; my right foot was putting down *Loves You.*

Now really, Louisa, you might be saying. Seriously. What's so bad about that? There's not a thing wrong with what he believes and he's just trying to be a good son. It doesn't seem like you appreciate him the way you should.

I can see how you'd say that. CarolSue says it all the time.

Get yourself some tea with a big splash of bourbon and I'll tell you the rest of the story. But be patient; there are some things you need to hear first. You know, I have to tell a story in my own way.

24
Brandon

It was harder than he'd thought, working for the farmer, but at least it hadn't gotten unbearably hot yet and he didn't hate the physical work once he got over being so stiff he felt like he was made of wood. Dud made a number of obscene jokes about stiffness that Brandon did not find amusing and he didn't want to think about what it would be like in August, but he was surprised to find he sort of liked being outside. He hadn't been able to find anything that involved working at a computer, which was what he was interested in doing. Not much of that in rural Indiana for a high school kid, his mother laughed when he told her that's what he wanted. She'd called Crazy Connie then because she was the Future Farmers of America Secretary of the Year or something and naturally had a list of area farmers who were looking to hire part-time and summer help. Of course, they all wanted FFA kids with some skill or another. One of them didn't specify that, the one who paid a buck an hour less and was in the next town over, not exactly close. Mr. Pelley said he'd taken on too much contract work and needed someone to pitch in around his own place and to give him a hand generally.

His mother said, "If he offers you the job, I think you should take it, honey. It's more than minimum wage, which is what you'll get someplace else, and he wants somebody part-time now, and full-time this summer. I bet he'd use you through harvest, too. I mean, he knows you're in school, he contacted FFA."

Brandon had sighed, made the call, gone to see the farmer, and gotten the job. Now, suddenly, he had no weekends, a sunburn, and was hauling, digging, cleaning, even mowing some lady's grass while his employer plowed her field. She'd been nice, though. Told him to take a break when he finished the front before he did the back.

"I'm not sure I'm supposed to do that, but thank you, ma'am."

"Nonsense. I insist. What's your name?"

"Brandon McNally, ma'am. Thank you. I'll just sit in the shade a minute."

"You have beautiful blue eyes, Brandon. May I ask how old you are?"

"Almost seventeen."

He'd felt terrible then, because her eyes got all watery and he had no idea if he'd done something, but he didn't see what it could have been. She went into her house, then a minute later came back out with a glass of lemonade and a cinnamon roll. It scared him that he'd lose his job, not that Mr. Pelley had said not to talk to a customer or take anything—it hadn't been mentioned one way or the other—but Brandon thought it might look like he'd asked for it.

"Ma'am, I shouldn't—" he said as she approached him, holding them out. Overhead the arms of an old sugar maple. His back rested on the thick trunk, his rear on the bump of a root. Tired as any grown man from work and thinking what's okay to do.

The lady, she was maybe his grandmother's age, walked through the brilliance of the day into the staggered circle of shade where Brandon sat. She wasn't fat like his grandmother or dressed in fancy pants and a matching print shirt with a lot of jewelry. She had some of the same turkey wattles under her arms and chin, but not so many as his grandmother, and her teeth weren't all yellow when she smiled at

him. She looked plain, hair stuck behind her ears, and she
wasn't covered in eye shadow and lipstick like his mother and
grandmother. Not too wrinkled up, but when she handed him
the glass, he saw her nails were dirty and her hands rough like
Mr. Pelley's.

"Nonsense. I know what boys like. You're doing a fine
job, and I appreciate it. I know how long Al will take, and
you'll finish the yard before he's back. Maybe you'd do me
the favor of spreading some compost then? Just till Al is
done, I mean."

"I'd be happy to do that. Thank you very much for the
lemonade. And the roll, too." He sat where she'd come up to
him beneath the tree, holding one in each hand, not wanting
to eat or drink while she was talking, afraid he would be
called on to answer. I was supposed to stand up when she
came out, he thought.

"You're a good boy. Do you like to read?"

"Yes, ma'am, actually, I do."

"That's a fine thing. Read any of the classics?"

"A few. My English teacher last year was suggesting American ones."

"Very good. I have quite a library of them. I hope you're
planning on college."

Her eyebrows went up while he tried to think what to answer. She said she had all those books so he guessed what she
wanted to hear. It was true anyway. "Well, I'd like to."

"I used to be a teacher," she said. "You can look at my
books, and if you want to borrow any of them, you may.
College is extremely important. You go ahead and drink that
now, and just bring the glass to the back door when you're
done. I'll be grateful for your help with the compost."

She was a nice lady. He spread the compost for her when
he finished mowing the lawn. It was no big deal, and he liked
the chickens pecking around in the back. The lady had come
out to show him what to do, and she'd talked to the chickens
like they understood. The chickens had names after charac-

ters in a novel, she said, and Brandon thought that was cool. While he worked, she asked him if he liked animals and he said yes, a lot, he loved animals. But when she asked if he had any, he had to think about what to say. The truth was that he'd asked his mother for a dog every year since forever, and she'd always said, "No, we don't have a yard and I'm allergic to cats so don't ask for one of those, either." Then one day she'd said, "Well, I guess if we do move in with Larry, since he's got a house and a yard—as long as you do all the work— would that make up for changing schools again?" and in the paper, Brandon found a free dog that needed a home and was already housebroken and everything, but then Larry said, *No way and no stupid discussion about it.* Brandon decided to just tell the lady that no animals were allowed where he lived. She said she was sorry about that and he could come see hers if he ever wanted to. Then she said the thing again about how he could borrow some books, especially since he wanted to go to college. Her eyes looked sort of wet again and he hoped he wasn't doing the compost wrong, but she said he was doing a fine job. He didn't borrow any books, though. He didn't think Mr. Pelley would like that since he'd said that if Brandon had to pee he should go behind the barn, and he wasn't sure how easy it would be to return them anyway.

He didn't tell Mr. Pelley he'd done the compost. He thought Mr. Pelley might charge her extra, and Brandon didn't want that. She was a nice lady.

25
Louisa

You need to know about the rest of the summer, and how The Plan moved on. The clover rose, first a pale haze and then an emerald blanket. When he planted the corn, I had Al leave a whole section of that same field empty for the winter food source for the deer. I'd plant those root crops myself in August. He was going to have to come back to turn it over again because the ground would harden over the summer. All the physical work I'd done had strengthened me, and the arthritis in my left knee was bothering me less. But then it always bothered me less in the summer, so maybe I was foolish to feel such hope.

This next may seem crazy to you. I don't care, I'll tell it anyway. I set up tin cans on long branches I stuck in the ground and took target practice with them. Often. It passed the weeks while I waited until it was time to start putting the rest of The Plan to work.

At first I got a little panicked because I was plain terrible, nothing like I used to be when Harold taught me to shoot, I don't know why. I guess he wanted the company when he practiced, but what he said was that a farm woman needed to know, living out where we did. But back then, I had a really good eye and The Plan—because I'd started to refine it—required that I have not just a really good eye but a spectacular one.

So I went to Dr. Rollins, the optometrist over in Tucker

City, and found out I need glasses for driving as well as reading now, which explains why they paint the street signs in such faint letters these days. Bifocals. First they cost me two months' worth of groceries and put me behind in the bills, then they were impossible to get used to. I kept looking through the wrong part at the wrong time and thinking I was having a stroke. It reminded me of the time Harold got himself a cell phone so I could call him out in the field. He put it in his shirt pocket where he'd hear it if it rang. He had no idea he'd accidentally set it to vibrate instead of ring. Don't you know the first time I did call him, he had such a sudden strange feeling in his chest that he zigged and zagged the tractor all crazy, certain he was having a heart attack. Started slapping all over his chest for his cell phone so he could call an ambulance, thinking he'd been pretty smart to get one after all. When he finally pulled the phone out of his pocket, it was amazing how that heart attack just quit and he felt fine. Oh, how we laughed about it, once he got over the embarrassment and told me. The memories come like that, like tender, sweet crumbs left after pie.

Revenge is even more expensive than glasses. Such a mistake I made not attending to the harvest when Harold died; that money would have been some cushion instead of the loss of plowing it under. "Stop worrying, Beth," I had to say, seeing her fidget as we talked it over. Amy agreed, and in a flurry of white flew up to where Jo was, on the couch, while Beth continued to pace around the living room carpet.

We'd put in a good day, and stopped for tea as the sun started to slide toward the treetops. The vegetables were coming in bountifully thanks to a long sunny spell, which the squash and tomatoes and green beans particularly loved. "We'll blanch and freeze vegetables for the winter, and we have our Social Security, unless, of course, that damn idiot Congress messes with it. Stupid talk about cuts again. Don't they know it's a trust fund of money we earned? But I can only take on Larry Ellis right now. Revenge is worth every cent." The girls had to agree with me. Except for Beth, who off and on got nervous, always thinking maybe there could be flaws in The Plan I just wasn't seeing, especially now that she knew my eyes had gone bad, even clucking that maybe I was just a batty old lady wearing worn-out pink house slippers with chicken poop on the left toe. I wondered how long that had been there, went to the sink, and cleaned my slipper off. Damn bifocals.

"I don't want to wear the new garden shoes in the house!" I said. "They're heavy with that waterproofing, and you know Gary took my old sneakers so I wouldn't wear them anymore. I am not batty. So I need some other shoes. Big deal. You're just having an anxiety attack, Beth. Be quiet or out you go."

Marvelle crossed the kitchen counter and sniffed the sponge I'd used to clean the poop off my slipper. Then she just stood there twitching her tail and staring me down.

"What?" I said. "What? Oh. Okay, you have a point. I'll put bleach on the sponge right now to sterilize it. Will that make you happy?"

Marvelle got that uppity look and sauntered away.

So June and then all of July passed: planting, target shooting, talking to CarolSue, gathering vegetables from the garden, freezing and canning vegetables from the garden. After the clover, the corn rose, silver and rippled like waves in morning sun. The girls pecked in the yard, flapping up onto my chair or the clothesline or the roof of the coop now and then if something startled them, but usually just doing their stiff-legged bobbing along the ground, their coos soothing and peaceful. Marvelle slept in the shade or made her stealthy way about the property, pretending she could still hunt when she wasn't criticizing me or being bossy. By mid-August, the heat nearly undid me, especially on canning days, the heat from the stove at six and seven in the morning cheating me of the few hours in the day that were bearable. But I knew the deer were coming. Their scat was between the corn rows, and I saw what they were already eating. Good. I hoped they knew they were safe. I stopped the target shooting, not wanting to alarm them. They came closer then, and as daylight shortened, I saw them more often.

Here's what you should know, though. I'd adjusted to my glasses. The hours and days of practice had steadied my hand again. I'd made the targets smaller and smaller. I almost never missed the mark anymore. I wasn't going to kill him, but he wasn't going to take any more trophies. Not ever again. I hadn't decided on whether it would be a knee or a hand. Whichever was the cleanest shot at the time, I guessed. Not that CarolSue knew any of this. CarolSue would never approve this version. No, The Plan she liked was a tame and impermanent iteration. When I considered how I'd lure Larry Ellis to hunt illegally, to poach from my land—which is abundant with deer because I've done everything to make it so—and having him arrested and charged, could I be sure he'd never take another trophy? Would he truly lose forever what he most loves? Would he know the meaning of grief?

I thought not.

And if I wasn't sure, what was the point of The Plan?

August was important for another reason, as you might remember. I called Al to come back and turn over the section of field I'd left fallow again. I told him I wanted it finely disked, too, but of course, I didn't say why, which I know topped off his opinion that I'd gone totally loony. It wasn't easy planting the root crops for the deer myself—so maybe I *was* a little loony—but I did it. The section still looked bare when I was finished, but I knew the secrets the earth and my heart held, and I was glad. All I needed now was rain, time, and luck.

26
Larry

"So, we're gonna go. I wanna join. The money'll even out because the dinner and drinks are way less for members, and I can find out where other guys are gonna set up," Larry said to LuAnn. "Stupid dicks can't keep their mouths shut. Works for me." He rolled onto his side, asking and not asking, his hand snaking under her short nightie. She slapped it away, wet her forefinger—provocative, provocative on purpose, he thought—and used it to turn a page of her magazine.

"I thought you always wanted to avoid those places," she said. "Where guys are hunting."

He sighed. "That's the point. If I know, I can avoid 'em. Most of 'em are lousy anyway. Bag one buck every ten years and think they're the Great White Hunter."

"When actually only you are." She flipped through the pages, stopped at one, and held it in his direction. "Would this look good on me?"

"Damn right. Sexy."

"Oh, I wasn't sure."

"Sure of what?"

"About the color. It's cobalt blue, and I usually wear—what are *you* talking about?"

"Come on, baby. You can buy any color dress you want, how about that? It's next Friday. They all take their women, and I don't want to look stupid. Last time I went as Chuck's guest, I had to sit with him and his wife like a third wheel."

He heard himself and stopped abruptly. He wasn't a man who'd beg for anything. He could be nice, or he could make her sorry. Her choice.

"Isn't it fifth wheel? You're obsessed with this stuff."

"What? Fifth . . . ?" But he decided it wasn't worth it to pursue what she was talking about. It had taken him the better part of a year to figure out that he could just let her asides float over like bubbles, whatever she meant not having to burst on his head, but he had it now. "So what. You're obsessed with shoes." He gentled his voice, nuzzled into her neck. She smelled faintly sweaty with an overlay of hair spray, or maybe it was cologne. When he'd first known her, she'd had hair that was sort of blond-and-brown striped. Now it was all blond. She said the sun did it, that it was natural. He didn't know about that, but her boobs were natural, he was pretty sure about that. "And me. You're obsessed with me," he said. Really what he thought was that she was obsessed with her son. LuAnn was crazy about the kid. She called that natural, too. He thought she was worse that way since the accident but maybe it was his imagination. She blamed the deer, not him, though. He was giving her time to come back to her senses. He did like her, the kid wouldn't be around forever, and he didn't like being alone. He'd had enough of that.

"In your wet dreams," she said now, but turned her head toward his and let the magazine fall to the bed. He slid his hand up her nightie again and she didn't slap it away. Not that he would have let that stop him.

"If I go with you, which I really don't want to do, even you said the chicken was all greasy when you went and the Lodge was a bunch of losers. If I do it, will you do something with Brandon again on Saturday? His father isn't going to do—"

"That asshole."

"So, will you?"

"I suppose."

"You have to put more effort in. He's a teenager." Her

hand went into his boxers. "I did pay your bond. And pay for the lawyer. You never would have gotten off without him."

"God, LuAnn, how long am I gonna be payin' you back for that?" He laughed. "I told him to wash my truck last week. I even said he could vacuum it." Squeezed a boob. Definitely real, he was ninety percent sure.

"Oh yes, an irresistible offer of a nonstop fun time. True bonding. Hey, I can stop if you want. I mean if you really don't want to meet effort with effort," she said, pulling off his boxers and working him harder with her hand.

"Believe me, I can meet effort with effort. That thing you're wearing is cute but get it off."

He swung a leg over both of hers. In the mood for a power position first. "So you'll go. . . ." He didn't wait for an answer. She wasn't the one in charge and she never would be.

27
Louisa

Have you ever noticed how elastic time is, stretching impossibly and then rushing to snap tight? More weeks passed. I walked the sections of my land in the mornings, leaving a written trail for wildlife and aliens about the affection of Jesus—but the shoes are comfortable—looking for signs and yes, yes, they were there. I saw the deer themselves, too, once a whole herd on the edge of one of my fields at dusk. There looked to be twelve, maybe fifteen, that time. More often I'd catch a glimpse of two or three, yearlings in tow, sometimes startled up out of their day beds. There was a buck, maybe more; I wasn't ever close enough to know if it was the same one I was seeing. Even with my glasses, I can't count the points on a rack at a distance or distinguish one set of antlers from another, and if you're thinking I should be competent at that, well, give it a try yourself. So, I just called him *my buck* and reminded him to stay on my land where he was safe, where they all were safe.

It was time for Phase II. "I can't chicken out now," I muttered to Amy, who clucked a protest and headed out of the kitchen. "Okay, I'm sorry," I called after her. "I know that expression is offensive. I'm sorry. I wasn't thinking." I'd been about to call Gus and set The Plan in action after waiting so long, but had put the phone back into the cradle on the wall before dialing. Now I just stood there and stared at the yellow-

and-peach print, tiny watering cans holding daisies, on the old wallpaper. Tired and fading. But I couldn't be. Not yet, not now.

I turned away from the wall. Even sweet Beth glared at me from where she sat on the counter. Marvelle was disgusted, though not by my having insulted chickens. (It's use of the term *scaredy-cat* that pushes her over the edge.) Hesitation always irritates her. I suppose it doesn't serve well when you're catching mice. Or a drunk driver who killed your grandson and your husband. "All right. I see your point. Both of you. All of you. This is no time to back down. I still wish Carol-Sue were here. But we can't think about that, can we? She'd never go for this. But we'll have a bit of tea and then I'll do it."

I endured all of them giving me accusing looks as I waited for the whistle of the kettle (a noise that usually makes Marvelle run for cover, but it was a measure of her annoyance that she sat her ground on the kitchen table, all the while giving me the evil eye). "Can't you just be nice?" I said, pouring Marvelle a saucer of milk and with a splash of bourbon for company and adjusting my tea to Plan Courage Strength. "There's no way I'm backing out. I could just use the support of my friends."

Marvelle swished her tail, which I took as assent. We drank our tea, and I had chocolate bourbon balls rolled in powdered sugar that were Mom's recipe (I made them yesterday after CarolSue asked me how much I was drinking) while the girls had grapes; then I went to the bathroom, put on some lipstick, and combed my hair. When I came out, I opened my arms and announced, grandly I thought, "It's time!" The moment was spoiled by JoJo squawking and flapping her way from the floor in front of the refrigerator to one of the straight-back chairs at the kitchen table, and then over to the top of the wingback chair, as if she'd suddenly reconsidered because I'd said something about which we should all be frightened to death.

"Gus? Hello, Gus, this is Louisa Hawkins calling. How are you?" At first, I had pressed the phone tightly to my ear, but the baritone that answered startled me into pulling it away from my head. Now I tried to figure how to put my mouth close enough that he could hear me but keep the receiver far enough away that I not go deaf when he responded. Nothing is ever simple. Have you noticed this about life? It's true. Don't make the mistake of thinking I only say that because I talk to chickens and a cat. If you're ever old and alone and you've lost everything, you'll talk to animals or birds, too, at least one. If you're smart, that is. Don't be fooled about me; I know exactly what I'm doing. And what I'm telling you about life is true: it's always got more layers than you expect, which is what I really mean when I say nothing is ever simple.

Maybe Gus is, though. His opening pleasantries boomed through the receiver, his voice deeper than I remembered it. Or just louder. "Yes, I'm doing quite well," I got in, "and I imagine you're happy that work on the bridge is finished. That detour was quite an inconvenience, wasn't it? Must have gotten your car all dusty." Did that sound sincere? It wasn't, but irritated teachers get practice sounding sweetly sincere by dealing with difficult parents and administrators, so I thought I pulled it off.

I took a swallow of tea, which wasn't nearly strong enough so I fixed that, and steadied myself while Gus waxed expansively about how the detour had interfered with his critical role in the county. You'd have seriously thought that bridge being out had deterred him from catching four or five of the fugitives on the FBI's Ten Most Wanted list.

Finally, I couldn't take anymore. "So, Gus, I've been think-ing. It's been a couple months since you mentioned it, and maybe it's not proper for me to bring it up, but . . ."

Thank heaven, he took the bait. "Dinner at the Lodge! Louisa, that would be an honor, a mighty honor if you would accompany me, in fact, the next monthly get-together is a week from tomorrow, it's the second Friday of the month, see, and that's a week from tomorrow if you'll check your calendar, you'll see that . . ."

Good grief. If he said it again my eardrum would explode and the calendar would self-immolate. Of course I knew. I cut him off, trying to disguise it as enthusiasm. "Oh! So soon! How lovely. That would be perfect! What time? Would you like me to meet you there?"

"I'll pick you up at five thirty. We're big-time, don't you know? Open bar." Chuckle, chuckle.

Open bar. Maybe there was hope. Having him pick me up was something of a relief to me, even though I'd rather have my own car. "Well, thank you very much. I'll look forward to it."

"And, Louisa, if you ever need any help around the place, you let me know, hear? I know Gary is real busy with the church."

"Oh yes, and such a good thing that he is, too. Bless his heart."

"Isn't it, though. You must be proud."

"You could say that." I don't know what I actually would say instead, though. "I'll see you a week from tomorrow. Thank you again, Gus."

CarolSue and I had a good laugh over the whole thing, although I know she worries about Gary. She says I'm going to need him and reminds me that she's older than I am, but I won't think about that. There's only so much a mind can hold, and then it's pointless as pouring water into a glass that's already full.

That week passed more slowly than I wished it would, even though the girls and I were busy. CarolSue coached me on what to wear ("No! Not that old blue thing! I've ordered a dress, a skirt, and two tops online, and they'll be there in the mail by Tuesday. All of them are in style, which I really can't say for anything else I saw in your closet when Harold died, and I certainly don't want you wearing your funeral dress. Try these on. They'll fit, unless you've lost more weight than you did between Cody and Harold.")

"Not much. I do eat." Not meat anymore, but why make a point of that?

"You have a nice shape, Louisa. You've always had a pretty figure. You don't have to dress like you live in a barn."

"Well, I sort of do live—"

"That's not the point," she interrupted. "Listen, you can wear either top with the skirt, but for God's sake, don't put a top over the dress. I wish you could send me a picture, and you could if you'd just kept Harold's cell phone. Then I could make sure you look okay."

"I'm not trying to impress Gus. Of all people."

"Nothing wrong with seeing who else is there you might meet."

"Pfft. Not interested. Wearing my rings anyway."

"This revenge thing is fine, sister, and I'm all with you. It's keeping you going. But we do need to think some about what happens after you get your revenge."

"I'll be fine. I'll be just fine."

She sighed through the receiver. "Just try on the clothes when they come."

The clothes came on Tuesday, just as she said they would, and I don't feel good telling you this because possibly it will lower your opinion of me, but I lied to CarolSue and told her they were beautiful and I loved them, but really, I never opened the box. I don't think I've ever outright lied to her before, as opposed to omitting information that might upset her, but I couldn't make myself get dressed up in something new to go to dinner at a hunting lodge with Gus, something I'd never do except for The Plan. It just seemed sacrilegious.

There was a time when I couldn't have lied to CarolSue. She's the only person who knows about The Plan at all, but part of me feels like the Lone Ranger without Tonto now that

I've gone off on my own and revised The Plan to one she'd never approve. Or maybe Dale Evans without Roy Rogers. I loved both those cowgirls, especially Annie Oakley, when I was a kid. My parents got a tiny black-and-white TV when I was maybe six. We were one of the first families to get one, too. My dad was so proud. *Meet the Press* was his idea of a religious experience. He made us all sit close circled around the little screen and watch; our reward was that we also got to watch Milton Berle. Later, Mom used to watch *Lassie* and *Rin Tin Tin* with me, both of us hiding our eyes when the dogs were in danger. But I can't think about all that's gone now. I'll just think about all the justice Annie Oakley saw to, and how she did it herself, no sidekick.

So yes, I was wearing "that old blue thing," which would have put CarolSue in a dead faint, when Gus's tires crunched down the gravel of my driveway on Friday. We'd had quite a dry September so far, making for some early leaf fall in spite of the daytime heat. Twilight was coming earlier, and the cicadas were loud as an engine whining the earth toward darkness and winter, my hard, sad time.

I had done the whole makeup job, the way CarolSue taught me—a touch of blue eye shadow, too—and put my hair up with the tendrils and soft bangs, also her flourishes. See, I'd done all that for Harold. Or CarolSue had, but either way, he'd seen me fixed up and taken great pleasure in it, too. How could I put on a beautiful new outfit for another man to see? CarolSue has such an eye for clothes: always fine, fashionable, flattering, and on sale. Before she moved away, she wouldn't let me go shopping alone. I'd stay in the dressing room and she'd bring things in for me to model and her to say *yes* or *no*. I'd get a vote, but often she'd override it either way. Whatever she'd sent would make me look better than I wanted to, better than I am now.

It didn't end up mattering that I wore the old blue thing anyway. Gus acted like Marilyn Monroe had opened my front door when he knocked. "Miss Louisa, you'll put all the other ladies to shame tonight," he said. I almost felt guilty for a moment about The Plan because he was possibly sincere and men are so fragile, but then I reminded myself how he'd frustrated my Harold all the way to the grave and positioned myself just slightly sideways as I opened the door so my boobs and hip would be evident. The blue thing might be old but it's not shapeless. After all, it was CarolSue who picked it out, even if it was ten years ago.

"Bless your heart. Step in for a minute, Gus, while I get my purse. I'm ready." Oh, was I ready. I have to admit Gus looked better out of his uniform. It had to be accidental that he smelled a bit like Harold, or maybe it was just that fresh-showered-man smell. He put his hand on the small of my back as he walked me out. I didn't want to like it.

The Lodge would be crowded, Gus warned on the way over. "Guys gearin' up for the season, y'know. Some of 'em plain dangerous, but most are the real thing."

"I guess the laws are pretty strict," I said, "or are they?"

He glanced over at me in the passenger seat and I kept my face that of an innocent woman. "I can't be everywhere," he said finally.

"You seem pretty good at it, though," I said, and my tone lied it into a compliment. I smiled at him and looked ahead at the road. We were passing fields of yet-uncut cornstalks, tall and weathered to brown now. Here and there we'd pass a pasture where cattle were scattered, lips to good grass, not knowing their luck would run out. FRESH EGGS, $1.25 DOZEN, said a hand-lettered sign in the yard of a white frame house with a porch like mine. It took me into memories. Harold had made my sign. LOUISA'S EGGS FOR SALE, it said, which I always found very unfortunately worded, but he'd painted it so carefully I just didn't have the heart to say anything. The sign was still somewhere in the barn, I was pretty sure. I'd not had the heart to get rid of one thing Harold had owned or made or given me.

We were driving into a melon fire sunset. Gus dodged a pothole. The roads were no better there than around home. The terrain became more wooded and remote as we headed west, toward Seeley Crossing. "There's a whitetail," Gus said once into the silence, pointing, his hand shooting just past my face toward the window. "Just watch. Where there's one, there's at least one more, usually two. That's a nice boy, that one. Look't that rack. We don't see many around here anymore." He put on the brakes, and I saw the buck, ahead on my right, emerging from the undergrowth, which was yellowing from both recent drought and the season, though honeysuckle is always the last to lose its color or leaves.

There weren't others, though. The loner stood watching us. Wishing Gus had been going slowly enough that I could have seen his eyes, I looked over my shoulder as we passed him. Only then did he turn and walk as if unafraid back into the forest, to safety. That just doesn't happen; deer don't stand around casually to observe passing traffic. They have a natural and well-founded flight instinct. So I took it as a sign from Harold that I was doing the right thing. I realize that believing in good signs is ridiculous because there are bad signs everywhere that I ignore. I've always thought that believing in signs is plain delusional. Give me a working tornado siren over some mysterious bad sign any old day. But there I was "seeing" Harold give me the A-OK by appearing in the form of a deer. It made me look forward to that full bar we were headed to. But it was a nice, natural opening.

"There are deer twice that size on my land."

"Really?!" Gus said. "No kidding?"

I couldn't decide if I should say more to him, but I didn't want to overplay my hand and there was a road marker for the Lodge. It noted PRIVATE PROPERTY.

Gus made a point of it, too. "It's a private club," he said, like it was a good thing, when we went in the door and I fanned the smoke odor away my face. "Didn't have to change anything when they banned smoking in public places," he said, and I thought he might be apologizing for a bad law. A good thing Harold didn't belong. He'd have died twenty years sooner just from the secondary smoke at the dinners. I wondered how Gus afforded it, on his sheriff's salary, which was public information, but CarolSue always says that what we don't know about people is a whole lot more than what we do. Maybe he inherited some money and being sheriff was his hobby. I reminded myself to concentrate on The Plan and looked around.

"Do all these people belong? It's much . . . bigger than I thought."

"No. Lotta guys come as guests. You can be a guest four times a year. Gets the cheap ones out of paying dues." He chuckled. "But we make money on 'em anyway, charge 'em almost double for drinks and dinner."

Red-faced men in sports coats with open-necked shirts and skirted women of almost every age were jammed in, holding plastic wineglasses, beer bottles, or swirling ice. The crowding was because there were tables set up for dinner all around the floor, which didn't make for comfortable mingling. The bar was to the left on two long tables set side to side, and it looked to be self-serve but there was also a smiley blond woman behind it taking money.

It took my eyes a bit to adjust to how the small windows cut the available light, and I was distracted by the smoke and people greeting Gus, Gus introducing me to people whose names I wouldn't and didn't care to remember. Then some shoulders parted and we were headed to the bar, Gus presuming I might like "a little white wine," and me trying to figure out how to get a hefty straight bourbon, forget the tea tonight, when I realized that close behind the woman at the bar was a deer. A buck's head. Mounted on the wall. No, two . . . three. More. When I looked around the room, wherever my view wasn't blocked, another head stared out. I was surrounded by a herd. I felt sick, even a little light-headed. *Oh my buck, my does, my yearlings in their day beds.*

"Where's the ladies' room?" The question was abrupt. I'd have to get control of myself.

"Far back, over there, right side. There's two. You go to the one by the doe." He threw a football pass gesture over the crowd diagonally across the room. I looked up automatically; the top of antlers were visible above heads. "You can't see it from here. Just head that way and it's the door by the doe."

I didn't move.

"You all right, Louisa?"

"Yes, of course. I'm just a little warm," I said, thrashing through my purse for a tissue. I was sweating, and not only my face. Gus's cheeks were red, but he was a beefy man and they always were. He'd not taken off his sports coat, and here I was, years past menopause and wanting to rip off my dress, anything for some air.

"I'll put some ice in that wine for you. How 'bout I wait for you by this end of the bar?"

I remember thinking, There's no way I can do this. But I made myself head toward that bathroom. It's a good thing I kept reminding myself to focus on The Plan, focus on The Plan, because I made it three-quarters of the way, which seemed like five miles, saying excuse me, pardon me, just trying to get through here, excuse me, as faces turned and lit in succession as people laughed and made way. Until one male, his back to me, had a scrawny ponytail in a weak curl that went just over the coat collar. It was less him I recognized, though, than the platinum Barbie doll in spike heels next to him. They stood hip to hip, her arm tight around his waist, his circling her back and his hand holding her bare upper arm.

You're wondering what I thought, what I felt? I didn't. Not then, not yet.

Another woman approached the Barbie, her arms open to hug her. The Barbie moved to reciprocate and Larry took steps to make space, blocking me as he did so. He raised his eyes as he turned, brushing them over me like a dust cloth. There was no logical reason to panic, but I did. There I was,

Lot's wife, paralyzed, when I most needed to move quickly. He widened his stance and shifted his belt under his belly. For just a second I thought our eyes met, but his were vacant. I recognized the too-close features crowded into the center of his face, but now I could better see the color of his hair—yes, exactly what my mother used to call dirty dishwater—and how scalp showed through in some spots. His mouth looked like the mug shot, thin straight lips closed, under a scraggly mustache. The Barbie tapped his shoulder, trying to get his attention to meet her friend.

I felt space close around me, like a lens slowly browning out the rest of the room and trapping me there alone with him, surrounded by a rushing white noise, Larry growing bigger and closer in front of me. I saw his Adam's apple and thought it moved. That movement must have been what galvanized me, because somehow I didn't faint or throw up. I averted my own eyes (as if I were the one who was guilty!) and forced my feet to move in a sideways dodge.

I made it to the bathroom, locked the door, and put the lid of the toilet down. I put my head between my legs until the dizziness seemed better, then sat up and tried to breathe normally. *Remember why you're here,* I said to myself. *You can do this. He has no idea who you are. Stay focused. He's the whole object of The Plan, and it's so much the better that he is actually here in person.* I stood, sat back down as another flush came, and stood again when it passed. I thought to wash my face, but that would take off my careful makeup job, and I hadn't brought anything but lipstick and a compact in my purse. Then I thought of how my mother used to put a towel with cold water on the back of her neck. There were paper towels, so I wet one and put it there. It helped me pull myself together.

Not for long. I went out of the bathroom intending to find Gus. I made a three-quarter turn to the right to get my bearings. Not eight feet from me, Larry was standing sideways—that skinny ponytail!—with nothing and no one between us.

I panicked again. How could he have been onto me? Had he
followed me to the bathroom? But no, he was staring up, as
if something were happening, and without thinking, I glanced
where his gaze was riveted, and of course—and I knew this, so
even looking was stupid, but it was some sort of involuntary
reflex—he was fixated on the head of the buck over the men's
room.

Trying to keep my breathing under control, I escaped back
to where I found Gus at the bar, talking to a broad-faced man
with corkscrew hair named Ronny. I positioned myself with
my back to the deer on the wall and pretended to focus on
their conversation. *Breathe,* I told myself. *Breathe. It's okay.
Remember The Plan.*

"Louisa is Reverend Gary's mother," Gus said.

Corkscrew Ronny's eyes widened and he took my hand.
He fizzed with enthusiasm. "Oh, ma'am. I am so looking forward to the revival. You must be so proud of your son. Your
generosity will be rewarded in heaven."

"Oh, no, really, I'm not doing anything. It's all Gary's . . .
doing." My heart was still beating too fast and I couldn't focus.
"Do you farm . . . Ronny?" It was a safe question to divert him.
Almost everyone had some connection with farming.

I don't remember what he answered. I completely wasted
the opportunity to set The Plan in motion before dinner—I
could have asked Ronny what his weapon of choice was—
but I was worrying about dinner seating, and if Larry Ellis
would be at our table, which I knew I couldn't handle. I'd
have to tell Gus I was ill and ask to leave. Two other men
joined us—one of them with a string tie and shaved head,
and the other with a brown beard down to his first button,
the kind that made me sure there was no woman in *his* life,
and they and Ronny got into an animated discussion about
how they retrieved their kill from thick cover, anyplace they
couldn't get a four-wheeler in. My attention wavered in and
out as one of them bragged he'd built a wheeled sled contrap-

tion, using parts cobbled from planks, a ladder, and a tricy-
cle, but he complained it was hard on his arms and he could
only manage a little over a hundred thirty pounds. They de-
bated the advantages of skids and sleds over any wheeled carrier, and what was easy to put in their truck beds. Gus didn't
add anything, I did notice that. Anywhere I looked, a deer
head was in my sight line. I tried to position myself so Gus's
chest was a block, but he'd move, and I'd see one or another,
its eyes appearing alive, sentient, suffering.

Larry Ellis wasn't at our table, but he was at the next one.
He and the Barbie doll sat down well after Gus and I did, and
I couldn't come up with any reason to ask Gus if we could
move, especially since we were sitting with his friends.

Dinner was a country cooking buffet of fried chicken,
green beans with ham, macaroni and cheese, mashed potatoes, coleslaw drowned in mayonnaise. Ambrosia. Rolls and
butter. Cherry pie, chocolate cake. I moved food around my
plate and tried not to look at any wall or toward Larry's
table so I wouldn't be sick then and there. At the same time,
I kept forcing myself to remember why I was here at all.

So finally, hoping that the deer on the wall would receive
the message I'd sent them by mental telepathy (very different
from believing in signs) and consult Harold The Buck for details of The Plan so they'd understand, I fired a scattershot
opening question at the men at the table. It took a few more
minutes for my brain to kick into action and realize that I
could deliberately try to let Larry Ellis eavesdrop. I wouldn't
have to just hope he'd happen to hear other hunters lament-
ing how there was a widow living on virgin territory who
wouldn't let it be hunted. And who talked about how many
deer roamed there unafraid.

"So, is this property where you all hunt?" I said, knowing
it wasn't; too many people, not that much land right around
the Lodge that they could own; it was adjacent to some resi-
dential spreads.

There was laughter from the men and polite smiles from the women. "Not that we wouldn't want to, but we'd kill each other if we tried," a pale crew-cut one with no neck said. "I'd be okay, because I'm the best shot," another said. "You all would be goners." That one was skinny, with a long slantwise nose, his beard shaved into an elaborate oval around his mouth, the way I pictured Ichabod Crane.

Gus leaned to me and said, "There's also too few deer. This whole area's pretty hunted out."

Ha! Thank you, Gus!

"Oh! I'm surprised to hear that. I have so many on my land I hardly know what to do. And that monster buck that's around! I suppose it's because it's never been hunted, though." I said this very softly, on purpose, and sure enough, Corkscrew Ronny obliged by saying, "Pardon me?" The shaved head with the string tie cupped his hand around his ear to indicate he'd not heard me, either. So, of course, I cleared my throat and repeated it at double the volume, hoping Larry Ellis could hear me clearly though I didn't trust myself to look away from Corkscrew Ronny, and Shaved Head across the large round table from me. Only when I repeated it all, I added, trilling in a little laugh, "Maybe it's more than one huge buck, though. I couldn't tell one from another."

Every man's head lifted to attention. I swear it was like corn popping all at once. "Is that right?" said the one who looked like Ichabod Crane. "Virgin territory? You want to open it up this season?" He could hardly contain his excitement.

"Oh, I don't think so."

"Now, seriously," said Corkscrew Ronny. "That's a waste. You've got a farm, you say. Don't you know they'll damage your crops?"

"Louisa's just widowed this year," Gus inserted. "She's not had to manage the farm herself until now." Mr. Helpful then turned to me. "You might want to think about it. You know, it's just a few days and it'll save crop."

I shrugged. "That's okay," I said. "I'd rather not. I'm there by myself." Shaved Head's eyebrows went up and I pretended it meant he hadn't been able to hear me. "Oh, sorry. I said I'd rather not have hunting on my land, being there by myself and all." I used teacher volume the second time.

"You know, they carry Lyme disease, don't you?" Ichabod said through a bite of chicken. "That's another problem, right, Gus?"

"True enough," said Mr. Helpful as he started in on his heaped-up side of macaroni and cheese, and Corkscrew and Shaved Head nodded in agreement. Gus needed to use his napkin but I wasn't going to let him know the way I would have my Harold.

"They're pests. Hunting's a service." That was Corkscrew Ronny, who gestured still holding a plastic glass with something that looked better than white wine in it. "So, Louise, how about—"

"It's *Louisa*," Gus interrupted. "How about we just let her think it over."

"Thank you all very much. I really don't want hunting on my farm, being there alone and all. But thank you." Teacher volume again, while maintaining a sad expression and shaking my head. This is a more tricky combination than you might think.

The men shook their heads, too. Ichabod shrugged and rolled his eyes at Corkscrew. Then, realizing I'd seen him, said, "Sorry, Louisa. Whatever you say. Up to you. Sorry about your husband."

One of the wives—she wore black-framed glasses and had farm hands like mine—changed the subject by saying, "Gus mentioned you're a retired teacher, Louisa. What district did you teach in?" and that got the table diverted to the subject of education. I got to hear a lot of very ignorant opinions about why schools are failing, none of which recognized that my last fifth-grade class had thirty-eight kids in it because four levies in a row were voted down and teachers had to be let go—but it was better than having those men go back to their talk about hunting techniques. It was okay, though. If Larry Ellis had overheard me, it was all worth it.

28

I could feel Gus wanting to bring the subject up on the way home. I could always tell when Harold wanted to say something and didn't quite know how, and I usually knew what the subject was, just as I did sitting in Gus's car, my window cracked an inch for the cool night air. I wanted to just put my head back and hope my stomach settled down, but I knew I had to stay on task. I hoped he'd get to it, because it was part of The Plan. I needed Gus, so I forced myself to act pert and make small talk.

It didn't take long. "Gotta watch for deer on these roads," he said. "They sure make a mess of cars. And people in them, sometimes. Getting on toward rut season, and they'll be on the move. Lotta accidents . . . Speaking of deer, you getting much crop damage?"

I laughed. "The deer consider my place a refuge."

"Hmm. Well, that can be a problem. If you might want to reconsider about letting the guys hunt, I'd be happy to come over and—"

"No, not really. Are you a big hunter yourself, Gus?"

"Well . . . I don't know as you'd call me that."

"What would I call you?" This was my attempt to be coy. Lord, am I out of practice.

"Miss Louisa, you can call me anything and anytime you want."

Damn. I'd completely blown the opportunity to subtly keep

him on the subject of the deer and hunting. "It was very kind of you to invite me tonight. I haven't gone out in a long time." As soon as I said it, I heard my own mistake. It's hard to be flirtatious, perky, and *smart* when you're stifling a belch.

"But you go out with your friends, and you're doing that volunteer work at the school."

". . . I meant in mixed company."

"Perhaps you'd go out with me again." He didn't say it as a question, but I'd just said it was nice to be in mixed company, so how could I say I'd realized it was too soon? Now I'd done it.

"Well, perhaps." Thank goodness he was turning onto my road. This was torture. I picked my purse off the floor of the car and pretended to look for something in it, just for something to do.

In a courtly, old-fashioned way, Gus walked me to my front door, where'd I'd left the porch light on. Insects buzzed and flitted around it. Gus's hand was scarcely there on the small of my back again, and again I didn't want to like it. We swished through dry leaves on my unswept walk. Harold always kept the stone path clear. The cicadas were loud, stitching down the night. I was grateful for their racket and the noise our feet made in the leaves; complete silence would have been more awkward. At the door, I stuck my hand out for him to shake it, so he wouldn't get any ideas. He pumped it enthusiastically, as though to bring up water, and went in for a cheek peck in spite of my clear signal.

Once I got the door shut, I told Marvelle in no uncertain terms: I know he's being nice, but he's still a puffy fat man who messed with my Harold, and I refuse to forgive him for that. Marvelle practically never agrees with anything, but she got on my chest after I was in bed, and I swear she actually purred.

*   *   *

"No!" CarolSue said the next morning, Saturday. I'd called at seven thirty, knowing she'd be up early to go to the Farmers' Market. She does like her fresh vegetables, not that she grows her own the way I do. "Sweet Jesus," she went on. "Not Larry Ellis. Did you recognize him right away? How could Gus do that? What a douche."

"Either he's completely oblivious or Larry was a guest. He said people can come as guests and they make money off them. I don't know if he even saw that he was there. He might have. He'd never have said anything to me, and I sure didn't say anything to him. Maybe everything that happened is just gone from his mind and I'm the only one who remembers." I felt tears pressing from behind my eyes and damn, I did not want to cry, so I blew my hair back out of my face and carried my coffee out to the front porch where my furniture was still set up. I was going to have to ask Gary to put it in the barn for the winter, even though I didn't want him getting the notion that I need his help. Maybe I could ask Al, or the boy who put me so in mind of Cody I could hardly breathe with his just being a boy, his voice too deep for his body, and blue, blue eyes. I do like this cordless phone thing Gary got me, though. He brought it so I could answer the prayer line calls. It means I have to come up with all kinds of new excuses not to. CarolSue's a big help with those. She's determined that his feelings don't get hurt.

"Well, dammit, I remember. You could have said you wanted to leave!" CarolSue can get pretty indignant.

"I'm sorry, I didn't mean it that way. I know you remember. I did want to leave. I never wanted to go in the first place. But I figured it was good he was there. He'd hear about the deer on my land for sure. The other way I was just counting on him hearing it from other hunters. But you should have seen me making sure he could overhear me."

"What if Larry and Gus are friends, though? I mean if they know each other from that Lodge? Could that be why Gus was so determined to stop Harold? Let's say it all works perfectly and you catch him poaching on your property . . . what if Gus doesn't arrest him?"

"I always thought it was because he's such a law-and-order type. I never once thought of that." I pulled the rocker to the far edge of the porch where there was a small swatch of sunlight, sat down with my coffee to think that one over.

Then I felt old and defeated, like if I really look in the mirror: there's my neck, lined as old tree bark, and that greyish tinge to my teeth, how the lids of my eyes droop now, like they're edging toward that final sleep.

What do you think you're doing? I asked myself. You're as delusional as Gary. You just thought Gus was who he seemed to you. A good man.

"Louisa? Louisa? Can you hear me? Are you still there?" CarolSue's voice came at me and I realized I was holding the receiver in my lap. Good grief.

"I never even thought of that, never even never even . . ." I said, realized I was repeating myself, and that made me wonder, not for the first time, if I was losing my mind as well as my looks. This just wasn't a good day and it wasn't even nine in the morning yet.

"Honey, it was only an idea. It's not like I know. I was asking you, not telling you." That's CarolSue. She'll say anything to make me feel better, but I can tell what's on her mind.

She had to get off the phone then; Charlie had a doctor appointment they had to go to. CarolSue isn't saying a lot about him, but I get the feeling she's worried. She kept saying, "They have to do follow-up," but she was never specific about exactly what that means even though yes, I question her. I ask her all the time, and she gives me short answers and then says I'm providing her only diversion. And it's not like her to be vague. By nature she's one of those definite people. "I'll come soon," she promised. "But you can come here, too. Anytime. Remember, I need Mom's marinara sauce recipe."

"I know. I already copied it and put it in the mail. And it's fine," I said. "You just take care of Charlie. I'm doing fine," I said before we hung up. I could never tell her not to come, but good Lord, it would make a mess of The Revised Plan if she came now. It's a good thing I never told her I've been target shooting, let alone how fine-tuned my aim is now. It would be one more thing on her worry list, and I could spare her that. It was a damn good thing she wasn't aware that The Real Plan didn't rely on Gus arresting Larry for poaching. That was now nothing but Plan B, but I would be hugely disappointed if it came down to that. I was going to stop short of killing Larry Ellis, but he was never going to be able to hunt again. I was still thinking whether to take out a kneecap or his trigger hand. Maybe I'd wait to decide on the cleanest shot at the moment. It didn't matter. I could hit either one. It would only take skill and will, and I had them both.

29
Brandon

Through the wall that separated his bedroom from theirs, Brandon had heard part of a fight between his mother and Larry on a Thursday night after Larry was late from work, and Brandon figured that's what they were fighting about. Larry's voice was sort of bleary, the way it got with booze, and bigger than his mother's, like he was bigger than she was. Scared that she might get hurt, he'd snuck out of his room to eavesdrop outside their door. Should he knock? Barge in? Shocked, he'd realized that he was what they were fighting about, Larry calling him a punk, and his mother sort of begging Larry, saying he was a good kid. "So can't you show him about tools or cars or something useful men do?" she said, keeping her voice down, pathetic and supplicating, but defending him, and he was glad she was but it made him feel like shit. Larry was the one who was a punk. He even looked like one with that stupid rat-tail hair. Someone ought to tell him that men who are going bald shouldn't try to have ponytails. And that mustache that looked like he couldn't really grow one. Brandon didn't get what his mother saw in him. She was pretty and nice. She deserved to be happy. Why did she always go with these losers? He couldn't see any reason except that she had a kid to support. The guys seemed to be ones with houses, he'd noticed. Not that his mother was much for cleaning, but they couldn't afford a house on what she made.

He'd also noticed that the guys didn't have kids, or if they did, they didn't admit it.

"Mom, do you care if I don't go to Grandma's with you? Me and Larry are going to Indy to look at some parts for my car, cool?" He didn't usually lie to her, oh maybe he shaded the truth so she wouldn't worry, but not like this. After Uncle Chuck blew most of his right foot off with his own rifle, his mother had been all about not being around guns even though the only people that didn't have guns around here were cemetery residents. Brandon didn't know what to think. Uncle Chuck's elevator didn't go all the way to the top, so maybe he'd just been an airhead.

The point, however, was that his mother would flip out batshit crazy if she thought he was having anything to do with hunting. What Larry was doing today was different, anyway, not that his mom would see that. But it would make her so happy that Larry was spending time getting to know her boy, as he'd heard her say. It would make her happy and it wasn't that big a lie.

"Sure, honey, that's fine." Her voice trying to mask that she meant *fantastic*!

After that, his mother left for Bardsville all cheerful, kissing them both and saying, "You men have a great time. Take care of each other. Don't forget you have to heat up that tuna casserole. I'll have dinner with Mom but I'll be back by eight thirty or so."

"Get outta here," Larry said, and slapped her ass, which gave Brandon the creeps. Then he had a sudden bad feeling that his mother wanted to marry Larry, thought there'd be some kind of trickle-down fairy dust that would make a mean, loud, pinch-faced dude with a rat-tail into a dad. Not gonna happen, Brandon thought. This guy hit his mother, Brandon was pretty sure. His mother confused him. Sometimes he felt like they were in one of the novels Mrs. Powell kept recommending last year, all the times she'd said, "Brandon, please think about a four-year college, get the degree. You can do it."

She'd recommended him for Honors English this year. But the characters in the novels were easier to understand than his mother. He thought about what novel Larry would fit in, and couldn't come up with one. Mrs. Powell said that characters had to have good and bad qualities to be real human beings in a novel because that was like life. She hadn't met Larry, though. He wanted to argue that maybe some people don't have much good in them. Or it's been so long since they've exercised it, that the good dried up and blew away long ago, like, say, dandelion fluff, and all that's left is dead. And a dandelion was a weed to begin with. That was Brandon's hypothesis, not that he saw a way to prove it like in geometry class. He hadn't said any of this to Mrs. Powell at the time. He hadn't been sure she'd like it if he hadn't thought it through well enough. His biology teacher would probably ask both Brandon and his mother if they'd gathered all possible relevant data. Okay, maybe he needed to work on that. But damn, was his mother even trying?

"What's that you've got on? Shorts? Jesus, kid, we're not goin' to the damn beach. Man, don't you have any boots? You can't hunt in sneakers." Larry snorted disdain.

"Thought you said we were just finding 'em."

"Well, not exactly finding *them*, but sort of. Never heard of scouting, huh? But, kid, you don't go out like that. Lookit you, lookit me." Larry displayed his camouflage with a sweeping hand, then pointed to his hunting boots.

For the first time Brandon heard himself go back at Larry hard, pissed off. "Sure, I got camouflage. I just told Mom to pick it up for me and she was so happy to do that. She asked your buddy there to help her get the right kind, being as how he's the expert." He pointed to one of the trophy bucks, the one mounted above the brown sofa. There was a picture of

Larry, all proud, overweening Mrs. Powell would call it, posed over the body with his gun, right across the room.

"Okay, back up, whoa. Didn't think of that. You gotta at least wear jeans. Lotta brambles, y'know."

"Too hot . . ." Mumbled, backing down because for once Larry had.

"I know what I'm talkin' about. At least go with jeans. Sleeves. Got any high-tops?"

"Old ones."

"Wear 'em. Ankle support. We're gonna check some new areas today. And here," he said, tossing him a can, "spray yourself down with this, too. It's so you don't leave a scent."

That day they'd hung three trail cameras, one of them new, out in an unhunted area Larry said no one knew about. The road had looked familiar to Brandon, but the roads around here all looked the same, always like déjà vu, pages of cornfields punctuated by silos and old houses. Mrs. Elzey, the Honors teacher, would like that he thought of that; maybe he could use it when she gave the next descriptive writing assignment.

He asked Larry where they were and Larry said some nutso old widow's woods, don't worry about it. Brandon hadn't been out in woods before, not really. Before they moved in with Larry, they'd lived in Elmont, and a while before that in Indy, buildings all around like crooked teeth. Out here, nothing but different trees and tangled underbrush that finally backed up to a wide creek, nearly a river. Across that, more of the same.

Larry was all happy when he said, Yep, nobody's been back here, he was sure of it, but Brandon didn't know how he knew. Larry had Brandon wear a pack that was pretty heavy because supposedly he had a bad back and his job was spotting deer trails, day beds, and scat, which was another word for deer shit. Wouldn't be many fresh rubs on trees now, he said, but he found a couple old ones. Brandon got interested when they scared up a doe with twins. "You gotta think of 'em as prey," Larry said. "You're the hunter, they're the prey."

"Why do you wanna kill 'em? Live and let live." He didn't really say it as a question.

"Not the idea," Larry said. "Not the idea at all. See, it's what we call a primal instinct. Say there was a wild boar—or a bear. It's hunt or be hunted. It's how the world works."

"I dunno." Brandon busied himself re-tying his battered high-top, which hadn't come undone.

The other thing Brandon got interested in was the trail cameras. "Cool," he said. "Low tech and high tech at once. Can I see?"

"Sorta like Nintendo, huh?"

"Lar, for the last time, it's an Xbox."

"Whatever. Same difference."

Brandon checked the playback on Larry's newest camera, a Moultrie Trace, making sure it was set right when Larry had trouble figuring it out and hadn't brought the manual.

The kid glanced up at him. "And not like Xbox. You just gotta set this here, and then this one here for the date and time stamp, see? The batteries go here. Cool. It gives a panoramic view. You want video or still?"

"Not like my other ones. Do video. So, anyway," Larry couldn't resist a dig, "better than sittin' on Grandma's little patio sippin' tea and listenin' to the ladies' fascinating discussion of fashion, shoes, and recipes, after all. Huh."

"Batteries won't last as long. Just so you know." After that, Brandon—overheated in jeans and long sleeves—set and hung the other cameras, following Larry through the woods as he second-guessed the habits of deer, looking for their secret places, where they felt safe. The guy was right about one thing, even though he was insane. The underbrush was wicked; he'd have been a mess in shorts and a T-shirt.

After the last camera was secured in the bifurcating tree trunk where Larry had followed what he said was a deer trail

to the creek, Larry had them move away from the spot and
told him to take the pack off again. He rooted around in it
and brought a six-pack up from the bottom. He'd wrapped it
in some kind of insulation with an ice pack.

"Smart, huh? That's the thing I had to ice it when my knee
was messed up. See, if ya gotta stay awake sittin' in a blind,
ya drink real Coke for the caffeine. Hangin'cameras? Movin'
around? Beer. Here ya go." And he'd tossed one to Brandon.
"Now, ya gotta say, this is way better than the wussy stuff
you do, huh. Readin' books and Nintendo. Gah." It wasn't a
question and Brandon didn't answer.

Brandon caught the beer, hoping it wouldn't explode in his
face. It wasn't his first. One more thing his mother would go
batshit crazy about. Then he wondered if she'd dump Larry
if she knew, if eventually he could use this. He filed the
thought in a shiny new drawer in his mind.

"We'll find out by the cameras where there's the most traffic. See, we'll build us a blind in the one or two best spots. A
little elevated. You gotta make sure there's cover behind you,
but you also gotta have something to lean against. So then ya
get some deadfall and make a little wall-like thing around us.
But not in the way of the shooting line. You listening?"

"Yeah," Brandon said, wondering who "we" was supposed to include. He popped the top of the beer. He'd gotten
a lot tougher since he'd been working for Mr. Pelley, and he'd
even bulked up a little. Well, his biceps were definitely bigger
and maybe his chest. Thinking of that made him wonder if he
could take Larry Ellis down if Larry tried to hurt his mother.

30
Louisa

The corn hadn't silked until August first so instead of reaching full dent around September first, here it was the middle of September and it wasn't ready for Al to harvest. We were going to leave it in until October for extra drying time. Al said he thought we might get as many as a hundred and sixty-two bushels to the acre; it had been a good season, and I was grateful. The drought had come late enough that the crop wasn't damaged, and then, just in time, a couple of drenching rains. The girls don't care much for rain because I leave them in the coop instead of giving them the whole yard, which borders the first field, to range in. They like teatime best, though, and now we begin it at two instead of four, the way we did in late spring and summer. To take advantage of the sunshine, of course. No other reason.

Most of the vegetables had quit producing so much. I was still getting some tomatoes, but the vines were tired and the leaves yellowing. The zucchini and beans had surrendered. I put in fall plants: lettuce, spinach, peas, kale, but it didn't take long. One widow doesn't eat all that much, you know.

It left me time to walk the land, checking different sections to look for sign. At the entrance to my driveway, I pounded a little notice I got at the Tractor Supply into the ground with Harold's mallet. PRIVATE PROPERTY. I put in two more that said NO HUNTING at the property lines between my land and the neighbors'. Enough that there'd be no question that it was legally and legibly marked. Although I dreaded winter, how I wanted the days to hurry to hunting season now. I had my own hunt in mind.

As much as I'd been looking, I couldn't believe it when I first realized I had a bite on the bait. If I hadn't looked up at the exact right moment, I'd have missed it. And worse, I'd have been seen myself. I was following a thready deer trail that went between Rush Run and the area of corn I wasn't letting Al harvest, leaving it for the deer. I'd been looking down, watching my step; it was pure luck that I looked up and ahead in time to see a brown strap around a tree trunk not five feet in front of me, right about eye level. Attached to the strap was what looked like a box with bark-colored camouflage covering. If I hadn't done all that research in the spring, I'd have had no idea what it was. But I did know, from pictures in the literature. It was a trail camera.

I'd approached it not quite from behind, but almost. It had been placed at something of an angle; another step and I'd have been in range. I didn't think the camera would have picked me up, although I couldn't be sure. I stepped back and stood rigid, thinking it would capture sound, too, but then I remembered, no, not unless this was a very unusual type. Still, I moved backward slowly, trying to be soundless. I didn't want the hunter who'd snuck onto my land to scout prey to know I'd so much as ventured beyond the chicken coop. I thought I knew who he was. I believed I did because I'd snuck onto his land and eavesdropped on him. Had he really eavesdropped on me exactly when I wanted him to? I needed to be right about this, so I silently gave thanks to Harold The Buck, who must have helped me that night at the Lodge after all.

I wanted to re-read the hunting laws I'd copied, even though I thought I remembered. It was only the third week of September. The firearm season didn't start until November 16.

And then it occurred to me: was he doing more than scouting? Could he be that greedy? That stupid? Could I be that lucky? Could The Plan actually work *that* well?

Once I cleared the area, I picked up the pace as much as I could while keeping a head up for another camera I might have missed. I didn't see any, but there were so many deer trails on my land now I knew I'd have to figure them out more systematically than I had so I could look. I was distracted enough thinking about how to map them and mark where I'd found the camera, that when the trail opened into the field where I'd planted the winter root crops for the deer at first I didn't see the man walking the perimeter opposite me. And when I did see him, I didn't recognize him. This is what happens when you don't wear your glasses.

I ducked back, but not quickly enough. And it wasn't the hunter anyway.

"Mom?" Gary shouted across the field. It was his voice I knew, then I realized who he was. (Well, to be honest, it was his calling me Mom that was the giveaway.) "Mom!" And he came toward me, crossing over and through my hand-planted rows with his heavy walk. Oaf! I thought. I know that's not very motherly, but I was really irritated. Anyone could see it had been planted. Behind him to the right, field corn rippled silver in the light breeze, the high sea waves. You can't imagine how much I wanted to call, "Don't mess with your mother's work! You'll be in over your head, boy."

"Watch where you're stepping," I called. "Go around," but of course he didn't.

"I was following you!" he called, pointing behind himself to the edge of the field. Indeed, that's how I had come. Dammit, of course, the garden shoes. Now he was much closer. "It was great. I could follow you and follow Jesus at the same time." He laughed, all pleased with himself, his cheeks red even though it was a cool afternoon. He doesn't exercise nearly enough, it's obvious. Right then he reminded me of Cody when he was first put in as a receiver and he couldn't help his own face from lighting up when he caught a pass, and oh, how love can mix itself into irritation and melt you like chocolate, just like warm chocolate. Even though it made me want to throw those comfortable garden shoes right into the trash bin. I probably hadn't left tracks on the deer trail—too many leaves down—but it was possible, and why on earth hadn't I thought of this? Stupid damn comfortable shoes.

"Why were you following me?" I said, and I'm afraid my tone didn't make him think I was happy about it.

Now we were almost face-to-face. The blue of his eyes was almost the color of the cornflowers that had fringed the sides of our back roads through August. Like CarolSue's. No, like Cody's. "Oh, I was just kidding. I was really just . . . visiting," he said. His voice was too hearty and something in me was uneasy.

"Visiting the field?" I said, though I wanted to put my arms around him to hold that moment that I'd seen our Cody.

"No, I—what are you doing in the woods?"

I should have realized at the time that he'd deflected my question with one of his own, but I was so busy not wanting to answer him that I didn't catch how much he'd not wanted to answer me. Clearly, he's learned from the best.

"It's time to feed the girls, son. Will you walk me back? I'll bet they are hopping mad I left them cooped up. They so prefer to have the whole yard as their run, but this time of year I worry. There's been a hawk I've seen a bunch of times, and, well, you know, hawks won't bother them if a person is right there, that person being me. . . ." I rambled on like this, taking his arm, and heading for the edge of the field.

"I'm glad you decided not to put corn in this field after all, Mom," he said. "Good decision." At the time, I was annoyed that he was walking over the winter root crops I'd planted, which were in the part of the field that wasn't in clover. Farther on were the oats, but they'd been cut once and I wasn't going to let Al do a second cutting. They, too, were for the deer now. I didn't answer that because I didn't want to open the subject of why I hadn't. So I babbled about how many bushels Al figured to get per acre this year, which was high. Gary walked alongside with his head down until we reached the edge.

"I've got Charlie on the prayer list. He'll be okay," Gary said then, a propos of nothing I'd been saying.

"I'm glad you think so. But did you send them a card like I asked you to?"

"I'll do that. Since she can't come here, I've been thinking, you should go visit Aunt CarolSue in a couple weeks. I know you miss her, and she must need you. How about it? I'll make your reservations online."

"Not right now. I don't have the extra money until after harvest, and I have things to do. I'll wait and see how he does."

"I'll pay your way."

This made me swing my head sideways to look at him. He just kept going.

"That's *very* nice of you. Not now, though. Later on would be wonderful. Why don't we both go for Thanksgiving?" Surely it would be over by then.

"It'll be okay, Mom. It'll be fine."

I let it go then. I shouldn't have, but I didn't know. Much later, too late, I registered that Gary's head had been down and he'd let me ramble on because he was counting his own steps, from the center where we'd come together, to the edge. I'd half noticed but not asked, figuring it was some sort of religious ritual. I doubt he'd have told me his plan for that very ground, though, since he hadn't given me the opportunity to say what he must have known I would: *over my dead body.* It was ridiculous, each of us busy hiding our own Grand Plan. But I'm getting ahead of the story, aren't I?

31

The next morning, I had to go out and buy a cheap pair of sneakers before I went back to where I'd found the trail camera. I brought a lightweight leafy branch with me, one from the maple tree Harold had planted in memory of his father, in case I needed to obliterate any ridiculous footprints I might have left. I didn't find any, except the ones all along the edge of the field. There were enough dry leaves down on the trail. Still, though, I was so mad at myself that I hadn't thought of something so obvious. What else was I overlooking? I couldn't afford any mistakes.

I stuffed down fear by telling myself one enemy was nothing compared to the number Harold had in Vietnam. For him, I went on reconnaissance missions for five days, looking for flattened areas where deer had made their day beds, for the telltale scrapes where antlers had been sharpened on trees, for scat on the faint and feathery new trails I found when I made my way along the edges of Rush Run. The deer were there; the signs were everywhere, and I saw the creatures themselves more and more often, too, though usually it was the arcing white of their upraised tails that would catch my eye as they leapt away from my approach. My buck stood still a few seconds, though, just once, in fleeting light. *I love you*, I whispered. *Tell them all.* Did I tell Mom and Harold and Cody enough? Does Gary know, after all? I'll tell him. And CarolSue, again and again. I need to help her more with Charlie—the minute this is over.

Will it surprise you to know that I found another trail camera? I did. Or it found me. And this time, I knew I hadn't avoided the lens. So what could I do? The only thing I could. I took it down, opened its waterproof casing, took it back to the creek, and submerged it. I held it underwater for at least two minutes. Then I dried it. To do that part, I had to take off my shirt and use it as a towel. Later I thought about how I must have looked: a wrinkled old woman out in the woods in her bra and ratty blue seersucker pants using her shirt to dry a camera she'd stolen off a tree. But then I thought, Hey, it's not stealing if it's on my farm. And I was just wearing a bikini top a little past the season. I thought these things and decided I was either a perfectly fine, confident, strong woman or stark raving mad. I preferred the first explanation and went with it. Besides, I'm really not that wrinkled.

I wiped the camera a last time and put it back on the tree exactly the way I'd found it. I left a little opening in the water-proofing, enough to make the hunter think he'd overlooked it when he set it up. Now I just had to hope for rain. It was enough, honestly, to make a body answer those prayer calls that were still coming every day.

He'd taken the bait. He was scouting seriously, maybe deciding where to hide himself. I wondered if he was one to climb a tree to wait for the buck with the biggest rack. He'd be back. His scouting would have revealed abundant prey, no competition, and it was evident that No Hunting and Private Property signs were no obstacle. Was he going to wait for deer season, which was still weeks away?

Even if I hadn't overheard what his girlfriend? wife? had said, I decided it was unlikely. I couldn't give him the chance to get any of the creatures I'd taken into my protection. It was time for me to do some hunting of my own.

*   *   *

"So exactly what is going on?" CarolSue demanded. I'd answered the phone when I saw it was her. We hadn't talked in two days. I'd been exceptionally busy. "Where have you been? I've been calling. I know you're not out in the garden twelve hours a day now. Something's up and I'm not sure I'm getting the whole story."

Well, so what if she wasn't? Before you judge me, think of this: how likely was she to approve of The Plan as it had, to my (accurate) way of thinking, naturally and necessarily evolved? Big fat chance! She'd get all bossy and threatening. I was really happy we didn't have videovision, or whatever you call that kind of phone where you can see the person you're talking to. I could just hear her. "Louisa, what are you doing cleaning that rifle? Why are you wearing Harold's camouflage? Have you been doctoring your tea again? Do you realize it's only two o'clock in the afternoon?" Blah blah blah. Why would I want to hear that? And I couldn't give her something to worry about either, not with Charlie on her mind.

"Heavens, sister. You know I tell you everything." Everything I want you to know, I added under my breath, so it wasn't strictly a lie. "I'm going to watch for that evil man, and the minute I see him on my property, I'll call Gus and have him arrested. Now I just have to figure out where he leaves his truck to get onto my land. But you know, I read that hunters start a half hour before dawn and twilight when the deer are most active, so I figure if I get out and drive around at dawn and dusk I'm bound to see when he's there. Then I just have to dash back to the house, call Gus, meet him there, and we catch him as he's coming out."

"Well . . ." She sounded unconvinced. "My main worry about this is that you'll get yourself shot. You'll remember to wear the orange hat when you're outside, just in case? You've got Harold's old one, right? I mean, he doesn't know your land. . . ."

Now you can see the flaw in that right away, can't you? If Larry Ellis saw me, wouldn't he hightail it right out of there? Could I count on just waving a friendly *Hi there*, which he could claim he construed as permission-granting anyway, and moseying back to the house to call Gus? Sometimes I briefly lose confidence in my sister's brain.

"Of course I do. But I'm not sure I like how you're implying that I resemble an enormous old buck. I haven't put on that much weight." I figured to distract her by teasing.

"Don't try to distract me. Do you have the hat?"

"Of course I do. I told you that." It was the absolute truth. I did have it. I winked at Marvelle, who looked away and yawned. She can be a drag sometimes. I added a bit of bourbon to her water, hoping to improve her participation. She'd been trying to cut down on her drinking, but I saw it was just making her grumpy. I set the bottle down on the kitchen table, sat, and patted my lap for her to jump up. Her response was to rise from the patch of sunlight she was lying in, stretch, and amble off in the opposite direction, tail high. Lord, how I missed having a dog. The minute The Plan was complete I was going to the shelter to get one; wouldn't that just put Miss Marvelle in her place!

"Louisa! Are you there? Louisa? Can you hear me?"

"Oh! The line sort of went quiet for a minute. I can hear you now, though. What were you saying?"

"Will you wear the hat? Listen, I'm all on board with getting Larry Ellis, but you can't do anything stupid or dangerous, you hear me?"

"I always hear you, sister. Always. How's Charlie doing today?"

"Napping again. It's wearing him out."

"Wearing both of you out, I think." And I'll tell you the truth, right then I thought I should tell her that I was abandoning The Plan and getting on a plane to Atlanta the next day. But I didn't. I was afraid she'd say, *Yes, come now*, and, as you know, The Plan was to finally do right by my husband (the way I hadn't when he was alive and maybe could have saved him). It was a terrible flash: was I failing to do right by my sister, trading one disaster for another? No, I could do right by both of them in the end, I told myself. So I didn't say it. Instead I just said, "You hangin' on?"

"Of course I am," she said, too heartily, but I let myself take comfort in it.

"So, Gus called me again. Asked me out."

"It took you long enough to tell me! You're serious? What did you say?"

"I sort of said yes."

"Sort of?"

"I want him on my side, but I don't want him around here, good grief, because it could scare Larry Ellis off. So I said I'd have dinner with him, but not this weekend because I was busy. Thank goodness he didn't ask me what I'm doing. I said next weekend. I'm hoping I'll have caught Larry Ellis by then and I won't have to actually do it. Just to be safe, though, if I haven't caught Larry, I'll say I'm busy and make it sometime well after dark when he'd be out of my woods anyway."

"So old Gus is putting the moves on you? Or . . . wait a minute, are you putting them on him?" She finally laughed then and sounded like herself. "Who are you and what have you done with Louisa?"

She was teasing but that almost made me put the phone down and cry. In a way I was whoring myself out so I could get revenge for Harold. I hoped that good man understood. But he'd expected me to understand suicide, when he knew how much I loved him. Sometimes love just doesn't do a lot of good, does it? No matter how much we want it to save us all.

So it had all come down to this. The next morning I got up at quarter to five. The girls were so surprised they must have thought old Bronson had come back to life. He never did wait for dawn. I made some tea and toast, ate one of the eggs I'd thought to hard-boil last night, and put on long johns.

How I do feel the cold now! But over those went my jeans, and then Harold's camouflage, rolled up, of course. An old brown shirt, and Harold's jacket. Then, the heaviest socks I could fit under the sneakers. My barn boots were no good for hiking. If there were such a thing as bag ladies who went hunting, I'd be their poster child. CarolSue would faint. I considered putting on some eyeliner and mascara in case I died out in the woods and she had to claim my body—maybe it would make her feel like I'd listened to at least something she said—but then I realized Gary was technically my next of kin, and he'd be way too busy praying over my corpse to ever tell people *Mom might have gone off her rocker, but she sure looked pretty when they found her body.*

I picked up the rifle. Strange, I remember how light it felt in my hands. Nothing felt quite real. You know how you can plan and plan for something, even dream about it, see it in your mind's eye, and then when the day comes, it doesn't seem like it could be. With my free hand, I stuffed a couple of granola bars in one oversize pocket and a bottle of water in the other. Uncomfortable; the water bounced against my thigh when I walked, so I took it back out. How do men do this stuff? I wondered. I opened the broom closet and made eye contact. "Wish me luck," I said to Glitter Jesus. "You stay inside. You too, Marvelle."

First grey light above the trees. Black ground. The underbrush when I reach the deer trail that I'd figured was most likely to intersect with the road, the second trail camera and Rush Run—the area I'd guessed Larry would hunt first—was wet with condensation when it grabbed at me from every side as I picked my way through, trying to be soundless. Don't step in a hole. Don't trip, I kept telling myself. Nobody knows you're out here. That's good and that's bad. I had to get out before dawn and hide.

You see the perfection of The Plan, I hope. A hunting accident. My land was posted NO HUNTING, but that didn't mean *I* couldn't hunt on it. It was, after all, my land. I would say I needed the meat. I'd say that if I'd been successful, I'd have called Gus to help me retrieve it. Was anyone going to charge this grieving widow who needed food with hunting out of season on her own land? Not in this county. Wouldn't ever happen.

Suddenly, something was over across my face. In a panic, I batted at the sheet, mostly stifling an instinctive scream. I tore at my face where it clung, sticky on my lips, eyelashes.

Cobweb. Squatting to avoid the residue, as best I can squat, which is questionable on a good day, I opened my jacket and wiped my face with my pulled-up shirt. In the next twenty steps, there must have been ten more. Clearly, no one had been this way before me this morning. Would the absence of cobwebs reveal that I had? Or would Larry think it meant deer had been? Did he even use deer trails to make his way through the woods? I knew he'd have been looking for day beds and scrapes on trees, but because the rut wouldn't be until mid-November, there wouldn't be the mating activity yet that distracts deer from the human danger. I was basing so much on conjecture, but really, isn't that the way we all make our way through life? This was just a more apparent enactment. What was there to do but go on? What is there ever to do but go on? If you've decided to go on, I mean.

And I had. I did. I wasn't going to let it all be for nothing.

It took much longer than it had during the daytime when I could see clearly, and when I wasn't trying to be silent. Even wearing my driving glasses, which I'd decided I better do. The leaves, so distinct and separate in daylight, especially as they had begun to vary into golds and burnt oranges, here and there even to flame toward red, were a monochromatic dark grey. There was smattered birdsong, probably cardinals if I recognized their call correctly, though nothing like their raucous morning joy in spring. These were the ones like me, who stayed, who wouldn't give up and move on. "Be strong and brave," I wanted to call up to them, but of course I didn't.

I noticed the birds and how the leaves were leeched of color because I was trying to be alert to everything: sound, movement, sign of animal or human life. The sky lightened in imperceptible immeasurable moments. I had so little time to pick a place, get into hiding. I took one wrong turn and had to double back when I realized there was no trail where I thought there was and I was thrashing into underbrush. As I've said, it was very hard to see, and I didn't want to advertise with a flashlight, however small, though I admit it would have been a lot more efficient and, doubtless, safer.

I reached the creek, and picked my way along the slanted rocky creekside about twenty yards to another deer trail. I wasn't entirely positive it was the same trail; there were many, but I was pretty sure. The unobstructed sky over the water was a faint pink and the air like wet wool as I pulled it into my lungs. Rain coming. I had nearly made it to where I'd found the trail camera when I heard it. I had been going to go off the deer trail it was on and set up a blind. I had shifted my rifle to my left shoulder to let my right arm be rested and ready.

From another part of the woods: gunfire. A shot. Three seconds. Another shot.

I turned, trying to locate the source, but I couldn't. The reverberation died quickly. My heart thudded and I leaned against a tree to stay upright, sick with failure. I couldn't believe I'd so miscalculated where he'd be. The second shot must mean he'd gotten one of my deer.

There was a mature hickory tree three feet from me and I reached for it to steady myself but couldn't. The tears came slowly at first, it had been so long, and then harder and from some deeper, sadder place until I sank to the cold ground, the ground that holds my Harold and my Cody, and cried for everything I loved and couldn't save. I was on my knees, my back hunched over in the ancient pose of prayer and supplication. But there was no prayer, nothing to beg for. There was only grief, raw and gasping as an open wound. That un-staunchable bleeding, the way a bullet kills.

The rifle was lying a foot from my knees. I understood my Harold then, how the weight of failure was beyond what he could lift again, how he was broken and couldn't stay on his feet. I forgave him. I reached for the rifle and turned it around to look directly into the muzzle, forgiving Harold. I leaned forward so the muzzle would be directly over my heart. It dug into my left breast, and I remembered my Harold's mouth there when we made love. I forgave him.

Yes. You're right. I didn't do it. Not because I thought to spare Gary and CarolSue. It wasn't because of anything but this: Larry Ellis wasn't going to take one more life. Not on my watch. Not off my land. He'd taken my grandson; he'd taken my husband. There wouldn't be any more deaths to hang on his wall. None. I don't know how long I knelt there, sobbing on the damp mulch of trodden leaves after I let the rifle fall to the side. Long enough for my feet to go to sleep, for my pants and socks to get thoroughly wet and grimy and for me to stiffen up enough so that it was pretty much impossible to stand back up. Long enough to decide that Larry Ellis was going to die. Then I'd help CarolSue, and then, I'd see if I wanted to go on.

I had to roll onto my backside and straighten my legs one at a time in front of myself, still shuddering with the end of my crying. This gave me a whole new thing to be furious about. By the time I put my glasses back on and got myself standing up again, I had worked myself into a frothing-at-the-mouth rage. It was also full daylight. Cloudy, but the greens, russets, yellows, and early reds splashes at the tops had appeared out of their silhouettes, the whole scene repainted. I folded from the waist to pick up the gun. I was sure it was too late to find the shooter, but I could try to find where he'd been.

He wasn't going to get another member of the Hawkins family; he wasn't going to kill anything more. Not ever. Plans change, and mine just had. Larry Ellis never hunting again wasn't enough. It wasn't enough now that I knew, really knew, the despair my Harold had felt.

The shots had seemed to come from west of me, the direction of the other trail camera, farther from the creek. I'd seen more deer in the area where I'd gone, but then I'd had the benefit of not having to sneak around, of leisure. And of no evil intent. Perhaps the deer knew. Or perhaps that's a silly idea. Harold would say it was, but CarolSue would say, "Of course they can tell who's not out to hurt them. Likewise, if he were unarmed for five minutes, even a small doe would plant one of her hoofs in that bastard's forehead."

Anyway, maybe that's where he'd been, maybe not, but I was too seething mad to go home so I went to look for whatever I could find. I was guessing it was about a half hour walk in the direction of the road, maybe forty minutes if I didn't skirt the two front fields and stayed in the woods. The sun broke through the clouds in slashes, warming and thickening the air into a watery cream soup. As I moved, rifle over my camouflaged shoulder, I thought about my Harold in that faraway war. As soon as you're mad enough, you can carry a gun and shoot it at something alive. I haven't gotten to understand how anyone does it without anger, like the trophy hunters, when nothing they care about is threatened.

I was getting quite tired by the time I got to the area of the second trail camera. And I'd realized: maybe there were more, ones I hadn't spotted. I told myself, Don't think about that now. He wouldn't necessarily hunt near the trail camera anyway. The camera might have made him think it wasn't a good area. I knew it was, I knew it was full of deer, but what had he seen? I couldn't know that.

I was dizzy trying to second- and third-guess the unknowable, checking up in the trees in case he'd put up a blind, checking the ground for signs of disturbance, stopping to listen. I needed that water I hadn't brought with me. (Who knew that crying was so dehydrating?) All I was running on then was anger and will.

I found a declivity with flattened leaves that I was pretty sure had just been used as a day bed. There was fresh scat in it. I'd been quiet and downwind but maybe they'd caught my presence. Instinctively, I hid the rifle behind me and stood still. I didn't want them to be afraid. "This is your refuge," I whispered. Then I backed out in the opposite direction from how they'd run off.

I have no idea what luck made me spot it because it was off the deer trail a good fifteen or twenty feet, if I'm any judge of distance, which I'm not, as Harold would have been happy to tell you. I blessed the name of the optometrist who got me the driving glasses because there's no chance I'd have seen it without them. And truth be told, when I did see it, I didn't know what it was. The tree looked wrong, that's all. Like it was freshly broken, but oddly, unnaturally. I picked my way through the brush, fighting it all the way, to investigate. Damn the honeysuckle, taking over the woods the way it is. But I got to the tree, which I thought was a chestnut sapling, the trunk about two inches in diameter. At first I couldn't figure it out, but then I worked around toward the back and saw: a bullet was lodged in it. What were the chances? It had hit with enough force to break the trunk and the weight of the top had made it tip.

I was sick. Sick. Had his first bullet wounded and he took a second shot and missed, or had his target escaped entirely? Was he still out here or had full daylight made him quit for now? He knew he was poaching. All he didn't know was that I was after him. He had the advantage, though. He knew where he was. He was likely after bucks. There were possibly at least a couple of bucks. I didn't know where he was, and there was only one of him.

I peed in the woods, which I'd finally become adept at doing, especially avoiding poison ivy, as the very thought of squatting in it was a horror. Please don't picture it. I licked my lips to wet them and kept going. I headed north, in the general direction of the road, the way I thought Larry would have had to come in. I should have figured he'd go to the area closer to the road, the lazy easy spot, not the one closer to the creek. What was I looking for now? I didn't know. As I said, it was only anger kept me going.

The deer trail I was following was hardly a trail, nothing humans would hike along. Branches grabbed at my body and face, and I had to climb over fallen limbs the deer easily jumped. But I could see where they'd been, the narrow path they'd worn as they moved and foraged, mated and slept. I knew I was leaving my scent. I didn't know if that meant they wouldn't use this trail again. I needed to do more reading. I didn't know if this was how Larry had come in, either. At least I didn't know until I got to the road. Again, it was only luck that I saw it. (Either that or I was getting close to earning a Girl Scout badge in Advanced Tracking.) Or maybe no luck was involved because it was bright red. A Coke can. Not even Diet. Tossed onto the berm into the taller grass. I went over and picked it up, gingerly as if it were dynamite. I know there was no proof it was his, but good grief. There were tire tracks still in the grass, and it was a short distance from the nearly invisible entrance to the deer trail. You'd have to really know what you were doing to have found it. Coming from the road, I wouldn't have. But I have to think an experienced hunter would.

I was tired, and my mouth was dry. I'd forgotten to put my watch on, but judging from the sun it could be as late as nine. It was shorter to head for home by walking the road than to retrace my steps back through the woods and then the two fields. Sometimes expediency overrides caution. I used to warn the boys in my class about taking stupid shortcuts (they were the ones who'd climb over tables in the cafeteria to beat one another to the playground). It briefly crossed my mind: what if someone I know drives by? Nah. How likely is that?

I should have known.

32

I didn't even see the black-and-white coming. I was watching my step because the ground was slanty and uneven on the grassy berm where I was walking. All I needed was to step in some hole and go down. It was the sound of the tires that finally made me look up. If I'd just been paying attention, especially since I was actually wearing my driving glasses and could see a mile down the road, I'd have been able to hide the evidence and come back for it later.

"Louisa! You all right? You have a breakdown or something?"

For a minute I thought he meant nervous breakdown and I panicked, thinking Gary had sent him.

"Where's your car?"

Then I realized what he meant and a momentary tide of relief washed over me, thinking I was home free. "Oh, no, car's fine. I'm fine, thanks, Gus. Everything's fine."

He looked at me and I saw his eyes go meaningfully to the rifle and then back to my face. Oh damn. Double damn.

"You packin' heat, Louisa?" He said it with a smile, but his eyes were serious.

"Geez, Gus," I said, moving next to the car and leaning into the open passenger-side window using one elbow. "You know how I feel about guns. Why? Some local murder this morning?" I never should have said that, I know, putting the idea in his head in advance. The minute I opened my mouth I could have slapped myself upside the head. Amy and Marvelle would be disgusted with me and even amiable Beth wouldn't be pleased. Why not just blab on the Internet? I could go to the library, use the free Internet access there, and it wouldn't even cost me anything the way paying for a billboard or radio advertising would. I know what you're thinking, and I don't need more criticism.

I gave him my brightest smile and made my eyes sparkle. At least I think I did. Or possibly I made myself look psychotic. Either way, it did seem to divert him. Meanwhile I was trying to think of whatever I could, anything I could, to say when he got back to his question.

"Oh my, not hardly, Louisa," he said, clearing his throat, getting the words out after a false start, one hand in the air. His neck and face had reddened, too. I pressed on.

"Good! I was so scared when you first came up behind me like that, all official-looking in your sheriff's car and all. Just when I was getting used to the idea of you in regular clothes and in your own truck! That was nice." I did the thing with my eyes again, and smiled with my mouth closed this time for variety, and to look demure and harmless.

"Didn't mean to scare you. Wouldn't want to do that. You need a hand? Didn't break down, did you?"

"Oh gosh no, I'm fine. Just headin' over to Helen's." I pointed toward the Atherton's driveway across the road about a quarter mile in the direction away from the one in which I was headed. "I was going through stuff of Harold's—you know, it's time I just let go of things!—and I thought that Ben would like Harold's rifle. You know what a hunter he is. And I don't want it around. But don't you know! Nobody was home, and I sure wasn't going to leave a gun, even an unloaded one, lying on the front porch. So I just headed right back home. But it's been a lovely walk, and next time I'll call her first."

Gus grinned, stretching the skin on the upper rounds of his cheeks. The bottom frame of his glasses sank into them. What hair he had was close-cropped, color-leeched. "Well, now, Miss Louisa . . ."

I thought he was going to question my story, especially given my ridiculous outfit, and I felt heat rising toward my face. I didn't know what else I could say, or maybe it was illegal to walk on the road with a gun. Especially a loaded one.

"I was going to stop by your place, and I'd have missed you. I've been trying to call you. You must be doing a lot of gaddin' around these days. You're never home. Been wantin' to ask you out to supper again. Get a date pinned down, I mean. You promised."

"I'm sorry I missed your calls," I lied. "You're right, I have been busy. Why don't you give me a call later today when I have my calendar right in front of me and we'll set it up?"

"I can give you a ride there now."

Oh, right. I'd love to get in your squad car and continue this conversation. "Thanks so much for the offer, but I need the exercise. Especially if we're going out to supper! A girl has to watch her figure, you know." I trilled off what I hoped was a coy laugh, trying imitate a little waterfall. I ended up sounding more like a sick crow. I am so out of practice.

Gus was unfazed by the bizarre sound. "Well, that's fine. You do that. You gettin' excited for the big event?"

"Oh yes, absolutely."

"Me too. I'll be doing security. Talk to you later. Have a nice walk." He nodded and I stepped back from the car. Two quick horn toots came as the car crawled back into the road. Gus's pudgy hand waved out the open window. I waved back as I held the rifle pointed to the ground, along my leg away from the road, hoping to block his rear view of it with my body. Out of sight, out of mind, right?

"Doing security" for a supper date he was calling "a big event"? That's what I heard, and what I thought was *Oh my, we do have an ego, don't we now.* How about you? Are you shouting, Wise up, Louisa! There's a neon-red flag flashing

WARNING with sparklers shooting out of it if I ever saw one. I'm telling you now, I swear I was so relieved to see that damn car drive off, I thought I was home free.

I would have loved not to have to trudge the rest of the way home after all the walking I'd already done. After Gus pulled off and I relaxed, I tried to get back to the angry place I'd been for the energy to walk the half mile or so I had left to go. The plug had been pulled and all I could feel was how tired I was, but since the side of the road lacked a comfy chair and a glass of cold water, I walked on.

At home, I lay down with a cloth on my head for an hour or so. Maybe it was longer. I dozed. When I got up, I felt better. I made tea and let the girls in. They were quite annoyed at having been confined to their coop all day. Marvelle wanted to go out, but I had her stay inside with us. As I've said, she used to be a world-class hunter, sneaky as they come, so I thought she might have a decent opinion about how Larry Ellis might think.

When was he likely to be back? I didn't think it would be that day. "Lord knows, girls, I don't think I can do this twice a day every day. We've got to try to get ahead of him."

Marvelle rolled her eyes, which I thought was rude and told her so. "No more special milk for you, missy, if you can't be nice and helpful. When will he be back?"

The girls made sympathetic noises. Their hunting experience was limited to insects, Amy said. Nothing warm-blooded, and not before dawn, since I never let them out of the coop until well after sunup. How were they supposed to contribute to this discussion? JoJo puffed up, flapped once, and said she would use her imagination if I happened to have a few cut-up grapes around to inspire her.

I was at the refrigerator when the phone rang. Gus, I figured, and didn't move. Marvelle flicked her tail hard in the direction of the phone like an insistent pointy finger. I took it as a sign, which I don't believe in, and looked at Caller ID. It was CarolSue.

"Sister! I thought Charlie had a doctor . . . thing today. I was going to call you at five." I was ashamed I couldn't remember.

"It was canceled. Or put off." I couldn't tell anything from her voice.

"That's good. Right? Or is that . . . bad?"

"His MRI on Wednesday didn't look the same, and the oncologist is considering other, or I guess additional, treatment options." She sounded as if she were putting quotation marks in the air with her fingers.

"Oh. Oh no."

"It'll be all right. We'll get through. We have an appointment with him next week, and I guess we'll find out more."

"Oh no." What was I, some kind of two-word puppet? I couldn't think of a thing to say. Not a thing. And she'd been so good in every way when Harold died. What was wrong with me? I shut the refrigerator door, got to a kitchen chair, and sat. There was dust on the end of the table where Harold used to sit. In the next few minutes I'd get up, get the sponge, and wipe it clean. "I'm sorry. I'm so sorry. You must be scared."

"We'll get through. It's hard to wait."

"Don't shut me out, sister. You were there for me."

"I know. I don't mean to. Sometimes I can't bear to think about it. I really love him, and then I feel bad telling you how scared I am of losing him because I know how that must make you feel."

"Bless your heart." I affected the Southern accent, which she doesn't know is what I blame for taking her away from me—Charlie's, I mean. Damn the whole state of Georgia anyway. "Such crap. You can talk to me about anything, you know that. No one can understand like I do."

The line was quiet for a bit. I knew to wait. But then she said, "Distract me for a little bit, will you? It's the waiting I can't stand. Not knowing anything. What's up with The Plan? Where are we at, honey chile?" She put on the drawl back at me and I knew it meant she couldn't talk about Charlie any more right then. She didn't want to cry.

"The bastard was here this morning, dawn, and took a shot. He got away before I could call Gus." Obviously, I left out a few details.

"No way. Really?"

"I'm trying to figure out when he'll be back. That's what I was just working out in my head when you called."

"But did you see his truck? I mean, now do you know where he parked?"

"Well, I figured it out from tire marks by a deer trail right into my land. And a fresh Coke can tossed just off trail." No need to mention that I'd followed him. Have you ever noticed that once you start lying there's no going back?

"You stay away from him, you hear? The minute you spot his truck again, you just call Gus and let him handle it. All Gus needs to do is catch him on your land with a gun."

"But . . ." I was going to say that's not technically poaching. I'm not letting him get one of my deer, so it's only trespassing. I stopped myself, though.

"But what?"

"No, you're right. Gus can handle it."

"Louisa, do not, I repeat, do not say or do anything yourself. I mean it. Don't lose your temper and confront him."

"Oh Lord, honey, I'm way too chicken for that. He's the one with a gun, after all." I even added a little laugh. Both JoJo and Amy, of course, were extremely miffed by my saying I was chicken and intending it as a pejorative. Sometimes I simply can't think of everything.

I wanted CarolSue to believe me, but it hurt me when she said, "Yeah, okay, I know. I was just making sure." She doesn't even really know me, what I'm capable of now. Of course, I hardly know myself anymore. That's how long she's lived a thousand miles away. Here I am, determined that none of the deer taking sanctuary on my land will be sacrificed, at the same time—since the moment CarolSue told me about Charlie's latest MRI—my mind whispers a tiny something like prayer that if Charlie dies, CarolSue will decide to come home. I have to shut that down. When Harold died, she asked me to move there, and would I?

Maybe I'll answer the phone tomorrow and let the God Squad strike it rich on that one!

I didn't go out hunting Larry Ellis that night. I wanted to, but my knees hurt, I was exhausted, and my logic told me that he wouldn't be back on the same day. As if to keep me from worrying about it, though, the weather report told me that thunderstorms were headed our way, and to expect flash flood warnings. Normally, this in itself would have worried me; Rush Run has risen far above its banks multiple times, to the point of rerouting itself over the years, but to me that day was like a sign (which I do not believe in) saying, Rest up! It will be all right. And it started to storm heavily at three thirty in the morning, keeping on past dawn.

The bad weather gave me time to reason things out. I'd known I couldn't go out and cover my land twice a day, guessing where an intent hunter might be, even though I'd found the two trail cameras. Maybe there were more. And how would I know when? It was too chancey.

"You didn't think of this sooner?" I knew what Marvelle's rolled eyes were accusing. "Mice are smarter than you."

"Look, I can't get help on this from CarolSue, and exactly what help have you been? What have you killed lately? I haven't seen you stalk a mouse for a good two years," I snapped at her.

The afternoon was dense, the air like a sodden hot towel, unseasonable. No power, not since seven in the morning. Dwayne County Rural Electric is not known for speed in restoring electricity when a transformer is knocked out.

When I said that, something flipped in my thinking. "Stalking. That's it, Marvelle. Right! If you want to hunt something, you have to stalk it." I stood up so fast the chair tipped backward. "Damn. Of course."

When the power flickered back on, I put the television on to catch the weather report on the local news. I plain needed to know more about old Larry Ellis, that was obvious. I could pretty much count on his coming back; I needed to be able to predict when.

That off-and-on heavy rain continued another full twenty-four hours. "Thank you, honey," I whispered to Harold on the off chance that he knows what I'm doing for his and Cody's sake and is helping me, not that I believe in that, but I don't claim certainty about much anymore and the storms did give me a chance to rest.

Even before dawn of the next day, when it would naturally be cooler, you could tell the day was going to be one big improvement. In the early morning darkness, the moon was round as an unbitten cookie with smooth white frosting. It was going to be a long day. I had to go out just as I had the first time, in case he came back right away, after whatever he'd shot at.

I had to choose an area, so I went to where he'd taken the shot. It was difficult to pick my way, the landscape in shades of dark grey as it was. I saw my buck, enormous, running through a section of forest where there was less undergrowth than in most. The sight lasted only a few seconds, then the white tail flashed up and over a rock formation. *Stay safe, be well,* I sent him in silent blessing.

Stopping short of the trail camera, I looked for a place to hide, to put myself in a natural blind. The ground was wet and I hadn't thought to bring plastic. Crouching was too hard on my knees, and standing, even behind a tree, left me too exposed. So there I was, lying on the wet ground, covering myself with soggy leaves, propping myself on one elbow to peek over a fallen, rotting tree toward the deer trail.

Absolutely nothing happened except that whatever parts

of my body didn't have arthritis were certainly encouraged to develop it quickly. I could hardly stand up by the time it was wholly daylight. On the way home I reminded myself over and over that I'd heard no shots, so he'd likely not come, or I'd startled at least the big buck out of the area, which was a fine thing. And now, I thought, after a nap, I could start the reconnaissance that should help me refine the hunt.

33
Larry

Larry had been careful not to go too often. He didn't want to take stupid chances; it was too good a site except there was no place to hide the truck, and even though the nearest house was maybe a half mile down the road, he didn't want anyone noticing. No one was likely to pay attention if they passed it once, but hell, pass the same truck parked there regularly, and it would look suspicious. The last thing he wanted was to attract attention.

So he'd gone just a couple of times more before or after his shift, getting in and out as fast as he could to check the cameras. The place was crawling with deer; he could hardly believe it. One of the trail cameras ended up useless. The kid must have messed up the waterproof covering, but the other two made it look like the whitetails were holding conventions or something. He'd only brought his rifle in once, before work, and taken shots—it had been plain irresistible, a buck running like that, the challenge of a moving target. For the first time in his life he'd been just as glad to miss; he'd have had to go back to the truck, bring in the deer drag, his shovel, knife, all that. How would he account for his time, with LuAnn thinking he had gone in before dawn to put in overtime? He would have had to call off sick and get the carcass over to the one guy near Waynesville who'd process an out-of-season deer for extra cash. He really hadn't thought that one through. He hadn't been able to get a clear look at how big the rack was, whether it was trophy-size. So it might not have even been worth the trouble, to say nothing of the fight with LuAnn. Not that she was going to tell him what he could and could not do.

But he didn't want to fight with her if he could avoid it. Having LuAnn around paid off even beyond the sex and getting him out of jail. She'd gone to that Lodge dinner when he'd wanted to join, and talked to the women the way she was good at, which let him hang out and see what he could pick up. Now he had virgin territory to himself. That Lodge was a trip and a half. Some asshole fat guy had sidled up to him and like it was a threat when no one was around, he'd said, "Don't ever come back here, you're not welcome." What was that about?

34
Louisa

As I mentioned, the weather turned that day; it went from being hungover August to freshly washed early October in one diurnal cycle. Still, the brilliance of the sky that could have been a blue plate holding a fried egg yolk dousing the house with light by nine o'clock wasn't enough to keep me from lapsing into a coma-like sleep. I awoke at twelve thirty with a sense that I'd missed something urgent.

I skipped a shower again and just stayed in the clothes I'd put on last night, so I'd be ready to get up and get right out ahead of Larry, in case he came again, which I had no way of knowing for sure.

"Wait for me, girls. I'll be back really soon, and then I'll let you out." I didn't know if I was lying or not. I was prepared to wait it out. Six beady, accusing eyes protested as I passed the coop on my way out to the car. Even Beth, who is usually the most empathic of the three, was clearly annoyed.

I guess I might not have mentioned that I was going back to Larry Ellis's house. I'm a little embarrassed to go into it, after what happened last time. You probably figured it out anyway, I suppose. You can see, can't you, that I had to? It's not like I was going to break in or anything. Not that again, even though I didn't plan it the time I did.

Remember those big silver uncovered trash barrels alongside the house? I hope you're not rolling your eyes like Marvelle right now because it wasn't like I was some dumpster-diving old bag lady. In fact, I thought of myself much more like a senior Nancy Drew. I was hoping that Larry Ellis was the sort who threw out all sorts of things like the envelope his paycheck came in (if he even had a job!), so I could find out where and when he worked. Anything I could glean that might help me predict his schedule, when he would be likely to be back on my property and after the lives that remained in my care.

To make sort of a pun, I'll cut to the chase. I failed.

Oh, I got to Larry's house fine, just like the other times, and parked across from it and down the road. I was going to cut in through that section of woods and undergrowth I'd used for escape. When I turned off the car, I checked the rearview mirror to make sure no one was around. I didn't mean to look at myself, too, but I did. Or at my eyes. Then I pulled away to see more of my face because the eyes didn't look like mine. They looked, well, deranged, for lack of a better word. I couldn't even tell their color, but that must have been the lighting there in the car, with the sun glinting off the hood. My eyebrows looked wild and unruly, like my grandmother's used to. There was a time I kept them plucked neat as a made bed. I need to do that tonight. What am I doing? I thought right then. *What am I doing?* Is CarolSue right?

I swear to you I didn't get out of the car. I just sat, a rag doll, only a rag doll wouldn't have been able to smell her unwashed self. I cried. A car passed.

I wiped my face on the hem of my shirt finally, started the car, turned around in the driveway of a white ranch house a quarter mile down the road, and headed through roads fringed with faded cornstalks toward home.

This is the truth: I have no idea if I would have quit The Plan entirely, or reverted to the nice, tame, legal version CarolSue knew and approved of in which I just finally caught Larry on my land, called Gus, and had him arrested for trespassing and—if Gus did his job—hunting out of season and where No Hunting was posted. I can only say that a plug had been pulled on my confidence, which really isn't like me. What if CarolSue is right? I thought, over and over. How can I know? Maybe this is just the wrong thing to do. You see? The plug had been pulled on my anger.

I've already told you I'm not one to believe in signs, but what happened next is a doozie and changed everything. How the world can flip over, and flip over again, all of it in your mind. Nothing happens, but everything changes.

I have a bladder the size of a pea. I may have told you this already. I'd have thought I'd cried out all the water in my body sitting there in the car, but no, as I drove back I thought there was no possibility I was going to make it home without exploding. It was a lot closer to detour to Sandy's Mini Mart in Rushville (not even a town, just a breath while you drive through, but they have a bathroom as well as the canned goods, bread, milk, beer, and wine that save the people out here a thirty-five-minute midweek drive to a real grocery store).

Now why would it catch my eye, having to pee the way I did, that computer-made sign in the window along with all the handmade ones saying things like TRUCK FOR SALE, and LOST DOG (BLACK, WHITE, AND BROWN), and BENE-FIT FOR SAMANTHA CALDWELL, and YARD SALE?

TENT REVIVAL
REV. GARY HAWKINS PREACHING ON

ENBALMBED BY GOD

AT SITE OF OUR FUTURE CHURCH HOME!
(in FIRST FIELD)
Saturday 7:00 P.M.
154 Rural Route 2
Shandon, INDIANA
REMEMBER! IT'S ALL ABOUT JESUS!

It was like it was meant to happen. The outrageous spelling caught my eye before the name. Even though I practically had to cross my legs, I stopped to read it on the weedy sidewalk in front of Jamie's. If I hadn't gone back to Larry's and felt that despair, I wouldn't have been there to see it. If I believed in signs, which I don't, this would have been a neon one saying, *Louisa, you have to go on.* Of course, you've already figured out that the preacher is my son. What you didn't know is that address is my farm; the first field has the winter root crops for the deer.

To know now that all that time he'd been planning to use my land—no, more: to take it, without asking, without a word to me, too impatient to wait for me to die.

It's so much easier, isn't it, when things are clear? Like a running stream, no murk, no algae, no debris, the smooth stones glistening on the bottom, graspable and clean as truth. The rage I felt again then was like that, unmuddied by second thoughts, not even by grief. I could put love for my son away, as if in the back of the dark closet in the spare bedroom with Glitter Jesus. What kind of mother can do that? I know you have that thought. Don't you think I have felt myself failing Gary these last months?

I used the bathroom at Sandy's, feeling almost faint with the blood in my head. Waving off a pimply boy at the counter who asked what I'd like—the bathroom supposed to be for customers, and I'd intended to buy a Hershey's bar—I leaned over a rack of snack cakes to tear the poster from the glass where it had been taped. "Ma'am," the boy started to say. I didn't hear the rest. The bell on the door rang as I let it drop behind me, poster crumpled in my hand, back to my car, to my home on my land, what used to be Harold's and my land. Our beloved land.

35

Now I needed to think about The Plan *and* what to do to save my land, so I did mindless tasks. Plucked my eyebrows, put clothes in the washer, dusted, moved the clothes to the dryer. I didn't even discuss it with Marvelle or the girls at first. CarolSue called, and though I intended to tell her about what I'd discovered at Sandy's Mini Mart, when I heard her voice, tired and disheartened, I didn't. I knew that to stay with The Plan I should go to the woods at dusk, though I didn't have any more notion about when Larry Ellis might come back or where he might head. The phone rang as the afternoon waned. I saw it was Gary, and didn't answer even though Beth bobbed her head emphatically that I should and waddled off in uncharacteristic disgust when I didn't.

I think she's psychic. I should have answered the phone. A half hour later I heard a car door slam outside. Gary. I barely had time to compose my face, and no time to imagine what was next. He came through the front door, without knocking, wearing a green plaid shirt that had been Harold's, and his toothy smile. He'd tamed his curly hair into a side part and slicked it down, making him look like a TV game show host.

"Mom! I tried to call, but you must have been outside. I brought you a surprise!"

He didn't wait for a reaction, but lumbered toward me holding out several papers. I assumed that it was another church tract and took it, knowing that was the quickest—indeed the only—way to get him to leave. Thank heaven I hadn't changed into hunting clothes before he showed up, I thought, but there wasn't much time before I'd have to go. I knew my odds weren't generous at tracking Larry, but I had the will. And the will to deal with Gary and his revival, but one thing at a time.

"It's lovely to see you, honey, but I'm getting ready to go out for supper." I kissed him and we stood in the living room. I didn't turn to lead him into the kitchen, the way I usually would have, and didn't ask him to sit down, either.

"Great!" He wasn't paying any attention obviously, or he would have asked questions necessitating more lies. I was preparing what to say, but he just went on. "Look at your surprise," he said, pointing at the papers in my hand.

It took me a moment to decipher what the papers—a computer printout—were. I hope I don't need new reading glasses, too, but I think it was just shock making my eyes blur: it was a receipt and itinerary for one passenger—me—to fly to Atlanta on Wednesday.

"Gary! This is very generous, but—"

"No buts about it, Mom. You're staying a week, a real visit. Hey, you know these chickens are pooping in the house, right? I need to see your driver's license to make sure it's valid. You can't fly without a current government photo ID, you know."

"Does your aunt know about this?" I couldn't keep suspicion out of my voice. Probably I didn't try.

"It's actually a present to both of you, so I wrote that card you've been telling me to and said I was sending you down to help. She'll get it today or tomorrow." He grinned, pleased with himself. "That's why I had to tell you today. I had to give you *some* notice. And don't worry. I'll come feed the chickens and the cat. I promise I'll take good care of them. Are you excited?"

Excited? Trying to get me out of town so he could use my

field for his revival. I looked out the side window. Flares of light glared above the treetops; it wasn't long at all until sunset. Already the western sky was taking on a pinkish tinge. I had to keep watch in the woods, but I couldn't let this stand.

"*Excited* isn't the word. I am flabbergasted. Why are you doing this? What is this really about?"

"It's all about Jesus, Mom," he started. "He said we have to—"

"Gary, stop. Just stop. What does that even mean? *What* is all about Jesus? It's a slogan. It answers nothing. It's meaningless. Cody's death was not about Jesus and neither was your father's. It was about a drunk driver who took no responsibility for actions that devastated our family. Our family. Jesus had not one thing to do with it."

"God has a Plan, Mom, and everything happens according to His Plan."

I could hear the capital letters in his voice and they enraged me. I knew I should stop. I had to get out into the woods before twilight. I should have let it go and I couldn't. Or just didn't. I started putting capital letters in my own voice, mine irreverent, angry.

"No, Gary. God and Jesus did not Plan to kill off Cody any more than they Plan our wars or what spiders die under our feet or what chickens get thrush. Oma made Plans about who was using what beds and menus and so did Grandma." I knew I was too loud, but I didn't dial it back. "I might be capable of making a Plan to kill someone off, but that's not *The Jesus Show*. It's not All About Jesus. It's All About Larry Ellis." Now I was furious. "Your father and I should have been able to watch *The Cody Show* for the rest of our lives, even after *The Gary, Nicole, and Cody Show* was canceled. It damn well wasn't God or Jesus who ended *The Cody Show*. Larry Ellis got drunk and smashed that TV. And it was *pointless*."

I'd gone too far, but not for the reason I thought. I thought I'd given myself away.

Gary was crying. He turned his shoulders sideways, one hand to his face, then the other, too. Then he walked away.

Of course I followed him. I'm his mother, and that's what mothers do in moments like these, filled with that toxic mixture of rage and guilt that most mothers know at various times. I tried to put my arms around him. He pulled away. He seemed like he was going to leave, heading for the front door, but then his sobbing made him unsteady and he sat on the couch, doubled over his knees.

"It's all I . . . Mom. Don't take . . . Jesus . . . away from me. I'm begging . . . you. Don't take Jesus away . . . from me."

I'm his mother. "Oh, son . . . Okay, son. Okay," I said, and rubbed his heaving back. "Okay, I'm sorry. I understand." What else could I say? We sat like that a long time, my arms around him.

I hugged him then until, face flushed and wet, voice ragged, he used one hand to smooth his hair and forced a half-smile as he sat himself upright. "I'm all right now. Ticket's non-refundable, so you gotta go." He didn't tell me why he'd bought the ticket. Even then. And I didn't tell him that I knew. I told myself I needed time to think, and there was truth in that. And it was a lie.

"It's a very generous gesture," I said. "Thank you."

I had no intention of going to CarolSue's. Not on Wednesday, I mean.

I got him out of there in another five minutes by dissembling and letting him think I'd be on the plane. I even showed him my license when he asked to see it, though it doesn't need to be renewed until my birthday in three more years and I told him that.

He said he'd take me to the Indianapolis airport, but I made up a story about how I'd want to shop for some underwear in Indy before I went, since it's an afternoon flight. Like I'd dream of wanting to shop, which I hate. Have you ever noticed that once someone you love has disappointed you, it becomes easy to say and do things that should make you disappointed in yourself, but they don't? Not at the time anyway. That had become the story of me and my son.

Anger is a powerful fuel. I suited up for hunting—not to hide myself, but for the protection from the underbrush this time—closed Marvelle in the house, and put the girls in the coop. This really annoyed Jo, who made me chase her around the yard first, leaving me winded before I set out along the edge of the fields to the entrance to the trail I knew Larry had been on. It was only a guess as to where he'd hunt, if he came at all that night, but I wouldn't forgive myself for not trying. I couldn't even think about the likelihood of being in the wrong place again.

It was way later than I wanted. The deer would be already out of their day beds and on the move, increasingly restless, increasingly closer to rut season as the daylight hours shortened.

The pinkish sky had deepened to scarlet with apricot streaks. It wouldn't last; the sun would set soon. "Red sky at night, sailors' delight," I said aloud, just as I found the entrance to the deer trail my own use had already made more distinct. I meant there'd be sunshine tomorrow and I'd have to be up before dawn to be out in the forest. Already the rifle was heavy, and I was hungry. I was so rushed, I'd left without bringing any food or water.

I was checking my watch and guessing that there was about an hour until dark. Strange how shocked, how unprepared I was at the moment it happened: a shot. And it was close. I started to run in the direction it had come from, slowed a minute, and fumbled in the jacket pocket for Harold's old orange hat and pulled it on hard. I wanted the next shot to be mine, a last one.

Running is a big exaggeration for what a woman my age wearing crappy sneakers and too-big hunting clothes while carrying a Winchester deer rifle can do on a deer trail, especially if it's not herself she's intending to kill, but I moved as fast as I could while trying to keep the thrashing down. I wasn't getting enormous cooperation from the underbrush, which continuously thwarted me. Desperate to find my target, I was making too much noise.

I was almost to the spot where I'd seen the first trail camera, the one I'd found before it could record me. I slowed down and looked intently for signs. Footprints weren't going to be useful; too many fallen leaves. Sound is deceptive, but I was sure the shot had been close ahead of me. One minute there was nothing to go on, then suddenly there was everything. Blood. On the ground and splattered on the brush and the trunk of a tree. Then a new trail: the one left by a wounded deer.

36
Larry

"Okay, now see, we get the drag cart. We wanna take that with us. Takes too long to come back for it." Larry was trying to get the kid to move faster, get the drag cart into the woods before someone came along and saw what they were up to. He hadn't said anything to the kid about in or out of season or posted property. Why go there?

"What for?"

"Ya think you can sling a dead whitetail over your shoulder and dance it out? Just do what I say." He tried to keep any impatience out of his voice but went ahead and moved the cart himself. "Grab the backpack, will ya? Let's go."

"I thought you said, I mean I thought you had to check the cameras, see what's on them. I thought that's what we came for."

"Oh, yeah. That too. Yeah, one of 'em's messed up. Just grab the pack now."

It was getting tiresome, having to explain everything. He had a feeling the kid was going to balk at the gloves and mask, but when it's for real, you make damn sure you're not leaving any scent. At least the kid picked up the pack with the flashlights, range finder, knives, deer grunt call, and rope. Larry had stuck some protein bars, which tasted like pressed chalk and cardboard dust, and several Cokes and his beer in there, too, already missing the ham-and-cheese sandwiches he usually talked LuAnn into packing for him, just not missing how she bitched about it and complained how she'd worry until he was back home. She was taking care of her mother again, staying overnight. LuAnn was loyal, he always gave her that much. She was getting her payback, though: thrilled because he'd said okay to the kid staying back with him since Mr. Pelley needed him both weekend days until two. So Larry was building up dirty sex points with LuAnn while scoring the kid to carry the pack. He'd tell LuAnn they'd bonded over auto parts. Whatever. Worked for him.

"This thing is heavy," the kid said.

"Ya wanna trade? You can take the drag cart." It was a taunt. "Yeah, I didn't think so. Quit soundin' like a little girl."

Larry wondered if it was going to dawn on the kid that without him Larry would have the backpack and the drag cart, as he usually did.

"We're only takin' the drag cart in a little way. We'll leave it and come back if we need it." Larry didn't want to leave it visible in the truck bed.

"Why not just leave it in the truck then?"

"Too far," he said. "I know what I'm doin'."

The kid sighed loudly. "Right."

Larry knew exactly how the kid meant that and wanted to slug him. "C'mon. We gotta be in place before sunset. They're active at dusk. No noise from here on out."

"You're the one doin' all the talking," the kid said, which made Larry want to slug him again. The kid was getting cocky, too big for his pants, or whatever that expression was. He might have to put him in his place.

Larry left off the drag cart, not all that far from the road. He'd lost a certain amount of enthusiasm for the company. They hiked on to the first blind, the kid behind him, blissfully quiet.

Twilight. There'd been plenty of sign, if you knew what you were looking for, and Larry did. Now they were in the blind, and he was signaling the kid to stay down and stop making noise as he rummaged in the backpack for a Coke and protein bar. Annoyed, he put his finger to his lips. The kid rolled his eyes.

It had only been an hour when the kid stood up. Larry signaled him to get down and the kid said, "Gotta take a leak."

"Told you to take care of that before," Larry whispered, hoping he'd get the point.

"Nature calls." Not whispered.

"Keep your voice down. Stop drinking Coke," Larry hissed. The kid had gone through a whole one, couldn't sit still, didn't even practice with the range finder to get the feel of it. He thought the sound of the deer grunt caller was "weird." And to completely piss Larry off, he'd taken his cell phone out of his pocket and started playing with it. There was no signal out here, but there were games on it. That's what the kid said, anyway. A couple of times Larry thought maybe he was deliberately doing what Larry told him not to, but then he remembered what a moron the kid was generally. He'd had to tell him to turn the game sound off, for chrissake.

"You gotta watch for whitetails," Larry said, forcing elaborate patience into his whisper.

"Tell me if you see any," the kid said.

Well, he guessed the whole thing had been a mistake except for the points he'd made with LuAnn.

"We could be up in a tree stand, y'know," Larry said, as the kid peed the stream of youth, long and strong and steady, right behind the blind. Crap, he thought, even I can smell it. Might as well pack it in early and give up for the day. Hope for a hard rain, come back without the kid.

Just after he'd given up in his head, there it was, upwind and to his right; he'd nearly missed the big boy while he was arguing with the damn kid. The rack an enormous thing of beauty, and the buck taking his sweet time headed toward the water just the way Larry had figured.

Making no sudden motions, Larry dropped to one knee

and braced his rifle. No time for the range finder. Experience told him twenty yards. A clean shot to the chest.

"NO!" The kid, coming from behind him and thrashing over the top of the blind toward the buck, yelling "Go!" just as Larry squeezed the trigger with pressure and absorbed the kick and the kid became a grotesque sound track underneath the explosion of the powder, the kicked-aside brush and the shouting muffled and tossed into the air with the reverberation.

"Goddamn, what the hell—" No blood he could see on the kid. Didn't know where the shot had hit, though. The buck was gone.

The kid turned around, shouting, "Don't kill him. Don't! He didn't do *anything* to you." His face was working like he wanted to cry.

"Christ! You fucking moron! You cost me that buck. I had a clean shot!" Furious, he picked his way through the underbrush to where the buck had been and yes, blood, and a trail of it.

Larry made his way back to the blind. The western sky still held some color but the land was getting thick with darkness. "Dammit, now I've gotta track him. Get the lights outta the pack."

"Whaddaya mean? He got away—"

"He didn't drop. Thanks to you. Just shut up and do what I tell you."

"What?"

"What is *wrong* with you? I gotta finish him, get the carcass, get the drag cart. It's gonna get dark. C'mon."

"He didn't get away?"

Larry pointed. "Go tell me if you see it on the ground. Move! That's a twelve-, maybe fourteen-point rack. I want him. Move!"

"Oh God, oh God."

When the kid just stood there looking like he was going to vomit, Larry ignored him and hustled to get out the two flashlights himself. He tossed one to the kid, who fumbled and dropped it. Carrying his rifle, he pointed to the pack.

"Put that on," he said, and waited to see that that the kid did, not trusting him to do the simplest thing right. He walked out to pick up the blood trail.

After a minute, the kid followed.

"Dammit, shut up. Jesus, what don't you get about *shut up*?" Larry wheeled around; the kid was sniveling and making a racket. He'd scare off any whitetail within a hundred miles, let alone one that was bleeding.

The kid had his head down. He smeared his sleeve across his face and shook his head. "I'm goin'."

"Goin' where?"

"Home," he said. He veered off through the underbrush, his flashlight on, bobbing ineffectively ahead. It wasn't even dark enough to need the damn flashlight. His eyes wouldn't adjust as well.

"Go then. You think I care? Put down the pack. I need my stuff." The kid let the pack slide off his back and thud to the ground. He veered off blindly, still sniveling. "Wrong direction," Larry was forced to call after the kid when he was trying to be silent, "wrong way," and went after him. LuAnn would shit a brick about this. He grabbed the kid by the arm. "God, you're a pain. Do you know how to read a compass?"

"Sorta." The kid sniffed. Watery blue eyes were ringed in red now. Looked like a big baby.

"Take this." Larry detached the compass from his key ring. "Make the arrow stay northwest. That's N and W, there. See?" He pointed, but gave up because his forefinger covered the whole face and what dumbass couldn't figure out N and W? Well, probably the kid, but whatever. "Try not to go in circles," he said. "It'd be just like you. You'll come to the highway. Unless you mess it up, you oughta see the truck if you head up to your right. If you mess it up, your problem. This is stupid, hear me, stupid. You are *stupid*."

As the kid left, Larry swore to himself again. The dumbass was using the flashlight. Which he didn't need now. Larry called, trying to direct his voice. "Hey! Stupid! Wait till it's darker, and hold the damn light down. At the ground."

The kid was an idiot and LuAnn was going to find out and flip out, even though it was her kid who was too dumb to live. He knew what would rain down: instead of being grateful that Larry was showing her stupid baby boy how to be a man, she was going to go crazy and he'd have to break up with her. First, though, he had to find that buck and finish it. He was not going to lose that trophy. If he was going to end it with LuAnn, it sure as hell wasn't going to be for nothing. He picked up his pack and put it on. Screw LuAnn and screw her kid.

37
Louisa

Larry would be following the blood, trying to finish his kill before dark. I could double back to the house, call Gus, drive to Larry's truck—almost certainly parked where it had been before—and Gus would nab him coming out of my woods. Who knew how he would drag the deer? He couldn't get the truck in there. Trespassing, poaching, hunting out of season might be enough to get him, in sort of a disappointing Plan B way. But he might be the kind of jerk who'd leave a suffering animal if it took off on a difficult trajectory or looked to be a long chase. He'd be gone before I got back to the house.

I paused there, surrounded by yellow woods, slant light coming from the west. The final sun was setting the treetops on fire now, or they were giving off their own scarlet glow. I'd like to tell you I pushed on and followed the blood trail because I wouldn't risk that an animal on my land was deliberately left to die in pain. But because so far I've told the plain truth I'll say I felt a dark joy at the thought I could stop Larry and accomplish Harold's revenge—which had become my own—and it would all look like a terrible "accident." For Gus's eyes, I'd be incoherent with crazy grief that I'd accidentally shot this unknown stranger! I didn't pause to wonder if I'd become no different from Larry, bloodthirsty, hell-bent on bagging my trophy.

I didn't know how far behind them I was, but in some

places the blood seemed heavier. I was afraid I'd lose my sense of direction and started breaking branches so I could find my way back by the raw tips. Some I couldn't break and had to climb over or step on or duck under. I needed two hands. I stuck the rifle under my right arm, squeezed to hold it against my side. It slipped several times, and I'd lurch to catch and shove it back in place.

Light faded. I couldn't distinguish the blood from darker leaves and had to get on my knees. I couldn't keep that up. I'd have to get back to a spot I recognized before it was fully dark and hope for good moonlight, but it was unbearable to come so close and to fail for want of an hour's light. I was on the losing side of some war. Harold, my Harold: how many times did he feel this? And where had he been when he did? When he stepped in front of the Dwayne County Waste Recycling truck, did it feel like the final failure or one battle he could win?

I steeled myself to turn back, dreading the sound of another shot—yet in a way wishing for it, too, when I thought I heard something to my right and ahead. I froze and listened, and yes, something else was breaking ground. I stood and moved ahead as silently as I could. There was a small hill over there, and less honeysuckle underbrush. It took me away from the blood trail, but I could move quickly. As I got toward the top of the rise, I had to crouch, joints protesting *I can't do this.* The noise kept up.

The buck must have doubled back. I reached the top. Just below me: Larry, in camouflage with a camouflage hat, too— not orange—raised his rifle and shot. His bullet thunked into a tree.

He hadn't seen me. One quick, silent motion. I raised my rifle and aimed for his head, a shot I'd practiced and damn near perfected from this distance.

Maybe you'll think I should be proud of what happened, but I'm ashamed. Oh, I want to blame the light, or my eyes, or an unsteady hand, but it was none of those. Nothing but failure. Did I not love Harold enough to carry out his mission? He'd have used this gun himself, I'm sure, except for his promise to Cody. Wasn't I strong enough to find in my rifle sights a target rather than a human being who had a blond Barbie-woman in ridiculous shoes who kissed him and slept with him and would grieve? The Barbie-woman and that boy of hers who lived with them. Could their pain be as great as mine? What was my conviction worth to me, after all? Do you remember that dime balanced on edge, rolling, beginning to teeter side to side as it slows?

Yes. I pulled the trigger. But here is my confession. In that final instant, I shifted the sights.

Larry spun around, eyes wild with shock and panic. He felt his head and then pulled his hat off. One end of the bill was blasted away. I hadn't thought I'd be that close. As he threw his cap on the ground, he spotted me. Stared hard. Rage.

I tried to shout but it was a garble of sobs. I wanted to tell him I was going to kill him, but it was too late because I hadn't, and I couldn't.

"Crazy old bitch!" he shouted. "Ya just missed *me*. That buck is *my* kill. Back off." He spat on the ground then raised his lips to show his teeth.

I was broken, lowering the rifle to my side. Did he see that I was crying? Did I just look like a pathetic old woman in ridiculous oversize camouflage and a hunter's orange hat? Something made him decide I was no danger because he let out a laugh then, loony and high. He threw back his head in that moment of hilarity and I flashed on the image I'd so often conjured and tried to obliterate: Larry drunk, Cody walking the highway in light like this, reflector strips on his backpack, Larry's truck weaving, impact, the lurch, the snap of Cody's neck. And then it didn't matter that I was a lone soldier with no commander, no comrades whose will I needed to match or raise. That dime? It fell clean and hard.

Instantly, I raised the rifle, aimed, squeezed the trigger.

Sound in the woods off to the right. Was it the buck? Or did Larry think it was? As my shot exploded, Larry had already pivoted, raising and firing his rifle into the woods. He ran then, forging fast in pursuit, forgetting his cap on the ground. The brush cracked for five, six seconds as he pursued, then the sound was swallowed by the forest.

I'd missed. Two chances and I'd failed both times. I couldn't let this happen. I'd have to lie down and die here in the woods if I couldn't do better.

I slid and stumbled down the shallow hill and retrieved his cap. I'd burn it with the trash. A backpack like one Harold had years ago was there, too, on the ground, off to the side of where he'd stood. I'd missed seeing it before. I decided not to touch it anyway; all it proved was where he'd been. I checked to make sure the chamber had a bullet and started after Larry. Was he on a deer trail? I couldn't make one out, and as darkness let down like a long skirt, I couldn't tell at all if or where there was blood on the ground. Sick with disappointment, my only choice was to make my way back up and over the hill and go for the lesser version of The Plan.

It's a good thing I've gotten nearsighted and can inspect brambles that are smack in front of my face. I'd made enough of a mess purposely breaking branches that I could retrace my own trail. Once I was back on the deer trail, it was easier. I turned left, parallel to the road, and headed as fast as my bones could move for my field and home. Oh, Plan B wasn't what Harold and Cody deserved, and the thought of my suffering buck made me sick. But Plan B was surely better than nothing. Wasn't it?

I hadn't even left a light on in the house! Marvelle meowed loudly. Her dish glared, empty. I ignored her and lifted the phone. Then I put it down again. Just a deputy on night duty wouldn't do. I knew what Harold would want. I looked up the number and called Gus at home.

"Gus, it's Louisa. I just got home," I said in a breathless, terrified voice. "Hurry. An intruder's around here, maybe a robber. Or worse. Please come. There's a strange truck parked on the road toward the Atherton's. On the berm of my property. I heard shots. I opened my front door and shot Harold's old deer rifle into the air to try to scare him away, but I heard another shot after that. Please hurry. Call the deputy, too, if you want, but after all that's happened, I really need you."

I knew he'd bite on that one. I didn't know if the truck was still there, but I had to try. I had to.

"I'll be right there, Louisa."

"Catch him and lock him up. I'm terrified. He's got a gun!"

"On my way now," he said, and hung up.

I waited. Paced. Finally, I remembered why Marvelle was mad and filled her bowl. I moistened her kibble with a little bourbon and put some real tuna fish on top to mollify her. She loved it. I wanted to check on the girls but couldn't leave the house because I figured Gus would at least call. Maybe I'd been wrong; the truck wasn't there and Gus had just gone home annoyed. I hadn't thought to check the clock when I came in, so I didn't know how much time had actually passed. Does it make sense if I tell you that I couldn't stand it anymore? I picked up the car keys and left. I knew it wasn't reasonable. Unless Larry was gutting my buck by the side of the road, he must be long gone by now.

I don't know what I thought I was going to see. I can only tell you what I did see: a roadblock. Not a hundred feet from my own driveway. A sheriff's car, red and blue lights careening in circles, parked across the road to keep anyone from passing. A second black-and-white, farther down, similarly parked facing the opposite direction, lights warning cars off. Orange cones. Flares. Between them, an ambulance, more lights. There must be a terrible accident. Glass shone up like pieces of fallen night on the highway. I glimpsed a heavy man with a broom, backlit, wearing a ball cap and a neon-orange safety vest. He laid the broom down, walked toward my car, and I opened the window.

"Road's closed for a while here. You'll have to turn arou . . . Louisa?"

"Gus?" I should have recognized him, but he was in jeans and a plaid shirt with his badge pinned to the safety vest. The ball cap had confused me, too.

"Oh my God. Louisa. Turn around now. You can't see this."

But I just had. My eyes were already wet.

Gus reached through my open window and put his hand on my shoulder. "I know. But if it helps at all, this guy didn't hit a person. Dunno. Driver was likely your intruder. Hit a buck . . ." He pointed, and then I saw the rack shining as if by sunlight or moon, as the lights glinted around, and the dark mound of the body on the side of the road.

I moaned. I put my head in my hands and whispered, "*I tried, Cody, I tried.*"

Gus touched my shoulder through the open window. "Wasn't coming after you, Louisa honey. The shots you heard? Guy's dressed for hunting, not that it's in season, and he's got a Winchester that's been fired in the truck. Poaching. Damn thing is, that buck's got a bullet in him, too. Billy noticed when he checked to see if he needed to be put down. Musta gotten too dark—there's a skid in the back of the truck he'd of used if he'd . . ." Gus glanced at the scene and then back at me. "Guy musta been going like a bat outta hell because that big boy bounced enough to shatter the windshield, and that's hard to do." He shook his head as if to stop himself from talking. "Please," he said. "You need to turn around and go home. I'll come by and check on you when I'm done here."

"Is it bad, Gus?"

"You don't need to hear." There were night sounds, cicadas and crickets, and in the distance, someone—a deputy maybe—called something to someone else. Above it all, the high yellow lights of a wrecker blinked their approach from the other side. Gus looked over at it, his cruiser lights reflecting in his glasses. "I should go check—"

I wiped my face with the back of my hand and got my voice under control. "I can't go without knowing."

He waited me out but I didn't move. Finally, he pulled off his ball cap and rubbed his hand over the top of his head, replaced the cap, and sighed. "I'm not supposed to say," he said. "Only a doc can pronounce him. EMTs gotta take him to the hospital. This has to be hard after what you've been through with Cody. And Harold. I'm real sorry." His voice was gentle. He reached through the open window and put his hand over mine where it was still on the steering wheel, and for just that moment he was exactly like Harold. He waited, maybe a minute while both of us were quiet, then he took his hand back when I finally looked up at him.

"Dead?"

He closed his eyes, then opened them, and his chin bobbed down once in a nearly invisible acknowledgment. "You turn around now."

"Gus, is it somebody local?"

"He's pretty messed up. We're running the plates. I don't know the vehicle."

But I knew I would.

Gus hit the top of my car with the palm of his hand. "You go home now. This has nothing to do with you, so you don't need to be afraid anymore." Of course he was dead wrong about that first part, and I think we are all rightly afraid of a lot of things, but it was nice of him to say that, don't you think? Harold used to think he was shielding me, too.

"Anyone else hurt?"

Gus shook his head. "Thank God." He reached in and patted the hand of mine that was closest to him. Like my other hand, it was tight and high on the steering wheel, my knuckles bumping up and down in odd, flashing silhouette. "A boy's on the berm down past Atherton's, nowhere near the scene," he said. "I passed him when I was coming to your house and stopped in case he was your intruder, but he's just a kid, real polite, no gun, waiting for a friend to pick him up. And right then dispatch called about the crash. You get yourself home now. I'll stop in to check on you after this is cleaned up. Gonna take a while."

"Athertons' nephew! Andrew spends time with them—"

"No. Brandon McSomething. A kid, honey. No gun."

"You didn't just leave him there?"

It took Gus a couple seconds to catch on. "Oh, the boy?" Another shake of his head then. "Someone's coming for him."

"Gus, that boy could get hit. No! You know how people speed on this road. You can't leave him." I couldn't help myself. The boy must have people who love him the way Harold and I loved Cody, people who wouldn't want him walking on the dark road, people who would want someone like me to look out for him. Someone who knows what can happen to a boy if no one takes care of him. "I'm going to go get him. He can wait at my house." I straightened in the driver's seat, and pointed at the dizzying maze of lights and vehicles that looked like a small city ahead on the night road. "Make them move out of the way!"

Gus was silent a minute, maybe trying to figure how to handle the crazy woman. But that's not fair; I know he remembered how Cody died. He just didn't know what to say. Then he came up with, "Louisa, honey, don't cry, now. That's a good thing to offer, but you can't get through. See, the road is closed. I don't have it cleared. Body's not out. The boy said someone was on the way. He's likely been picked up already."

Poor Gus. My Harold could have told him he was never going to win against a determined Louisa. "Where's *your* car?" I said, unfastening my seat belt.

"Over there, Atherton's side," he said, pointing. "My lights are going. The blue-and-red set." Then he realized where I was headed and blocked my opening the car door. "Right," he said. "But I can't let you drive it. You can't *be* here." If I'd closed my eyes, I might have dreamed Harold had come back to take care of Cody, to go pick him up after practice that last twilight, because Gus's voice was that kind as he bent to speak through the window while he wouldn't let me out of the car. "Look, I can't leave the scene, but, tell you what, how about I send Billy down right now, see if the boy's still there. If he is, I'll have Billy follow up," he said.

But my eyes stayed open because I had to go on. There are mistakes we don't have to live again, and we can help to save others from making them. At least sometimes. "What does 'follow up' mean?" I did not want tears on my face, but of course, there they were. I swiped at them and tried to stare Gus down. "Follow up exactly how?"

Gus's hand went to my shoulder and stayed there, but not too heavy. It was big like Harold's. More puffy, not callused like a farmer's, but I can't say that bothered me. "Exactly by calling his parents and staying with him just to be safe until he's picked up," he said. "We won't leave him to walk or wait alone. We'll make sure he's safe, I promise. Don't cry, honey. We'll take care of the boy, I promise. Will that do it? If you watch me go and send Billy right now, will you turn around and go home?"

"You'll send him right now."

"Right now."

"Okay. Thank you." I managed to get it out. He was a man who would keep his word. He stood by the car while I fastened my seat belt again and put the window back up. Then he motioned to me to lock the door, and he turned. But I did stay to make sure, even though I believed him. Gus made his way past the ambulance, the EMTs, and the driver of the wrecker, picked his way around the mess on the highway. By the streaking lights, I saw him in the distance. Within a minute, the second squad car headed the other direction, down the highway toward Atherton's, to keep a boy out of harm's way. The boy wasn't Cody, but he was a boy and I could love him and other boys, bless their wild hearts, bless the yet-unlit Independence Day fireworks of their lives, and I could be grateful that there are still boys in the world with wild hearts and dangerous, glorious futures. Maybe I can be of use. Maybe I can watch out for some of them.

Like CarolSue says, sometimes you have to come up with an entirely new Plan. I really hate it when she's right.

By late the next day, word had spread. There really wasn't a way to make the story larger than life as it passed among my neighbors; once Larry Ellis was identified, the sheer ballsy improbability that he'd been poaching out of season on land owned by the widowed grandmother of the boy he'd killed, shot a buck and left it to suffer, but then the buck had appeared—it must have seemed an apparition as he sped down the road!—and used the last of its life to take Larry's. Well, it's not really a tale anyone can exaggerate much, so people got it the way it happened, and they marveled at it, the mystery of how things sometimes work out making you believe in the unseen.

Helen Atherton even picked up a copy of the *Dwayne Weekly* and found Larry Ellis's obituary, which was unusually short for a paper that typically finds an excuse to go on and on about life accomplishments of the "She brushed her teeth well" variety. Helen brought it to me, pleased as punch, saying the buck was a hero and Ellis being dead restored her faith in the possibility of cosmic order. Helen's loyal that way, but I didn't want that clipping. Before I got rid of it, though, I looked, double-checking that it had really happened and something was over.

The notice said Ellis was survived by his girlfriend, LuAnn McNally, and her son, Brandon McNally. Something pinged in my mind when I read it, but that's all it was. A little warning ping that resonated with something from earlier. Not loud. I threw the clipping away as I had the rest, satisfied by Larry's name and address. It was true.

Remember I suggested you get yourself some tea with a splash of bourbon to hear the rest of the story? If you did, I imagine you're glad and you may have gotten yourself a second, too. Perhaps you are satisfied, and think The Plan completed itself, without my action. Or perhaps you trace a convoluted thread between the intentions of my heart and what became of them. Don't think I haven't considered it. It's all right with me. You've stuck with me this long, which was kind. All I can do is tell you what happened; it's for you to decide what it means. You probably have questions. That makes two of us. I can answer your small ones. The large questions, the ones about life itself that roam like ghosts to disturb the night: I am no closer to putting those to sleep. Was it justice after all? Who are the innocent and who the guilty?

I rise and take responsibility at the same time I look at how I made my great Plan, and then life took over with its own Plan that was far bigger than the one I'd conceived. Maybe I glimpsed just one piece of it tumbling into place. None of us really knows what comes next, do we? But perhaps you can see better than I where this story truly began, and when or if it will end.

Here's one thing I do know: life changes us in ways we never foresee. It even sends our hearts to places we were once determined not to go. No, Glitter Jesus isn't hanging on my bedroom or living room wall. Nor will Gary's church be constructed on my land after I'm dead. I suppose I ought to tell him that I've deeded my land to a conservation easement to protect it for the deer and other wildlife. The land, the wide clear creek that runs through it, the animals and birds are sacred, and that's enough church for me.

Did I ever tell you that great blue heron nest around my little river every year? how glorious the span of their wings is against a late afternoon sky? Yes, my spirit flies, too, then, just as it rides the backs of my deer, and I feel connected to everything that lives and perhaps has ever lived, or will, and my love for life is as tender as a first green shoot coming up in my garden after the winter kill.

Here's what I mean, though: I'm letting Gary have his tent revival. I'm taking the plane ticket he bought me and going to CarolSue's to help out there. It's a decent trade, and more; I see that my son is only finding his way, like all of us. Like I am. Who am I to say what someone else should find holy? Who's to say what or who someone else should love? Carol-Sue says I am trying to understand Gary more, and that will help our relationship. I hate it when she's right, but the revival is a one-time thing, and I've hired Alyssa, the Atherton's reliable daughter, to stay in the house while I'm gone to take care of the girls and Marvelle, plus guard them during the event. I don't think one night will hurt the root crops I planted for the deer, though I admit to hoping not too many people show up. Alyssa's dad will come over that night so she's not alone, even though she's nineteen and says she doesn't need him to baby her. Gus will be around, too. Not that I imagine the people who come to a tent revival are generally vandals or drunk and disorderly, but on the other hand, you never know what behavior religious fervor will excuse, do you? Alyssa's mother thinks it's a good idea, though, and I agree. They're good, sensible folk who don't truck with nonsense.

Speaking of Gus, I was relieved to hear he isn't a member of Gary's or any cult. He helps him out because he's always felt so bad about Harold, he said. That's why he agreed to do security for the revival, but he said he had no idea that I wasn't on board with the whole thing. I believe him. Gary wouldn't have told Gus that he was going behind my back. When I return from CarolSue's, Gus is taking me out to supper. At a real restaurant in Elmont, not that death museum they call a lodge. When I told him I never want to see another deer that didn't die naturally if I can help it, he said, "I can live with that." He thinks he understands, bless his heart. I haven't told him that I don't eat meat anymore. Based on his girth, I'd say Gus is definitely a meat-and-potatoes man, but, as CarolSue says, one blow at a time. Plenty of time to get to know each other, she says. That's my sister for you. Have I mentioned how much I hate it when she's right?

And, about CarolSue: She is really excited I'm visiting. It'll be a distraction from what they've been through with Charlie. She needs some fun, she says, so she's going to give me a makeover (again) and we're going shopping. I hate shopping, but she'll pick everything out. She says I have to bring "that old blue thing" so she can personally put it in the trash. Then we'll come home and have tea. She can dress me, and I'll teach her how to fix tea the right way. It's my turn to help her. We lean on each other, as you've seen.

I've been thinking about the new Plan. Details. If you have a bit more tea left in your cup, you might refresh it with a couple drops more flavoring. Marvelle needed it when I announced that when I get back, I'm getting us a dog from the rescue shelter over in Elmont. I told her it's nothing personal, but I miss Emerson and Thoreau, and another Lab can go walking with me come spring. I told her "Marvelle, it's time." The does will be dropping their wobbly-legged fawns by April, and I want to glimpse their spotted backs as they try to keep up with their mothers. We could use another little goat on the farm, too. Goodness knows the grass needs to be kept in check.

I've already talked to the girls about starting with some chicks again, too. JoJo pooped on the back step at the mention, but Beth liked it, as I'd expect. She's a nurturing sort. Amy was nonchalant. She'll adjust. It's surprising what you can finally adjust to and go on. Not only that, you may be glad of it, as I explained to Marvelle. The dog and goat and chicks could become her new friends and she might be surprised by gladness, yes, and grateful to discover that she's glad when she'd thought that was impossible. (I will admit here and now that Marvelle hasn't shown cheer or gratitude for anything except a patch of sunlight to sleep in or getting fed on time since her retirement from mousing, though she's gotten pretty fond of her bourbon. I best cut her back some now.)

And since young wildlife is part of my Plan, I keep thinking about helping some boys. Cody would like that, and I think Gary will, too. I'll give some hapless beginning teacher a hand with the unruly ones on the playground at my old school, bless their wild hearts. And I can tutor the ones fallen behind in reading. I imagine some high schoolers could use a boost with their college applications. I'm good at that, especially the personal essays. Cody would like that, too. He'd been working on his when he died. I'd already thought of offering to help that boy Brandon who works for Al when it's time for him to apply. It did my heart good when he said he liked to read. And I know how to apply for scholarships and other financial aid. From what Al said, I gather Brandon might need a lot of that.

It was that thought that led me to another the night before last. Even if the new goat can handle all the grass, which isn't likely, I could use a hand planting the vegetables and the flowers come spring. Spreading the compost, too. Then I thought maybe Brandon could clean porch furniture. Al said he didn't have enough to keep him busy full-time last summer so it came to me that maybe I can hire Brandon to help me, and I can help him in return. So the next logical thing was to call Al to ask him for Brandon's phone number.

"Well, Louisa, the boy could use the work, I'm sure, but he called off on Saturday, said his mother's boyfriend died. You might want to give 'em a couple days. Lives way over outside Elmont, so you gotta put in the area code, don't you know, even though it's the same as ours."

Again, a ping went off in my mind and, after I hung up, that little bell harmonized with the others I'd heard, Brandon, Brandon, Brandon.

Did Al know who that dead boyfriend of Brandon's

mother was? Al's never cared much for human details; his life is about the land, the weather, and the cost. If he had known, he'd have blurted out his opinion, too. He wouldn't have been one to try to protect me by making something up, like, Oh, that boy's family is moving to Indy, so he won't be around. Not like my Harold. Or like Gus. But while Al rattled on with his irritation that it cost twenty cents to call over there and it was greedy and stupid of the phone company to charge extra in the same area code, I knew.

I waited a day. Then, yes, I called that number. Remember, I was a teacher. I can smell a cheater from across a classroom, and likewise, I recognize an honest heart in a boy who loves books, who loves animals, who tries his best.

Don't worry. I know another boy won't be our Cody. It'll just be nice to have a boy around again. Brandon does have beautiful blue eyes, and maybe it's good that they aren't either hydrangea blue or cornflower blue, but something darker, as I recall, as if they held a sapphire memory. Anyway, it's a different kind of sight I always looked to nurture in my students, through the lens of character, kindness, and thinking. You want to catch boys while they're young and help them grow into good men, like my Harold was. And, yes, like Gus, even if he is a puffy sheriff.

Just don't start thinking I'll end up marrying Gus even if we keep company and get close, as CarolSue foresees. I'll always be Harold's wife.

THE TESTAMENT OF HAROLD'S WIFE

Lynne Hugo

ABOUT THIS GUIDE

The suggested questions are included
to enhance your group's reading
of
Lynne Hugo's *The Testament of Harold's Wife*

(Please be aware that there are "spoilers"
in this guide, so you may not want to read
the questions before finishing the book.)

DISCUSSION QUESTIONS

1. What is your image of a woman in her sixties or seventies? In what ways does Louisa challenge or confirm that?

2. How did you assess Gary? Did he evoke sympathy, anger, or some other emotion?

3. What was your reaction to CarolSue? Do you have a relationship with a sibling or very close friend who has a similar role in your life? Do you think this sort of relationship is unique to women or do men develop it with other men, too?

4. Did your reaction to Gus change during the course of the novel?

5. How do you see the different notions of religion and/or spirituality in this novel? Do any of them fit with your own?

6. Louisa is extremely bothered by trophy hunting. How does this match your own feelings about hunting for the purpose of sport as opposed to hunting for food? Do you have thoughts or feelings about the notion of animal rights? If so, how do you define them and what do they mean?

7. Do you prefer a novel that has a few "loose ends" or do you like one that ties everything up neatly at the close? What do you imagine will happen after Louisa comes home from visiting CarolSue?

8. What do you imagine to be the author's intention as she wrote *The Testament of Harold's Wife*?

If your book club or group would enjoy having the author Skype or FaceTime with you during any part of your discussion of these questions, or to respond to any questions you might have about her work, she'd be delighted to do so. You may contact her through her website (LynneHugo.com), the publisher (Kensington Books), or Writers House literary agency.

Connect with U(s)

Visit us online at
KensingtonBooks.com
to read more from your favorite authors, see books
by series, view reading group guides, and more.

Join us on social media
for sneak peeks, chances to win books and prize packs,
and to share your thoughts with other readers.

facebook.com/kensingtonpublishing
twitter.com/kensingtonbooks

Tell us what you think!

To share your thoughts, submit a review,
or sign up for our eNewsletters, please visit:
KensingtonBooks.com/TellUs.